Rhapsody

Cassandra Frew

This is dedicated to my late husband Chris, my expert on surfing and how teenage males think.

Without your love and support, this series of books would never have eventuated.

Commenced 31 October 2009
Completed 13 December 2009

Cover designed by Microsoft® Clip Art and used with permission by Microsoft.
Microsoft, Encarta, MSN, and Windows are either registered trademarks or trademarks of Microsoft Corporation in the United States and/or other countries.

TABLE OF CONTENTS

PREFACE

SOMMERSETT is on the western coastline of Lake Macquarie in NSW. My Gran had lived there for as long as I could remember, well close enough – she was on the shores of Sommersett Park in the suburb of Glassread. We moved to Warden, a fifteen-minute drive from Glassread, when I was ten years old. Gran had become old and infirm by then and needed her family near her. Sadly, she died within two years of us moving to the area.

My earliest memories of Gran were the wonderful times I had spent staying with her over school holidays - setting crab traps from the old rusty runabout, prawning with a torch and a net when the sun had set. Gran had often told me that Lake Macquarie was 365 miles in circumference, one mile for each day of the year. Now that imperial measurements had gone by the wayside, these calculations were not quite so romantic in kilometres, but I adored the analogy, and it was something I always had with me as a gift from her. Let's face it, material possessions are wasted on youth. It's the values we gain as children that makes us worthy of being accepted as well-adjusted adults. I understood that now.

By the time Gran passed away, I was settled in school and my parents were opposed to uprooting us, therefore in Warden we stayed. I was unaware at the tender age of twelve this would turn out to be the most fortunate decision my parents would ever make on my behalf; it laid the foundation that would cement my life …

TERM 4

New Arrivals

Music Selection: Abba, 'Super Trooper'
Diary Entry: It's when we least expect it, there he is in the crowd and I didn't even know I was looking for him.

IT WAS LAST PERIOD on the first day back from the October school holidays and I was sitting in History class, eyeing off the new teacher. Minor irritation knitted her brow as she looked over the class, although I could not see the problem. The classroom seating was random at Sommersett High; the students could sit wherever they chose. The cleaners always set the desks up in singular columns at the end of the day I assumed. Students would drag two desks together as they wanted, especially when they were best friends or boyfriend and girlfriend. I sat at a single desk, second from the back row, second column from the windows on the left-hand side of the room. The reason I sat alone was my best girlfriend Bree sat with her boyfriend Simon Nobel, and my best male friend, Michael Lennox, was in class 2.

Mrs Standish wrote her name on the board in large cursive script. As she turned to address us, a brunette, God-like creature darted into the room, taking the only vacant seat in the front row. "Sorry I'm late Mum," he muttered as he sat down. I had noticed him in my other classes during the day, how could I not? In fact, I don't think my eyes had left his form at any stage, during any period.

"As you may have ascertained by the late arrival of my first-born son…" the class laughed in a somewhat controlled manner, we didn't know this teacher, "my family and I recently moved here over the October school holidays. You have no doubt met my two sons during the course of the day, but for those of you who have *not* had the pleasure," Mrs Standish looked over her glasses at her 'first-born son', "my sons Elijah", she said pointing to the God, "and Lorien."

At first I thought the rest of my class had gone crazy as they looked in my direction, and then realised they were checking out the other new student sitting to my left. I hadn't noticed him earlier as my gaze was angled toward the teacher. I also hadn't noticed him when I first entered the class. This may seem strange as a normal occurrence, but Sommersett was near the coal-mining sector of the Hunter Valley and we often had new students, moving here for their families to work in the mines. Sommersett was close enough for their parents to commute to the Valley, but near enough to Sydney that it was only an hour and a half by car or train if you were inclined to visit the 'big smoke'.

I heard sniggering from the boys sitting behind me, no doubt at the two names, Elijah and Lorien Standish. I glanced at Lorien to see if he'd noticed their amusement. He was already looking at me and smiling. I smiled back and introduced myself in a whisper. "Hi Lorien, I'm Ash. Ignore the fools in the back row," I said, looking over my shoulder at them with a grimace. "Even though we're all in class 1, they seem to think they need to swing on their chairs and be *clever*. It's all a charade." Lorien smiled at me and then looked over his shoulder at the mirth-makers, Joel Naismith and Billy Hall, then dismissed them. "Are you and Elijah very close births or twins?" They didn't *really* look anything alike so either option was a possibility. I swooned a little, saying Elijah's name and tried once again to catch a glance at his older brother.

"We're fraternal twins," he said, "he's four minutes older," and then that smile again.

"So, if I can have your attention," Mrs Standish interjected, this time looking at me and Lorien over the top of her glasses, "we no doubt have a lot of material to cover before you sit your end of year exams on the ninth of November, that's three weeks to you and me people!" She gave us one further eyeballing and continued to address the class.

When class ended, I walked out with Bree and Simon and hung out with them in the canteen whilst Bree waited on Michael. The twins had been following closely behind us it would seem, as Simon stopped them on their way past, starting a conversation. "Yum Yum," I whispered to Bree, checking out Elijah. It was the first decent look I'd managed to get of him, and I wasn't disappointed. Bree and I were just standing there watching the trio when Michael romped through the canteen.

"Hey gals," he greeted us and when we didn't reply he followed our gaze to where the boys were standing. "Bree, I am *so* going to tell Simon!" he laughed.

"I'm just scoping them out on Ash's behalf," she said.

"Sure!" At that moment, all three of them looked in our direction. We whipped around, making our staring even more obvious and I shot my friends a quick goodbye, darting off to the parking lot. We'd been *so* busted.

I had a lot of final preparation to do over the next three weeks for the end of year exams; however, I felt prepared considering the effort I'd put in all year, all-but ready for the final exams. I lay on my bed, stroking

'George', my fourteen-year-old tabby Persian. I wondered again for the millionth time why I hadn't called him something more exotic as the beautiful markings around his grey eyes were that of Egyptian eyeliner. The phone rang, interrupting my reflections. "I'll get it!" I called. That was one of the benefits of being an only child, no one to fight over the phone with you. It was Michael.

"Hey Ash," he gushed, "what did you think of the new 'paper' and 'plastic', 'search' and 'destroy', 'debit' and 'credit'..."

"Whoa Michael," I interrupted, "*what* are you on about?"

"The new *twins* dopey. I can't believe you sat next to one of them in History and you're *so* not into where I'm *coming* from, girl!"

Michael was a little dramatic and over the top at times. One of the most popular guys at school, definitely the best dancer, smart, great dresser, the source of many a crush from the sighing, giddy girls that always seemed to be on his heels from one classroom to another. Others in our group used to think it strange that at no time he'd ever gone out with anyone, nor even laid a kiss on any of the eager young volunteers. I was certain that their speculations were now a little more contemplated. Bree and I had discussed it a few times, both of us already indifferent to the unquestioned answer. I myself had realised about two years ago it was *very* possible Michael was gay. I loved Michael dearly but never thought of him as anything but a best friend. I would never make him uncomfortable in any way, although I was sure Michael knew I was no fool. However, he'd never brought it up and I did not intend to do so either. He would get around to it when he was ready, if it actually was the case *and* he considered it my business. "How did you find out I sat next to

Lorien in History anyway?" I asked, and knew right away that he sat with Bree on the school bus.

"You *know* that Bree will be ringing to tell you the goss too and I wanted to beat her to it. What do you already know?"

"I can't tell you much about either of them," I admitted. "I only spoke to Lorien for a few seconds, and I couldn't even *see* Elijah through the mass of female heads *also* craning in his direction," I laughed. "They're fraternal twins, that's all I know."

"I know more than you," Michael sing-songed. "Wanna know?"

"Hell yeah, give me the dirt on Elijah!" I sat waiting on some information, any information, I was hungry for news. *Especially whether he has a girlfriend left behind, missing her, emailing her, wanting her...* I thought, and then shook myself a little; I didn't even *know* this guy.

"Well, ahhh," stammered Michael. "I don't have that kind of information," he said a little awkwardly, "just boring facts for now."

"Well come on," I prodded, "give me something."

"They moved here from Sydney over the school holidays," he started.

"I already knew that," I said, hoping to speed this up into something new, something more than I already had.

"Let me *finish*," he said, and without missing a beat, launched into a list of known entities about the family.

I spoke with Michael for another ten minutes before hanging up. The wonderfulness of speaking Elijah's name repeatedly in conversation was not getting me closer to studying. No sooner had the call ended when the phone rang again. "Mum," I called, "can you get that? If it's Bree, can you ask her to call Michael? I don't have time at the moment."

It sounded funny to hear the landline ringing so frequently. I had turned my mobile phone off.

"'Kay Honey," Mum responded, and the ringing fell silent.

Dom and Anna Mercy were pretty cool for being in their late 30s. They had me when they were barely in their 20s - I was their 'little surprise'. Apparently, there was a difference between being a surprise and a mistake. A mistake was something you wouldn't do over whereas a surprise was something you didn't know was missing until it was there. Not that it worried me about being a 'surprise', I loved my family very much, and more importantly, they trusted me. Being six to twelve months older than the rest of my friends helped. I repeated fifth grade, which was utterly embarrassing at the time. I supposed it was worth it in the end as I'd been in all 1 classes since I started at Sommersett High; I even had my P1s since July this year. No one else in Year 10 had this distinct pleasure.

I had my own car too. Dad was a mechanic and had found me a great deal. I bought it with the money I'd earned over the last Christmas holidays working with Mum at the local doctors. She was a part-time receptionist there and I was employed to get the accumulation of back filing completed. A cool $2,500 I had earned, enough to buy the car, comprehensively insure it, and pay my subscription to road service – *just* in case.

I sighed, nothing was getting me into the mood for studying tonight, and I knew it was a lost cause. "I wish I was a cat," I told George, rubbing his tummy. He rolled over so I could continue the job more thoroughly. I smiled, "You don't care about *love*," I said and recalled the noise when the local toms mated with the shes. "In fact, I don't think you care about anything but boo-tay," I laughed, slamming my books shut. I gave up and went to shower and put on my pyjamas before heading to bed.

When lying in the dark, there was no option but to allow my mind to drift and rerun the conversation I had with Michael that evening. Elijah. Elijah Standish. What a regal sounding name. *Mrs Ashlyn Standish*. The thought made me laugh, seventeen years old and imagining married life already. This was not the first time I had a major crush on a boy at school, however most of them had ended up being unrequited love that left me shy, and not wanting to throw myself readily onto the playing field. I hadn't had much experience with boys over my tender years and none of our group ventured much past our own invisible barricade, Michael and I being single by choice, so we said. However, now that Elijah had turned up out of the blue, I could feel him drawing me in a way I'd never felt before - not that I would *do* anything about it...

Michael said that they'd bought the old school residence across from our high school. It hadn't been operating as a school residence since the late 1970s and had been bought and sold several times over; now it belonged to the Standish family. I already knew that Cara Standish was our new History teacher, but didn't know that their dad, Nick Standish, was a Mine Manager of coal operations in the Hunter Valley.

The reason the family had moved from the Eastern Suburbs of Sydney was due to Mr Standish's career. The closest coalfields to Sydney were located in the Wollongong area. With the infinite road traffic and being on-call, it was inconvenient for Mr Standish to commute so he lived away from the family Monday to Friday. Apparently, this was becoming more difficult for Mrs Standish and the twins, as theirs was a close family. When the decision was made to move to the Hunter Valley for work, Sommersett became their new home. Mr Standish easily accomplished a daily commute with nowhere near the traffic to contend with, even when on-call. How fortunate it was for Mrs Standish to work across the street. I had asked Michael how he had gleaned this information in the first place, and Elijah, *Elijah - swoon*, had already become close mates with Bree's boyfriend Simon. Simon had told Bree, Bree told Michael on the bus. The ever-vigilant bush telegraph was rarely silent.

It was hard to work out what *wasn't* attractive about Elijah. I felt a little ashamed that I could *not* get his face out of my head. He wasn't quite 'movie star' material but was naturally good looking and had everything in the right place. His nose was straight and slender, his mouth a sexy pout defined by a set of full, well-shaped lips. He had blue smiling eyes and a gorgeous thick head of short-cropped brunette waves, not quite curls. A dimple in one cheek played in and out depending on his smile. His tanned skin complemented his well-developed muscles, and I do mean *well* developed. He held an enthusiastic aura of confidence about him, pure quality all the way. "Tall, strong, self-assured and handsome. Mumma, I gotta get me some of that!" I growled to myself.

It was no surprise that he *was* so handsome, his mother and brother were equally attractive. Lorien was similar to Elijah only in the colour and texture of his hair. I had noticed in History class that his eyes were a dark brown, so dark they appeared black. Those eyes, not smiling eyes, but deep and intricate, holding many souls and secrets I was sure. A mop of the same brunette hair curled down the nape of his neck ending well past his collar, the fringe hanging partially in his eyes. At times, he would muss it toward the back of his head; he didn't keep it short like his twin. His lips were also well shaped, but his lower lip was much fuller than the top. No dimples worked on his face at all, but his cheekbones were high and wide, accentuating his dark features. Although also well-muscled, he was leaner and lither than his brother. If Elijah weren't so intriguing and handsome, I would consider Lorien to be an exceptional catch. I was to find out that other girls were thinking the same about the Standish twins.

I scrutinised my body, my mind, myself, comparing my pluses against the Standish twins. Well, more specifically to Elijah. I was tall for a girl, 170 centimetres, but nowhere near the approximate 185 centimetres of the twins. *Lovely kissing height*, I mused. I had what you would call a classic hourglass figure but with a little more 'junk in the trunk' than I thought necessary. The hourglass had a little more sand in the lower half than the top. I laughed at my thoughts, as I'd never really been *all* that self-conscious of my body. My chest was in proportion to my hips, and my legs were good I thought, shapely and slender, once you got past the pad of fat on the thighs. I was happy enough with my lot, but *no* girl was ever content in swimmers. Luckily for us, fashion dictated that 'boardies' were an acceptable bottom to a bikini, tank, or one-piece suit underneath. I also had a pretty face; no acne, clear blue eyes and my chestnut hair hung straight down my back, the shade balancing my eye colour nicely. *What lovely babies we would have*, I thought, a little shamefully.

I wouldn't say I was the most athletic person in the year either. Although as a child I was an avid gymnast, jump-rope skipper and hopscotch player, as I matured, I found I had the opposite of pigeon toes -

duck footed was I. My feet stuck out at nearly 45-degree angles from my shins thus giving me very little balance. I was shocking on a bicycle, could not run fast or jump, and don't even have rollerblades in the same room as me. I could dance well enough to get me through social occasions and I could walk without falling over. This was enough to make me happy.

As I fell into a sleepy oblivion, my final thoughts were of circling gracefully around the floor at the end of year dance in Elijah's arms. I could feel myself smiling.

Rituals

Music Selection: Kylie Minogue, 'I Should Be So Lucky'
Diary Entry: Nothing could be more simplistic in my own mind, daydreaming about you. The most glorious sensations can be created within my own thoughts, seeing us together.

I WAS *SO* GLAD I had my driver's licence. It meant I didn't have to ride the bus to school and back every day. I was free to come and go at my own pace and not have to comply with the rigid schedule of pick up and drop off. I didn't drive Michael and Bree to school unless I'd been staying at one of their places. They both lived in Gracey, which was roughly a twenty-minute drive to Sommersett.

I'd decided to come to school early this morning to make use of some time in the library before the first bell. As I pulled into the school driveway, which nearly exactly divided the grounds into two, I looked towards the old school residence. There was no buzz happening around the house, but it was only 8.00 am.

The driveway went all the way to the rear of the school, with only the oval and basketball courts continuing past it; our school had been neatly set out when built. To the right of the driveway was the 'serious' side of the grounds. You entered through the canteen into quad one, bordered on three sides by two-storey, typical brick buildings. The rooms consisted of the English, History and Maths classrooms and included the administrative sectors: school reception, sickbay and headmaster offices.

When one went screaming through quad one during breaks, one was bound to be caught.

Adjacent to quad one was quad two. The same setup as the first as far as the building formation, but was home to the Science, Geography, and Economics departments; the two quads sat abutted like giant horseshoes. The accessible end of the quads opened onto a grassy area and further down, a scattering of demountable buildings. These classrooms held the same subjects as did the brick buildings, forming a grin configuration sealing in the students, edging their way to the outer edges of the adjacent quads like a train of circus caravans. Past any of these borders was 'out of bounds'.

The driveway I now walked back down would take me to the left-hand side of the grounds, when looking from street view. I trotted up the flight of concrete stairs, running my palm over the handrail; its aged and peeling paint a coarse comparison to the shiny smoothness of the metal peeking through - buffed to ebony satin from the myriad of palms spanning the generations. The resulting sun-brightened alcove was a massive archway opening onto the rest of the grounds. This section was made up mostly of demountables and the old wooden classrooms we inherited from what used to be Sommersett Primary School, before the high school population became too big. The other factions of the curriculum were situated in this area - the home sciences, language, music, and technical works like woodwork, art, IT and industrial technology. Ms Moyet, my French teacher, *abhorred* being in this vicinity of the grounds. She did not believe that a language as beautiful as French should be surrounded by the clashing of pots and pans, grinding saws and blatting trumpets. *"Mon Dieu"*, she would often complain, *"le bruit!"* Which translated into English was *My God, the noise*!

To my left was the library, including the AV room; the students *loved* being in the AV room. It was a popular holding cell for any lazy teacher who didn't like creating a lesson plan for the day. Although we were supposed to be watching the screen and taking notes, many students took the opportunity to make out or fool around in other more disruptive ways; the teachers rarely stayed with us. God forbid 'Thunderfoot' Kershaw, the aging female librarian, came in to break up the tomfoolery!

To the right of the enclosed concrete area and down a flight of stairs was the MPC, the multi-purpose centre. It was not only the indoor courts, but also the drama stage, where the dances were held and the venue for any other entire school-body requirement took place. In a matter of only a few more weeks, I would be dancing in there with my peers at the end of school formal. This realisation brought me back to the musings I'd had last night involving Elijah. I smiled and walked into the library.

Thunderfoot was hot on my tail. "What *is* it with the early morning incomers today?" she asked, not all that kindly. Fortunately, all Year 10 and upward aged students could use the library before and after school as long as they had a signed note from one of their teachers. I produced mine from Ms Moyet, which Thunderfoot scrutinised carefully before handing back. "I would appreciate it if you stayed at one table Miss Mercy, I don't want to be chasing people all over the library at this time of the morning." She stomped off.

Nice… quiet… Way to obey your own rules Thunderfoot, I thought whilst I sought out the 'other' library intruders, of which there was only one.

There he sat, God-like; the natural light streaming in through the ceiling skylights was enveloping him in a hazy, golden pool. He may have chosen this seat subconsciously, his senses drawing him to the central Eden of the room. I prayed my face would not betray the less-than-religious thoughts I was having. He looked up as I approached the desk. "Hi, Mercy isn't it?" asked Elijah. I nearly laughed aloud when he spoke my last name instead of my first. I quickly looked up to see Thunderfoot leaving the room. I was glad he'd picked a grouping of desks at the rear of the library. It would make talking to him easier, assuming he had time to talk.

"Ah, actually it's Ashlyn, Ash for short." I stuck my hand out to shake his and wondered what I was doing. He seemed nonplussed, took it, shook it, and then kissed the back of my hand. I just stood there ogling at him feeling like time had stopped. "Ah, ah, ah…" I stammered.

"Unless you're about to break into the hit songs from 'Saturday Night Fever', I think you should take a seat. I doubt Mrs Kershaw will be gone for long." He looked at me and smiled, pulling out the chair next to him. I took a second, composed myself, and sat down, taking the books from my bag.

"I missed your point." I looked at him, my forehead crinkling. I was unsure what he'd meant from his comment.

"My parents are big fans of anything 70s and 80s and unfortunately my brother and I have *vast* knowledge on both of those decades." I must have still looked bewildered, because he continued,

"The beginning of the chorus to 'Stayin' Alive' by the Bee Gees, you know, the big hit from the movie 'Saturday Night Fever'?" I had a vague recollection of what he was talking about insofar as the movie, but was somewhat aware of the Bee Gees and their more recent hits. Mum was a huge fan and neither of my parents had really progressed past the 80s with their music and taste in movies, but I rarely took much notice of it. I lumped it all into what I considered '*80s – Gag me with a spoon, OK*'. I obviously made no recognition, in fact I know I didn't as I was too busy taking in his face, his hands, and the timbre of his voice. "I see I've met an 80s novice, this must be rectified immediately," he said. He looked thoughtful saying, "The theatre in Castlebrook is playing retro flicks all weekend. Would you like to go and see 'Saturday Night Fever' with me on Saturday," he asked, "assuming you are free?"

"Sure, I'm not doing anything Elijah, that would be great." It *would* be great. We could be hanging from the rooftops by our feet like bats for all I cared; he had *asked me out*!

"I'm glad you know who I am, I was wondering if I was being a little presumptuous by asking you before introducing myself. I wasn't sure you'd noticed me in class yesterday," he said.

"How could I not with your elegant arrival in History," I laughed, and he joined me. Mrs Kershaw walked back into the room at that point, and we realised our voices had been starting to carry.

"How do you want to do this?" he whispered.

"Can I get back to you at lunch?" I said in a hushed tone, motioning to Thunderfoot. Elijah nodded and went back to work.

It was nearly 8.30 am by this time. I knew the school buses would be arriving in about ten minutes. I wanted desperately to meet Michael and Bree's bus to tell them the news, but I couldn't just jump up and race out of the library, singing at the top of my lungs. In the vain attempt to cover my watching him through my down-turned lids, I faked several minutes of study. When 8.35 rolled around, I could sit there no longer. I tapped his hand and mouthed, *I have to go*.

Speak to you at lunch, he mouthed back with a wink. I nodded and scraped together my gear, dumping it unceremoniously into my bag. I sighed dreamily as I left the library. Knowing that Elijah and Lorien were 'A' students, I would see him in every one of my classes until lunch, except my electives. I wondered whether he had taken Music or French.

"Michael! Bree!" I called as soon as I saw them alight off the bus, the two of them chatting very animatedly. They looked up and waved, veering toward me.

"Not often we get a welcome from you," Bree said, looking over my shoulder for Simon. Simon lived in Woodbine, not far from Gracey, but they had a separate bus route, so Simon and Bree didn't travel together. A smile warmed her face, and I knew Simon was behind me. We all walked the few metres to the canteen, found a bench, and sat down.

"You will *never* guess what just happened," I challenged them. Michael looked at Bree and raised his eyebrows, Bree shrugged back.

"No idea Babe," Michael smiled. "You'd better tell us before you explode."

"Guess who I'm going to Castlebrook with this Saturday to see 'Saturday Night Fever'?" Peals of laughter were their immediate reaction, turning my excitement into confusion. "What?" I asked, a little taken aback.

"You… you…," sputtered Michael, "retro!" he finally managed to guffaw. Bree just sat there looking at me and laughing.

"Sorry Ash," she started, trying to get herself under control, "it's not something I've ever heard come out of your mouth," she said. Michael had managed to calm himself down and then they both realised I had a date.

"Who?" they chorused together.

"Elijah Standish," I said smugly. They looked at each other, eyes wide.

"Awright!" Michael said, standing to give me a high five. Simon sat there smirking.

"What?" I asked. "What do you know about him that I don't? I realise you two are *already* friends apparently."

"Nothing Ash," Simon started, "he's really a great guy, seems very genuine, both him and his brother. You're actually going out on a date; that has surprised me. I thought you may be batting for the other team," he finished, chuckling. Michael looked away, feigning interest in some thing or other in a nearby tree. *Brrriiiiinnnnnnnggggggg* the first bell of the morning sounded, right on 8.55 am.

"Well that's me off to French, see you guys later." With that, I headed back up to the left-hand side of the grounds.

Two periods, then a five-minute break, two more periods and then recess. Two *more* periods and then lunch. Would I ever get there? Why hadn't I thought to say recess instead of lunch? *But*, thinking further, *lunch would give us more time to talk.*

It was timetabled that I always had Music directly before or after lunch. Not good to be tormenting a violin with an empty stomach, nor a full one. I looked around the room, as I had in French, to see if my new love interest was seated anywhere. "Hey Ash, haven't seen you around today," greeted Keren as I took a seat beside her. She was another who formed part of our group.

"Hiya, K," I answered, "I was in early today, went to the library and then waited on Bree and Michael's bus to arrive." I neglected to tell her I had spent recess in the library, avoiding Elijah until lunch rolled around. Keren giggled.

"Yes, I heard quite quickly through the grapevine about your morning," she giggled again. "They're just *gorgeous* aren't they, you lucky thing!" She was looking distractedly over my shoulder and I turned abruptly, thinking I'd missed Elijah. I scanned the room, meeting the gaze of his twin instead. He offered a small wave and a smile. I returned the smile and twisted back around in my seat. Mr O'Dowd had just arrived.

"Afternoon class," he looked around the room. "Ah, I see we have one of the talented Standish twins in our presence," he noted, glancing at Lorien. "And which one might this be?" He looked to Lorien for a reply, but he didn't get the chance.

"It's Lorien Standish, Sir." Keren fidgeted around guiltily at the sound of her own voice answering his question.

"Thank you, Miss Kelly, I'm sure the young man knows who he is." With that, class commenced. I snuck a look over my shoulder to see Lorien's reaction. He shrugged his shoulders and raised his eyebrows, obviously unaware of Keren's crush on him.

"What was that all about?" I whispered to her. Mr O'Dowd was not the tyrant Thunderfoot was, but you didn't muck around in his class either.

"I like Elijah, but knowing he's taken..." Keren stared pointedly, if not amusingly, at me. "Lorien is also quite the dish don't you think?" her face revealing that she was wondering if others felt the same, already calculating her competition.

"One is enough for me," I grinned at her.

"Miss Mercy and Miss Kelly!" Mr O'Dowd yelled at us. "Do we need to cover this lesson over lunch?"

"No Sir," we both stammered and stuck our noses back into our theory books. I was *not* missing lunch for anything today.

As soon as the bell rang, I went to dash out of class. However, Mr O'Dowd asked to see me before I left. "Yes Sir?" I asked, thinking it was about the incident at the onset of the period.

"I am once again going to try and convince you to take part in our end of year festivities," he harrumphed. "As you know, you are the only violin in the school at an advanced enough level capable of partaking in the orchestral arrangements we wish to plan." I sighed.

"Sir, we've been through this so many times, I only took up an instrument in the first place because I *had* to as a requirement to take Music as an elective. I have no interest in public performances." I also neglected to mention that another reason I took Music was due to the massive crush I had on Scott Markham in Year 8. He was a brilliant clarinettist, and I worked every opportunity to be near him whenever I could. Yes, one of those unrequited loves, alas.

He looked at me, knocking a pen against his teeth. "Yes, I know Ashlyn. I was hoping however, I might have been able to change your mind. Have you decided on whether you're coming back next year?" he asked, taking me by surprise. I didn't see how the two conversations were not mutually exclusive.

"Ah, not really Mr O'Dowd, I'm still thinking on careers, and if I *do* choose teaching music, I'll still have the option of completing it through TAFE."

"I see," he sighed, "well at least it's something that you're still considering teaching as a career. See you tomorrow Miss Mercy." I bolted out the door.

I was in such a rush I didn't notice Lorien standing by the door outside. As I dashed past, fumbling in the process of trying to secure my bag, he grabbed my arm. "Where's the fire?" he asked.

"Hi Lorien, just trying to get to lunch with the gang," I answered, my voice sounding a little high and strained.

"Can I walk with you? If my brother has led me to understand correctly, we'll be both joining you all from now on. I hope that's OK?" he said.

"Oh, of course." This slowed my speed down to the usual playground pace. Our group of seven, now nine apparently, normally sat on the grassy area at the base of quad two near one of the Science demountables. It was our standard seating area and other junior students knew not to even try it on. Most of the Year 11 and 12s used the senior study, so technically, as far as outside during breaks went, we owned the school. I laughed to myself.

"Funny?" asked Lorien, looking at me with raised eyebrows. "Want to share?"

"Nothing in particular." He ran his hand through his tousled locks, pulling it back from his forehead. Within a few seconds, they were back in their original placement.

"I'm glad I had a chance to speak to you alone Ash, I wanted to ask you something." I looked at him inquisitively. "Are you going to Bree's party on Saturday night and if so, would you like to come with me?" Wow, what was it with these Standish twins? Neither of them ever seemed to have a nervous or stuttering moment in their life. It was as if they expected lemonade, not lemons - truly unique teens.

"Oh damn!" I answered and caught the puzzled look on his face. "Sorry Lorien, bad response to an acceptable question, I'd completely forgotten about Bree's party." My brow furrowed as I thought about how I was going to get out of this one with Bree. Strange that she hadn't mentioned it this morning when I told her about my date with Elijah. I continued to contemplate the issue in case she herself had overlooked it too. Bree was great, but she did not believe in breaking dates with her friends to spend time alone with Simon, and I knew she would expect the same consideration in return.

"So, does your silence mean yes or no?" Lorien pressed.

"I'm sorry Lorien, but it will have to be no, I already have plans."

"I thought that may be the case, being Wednesday already. I wish term had started a few weeks ago so I had the chance to be the first to ask," he said.

"Well, it's not that I already *have* a date for the party, I have other plans altogether. As I said, I'd forgotten about it." It was strange talking about dates for a party. It was usually just the seven of us with the occasional extra person or two. None of us ever brought 'dates' to any parties, it was just a group thing consisting of the already established couples and the rest of us.

We had nearly reached the other side of the grounds; Music to Science was always the greatest stretch. I could see Bree waving in the distance. "Will I see you there?" Lorien asked. "Perhaps you and your date can come after you've finished with your plans?" I could see Keren looking at us rather strangely, and then in a whoosh, Elijah was at our sides.

"Hey bro," he tousled Lorien's hair before turning to me with a smile. "Can we go over there for a few minutes before we join the rest of the group?"

"I see," Lorien smirked, "big brother beats me to it again." Before I had a chance to answer, Lorien joined the rest of my friends, sitting next to Cyndi Ashton, the last girl in our little collection. As always, she was joined at the hip to Frankie Oates, the other permanent couple in our group. Cyndi and Frankie rode the same bus as Simon. The two of them started chatting to Lorien and the others joined in.

"So," Elijah exhaled. He leant against the side of the Science demountable, his fingers resting in his pockets, one leg casually crossed over the other at the ankle. "What time, where do I pick you up, et cetera, et cetera, and so on..." He smiled as he waited on my answer.

"Well," I started, "firstly..."

"Firstly?" he said, his smile making the dimple play on his cheek.

"Yes, firstly," I continued, smiling back, "do you have your licence, would we be going with one of your parents, or possibly catching the train?" Castlebrook was about a forty-five minute car or train ride and I doubted he would have his Ps.

"In answer to your 'firstly', no, I don't get my licence until at least February and I would never *dream* of asking my parents. I thought we'd take the train if that's OK with you, unless you want to drive of course." He had obviously done his homework - I was impressed.

"This is your date Elijah. We can go in my car if you like, it would be more convenient."

"Actually, Miss Mercy, this is *our* date, and on second thought I would rather take the train, more time to talk and such," he concluded. "Now, what is the 'secondly' you were getting to?"

"I was wondering what time the movie starts. When I accepted your invitation this morning I'd forgotten about Bree's party the same evening." Could it have only been a few hours since Elijah asked me to go with him to the movies in three short days?

"Simon told me about the party in PE this morning, *also* mentioning our date that he seemed to know all about." I ducked my head, blushing. "I suggested we go to the matinee and we'd still have plenty of time to eat afterwards and make it back for the 8.00 pm kick off. How's that sound to you?"

"Wonderful," I breathed. He was looking into my eyes so deeply, I wasn't actually sure I'd responded. I cleared my throat and told him it was fine. "Shall I pick you up or would you rather meet me at the station?"

"I'll walk from home, it's not that far, but I'll need a ride home from the party, if *that* is OK." While waiting for my answer, he reached up casually and brushed my cheek with his fingertips. "I'm really looking forward to this Ash."

"Me too."

"Hey Standish!" called Frankie. "Are you gonna choke down some chow and join us or stand there hanging off Mercy all afternoon?" Frankie started throwing the football he held to Simon, and Lorien got up to join the game, spacing themselves across the grassy expanse.

"Coming!" yelled Elijah, about to speed off to the boys. He hesitated, turning briefly back to me. "10.30 am at the station then?" he confirmed. I nodded. He leant down to kiss my lips gently; I couldn't believe what was happening. He drew back grinning, still looking at me as he started to run over to the boys. Regardless of my state of euphoria, I noticed the look on Lorien's face, and I felt a little bad. But, what could I do? *Keren will fix him up*, I consoled myself as I walked back to the table, joining the girls and Michael.

Before I'd even had a chance to sit down, Keren asked why Lorien waited for me after Music. I didn't want to hurt her feelings so told her a small white lie about catching up with some of the theory he'd missed. "Whew," she said, "I thought you were going to monopolise them both for a minute."

"She wishes," Michael said, and I smacked him with my lunchbox.

It was difficult to sit there and eat, knowing such an Adonis was behind me playing football, but I refused to look around and stare as the rest of the table was doing - even the taken girls. I laughed to myself, smiling only fleetingly on the outside. Saturday was going to take *forever* to arrive.

At the Flicks

Music Selection: Lionel Ritchie, 'Hello'
Diary Entry: We have shared so much in my daydreams, capturing the solitariness of being together. When I let my mind wander, I imagine the kisses we share, simply thousands of them.

I PULLED INTO THE TRAIN STATION CARPARK at 10.15 am on Saturday, knowing that I was a little too early. Too early, too eager... but Elijah was already there. "Hey Ash," he called, approaching the car.

"Hi," I said as I got out, the door held open ceremoniously by Elijah. I turned and locked it manually, no central locking on this baby. "Have you been waiting long?"

"Just got here. I left a little earlier in case it took me longer than I expected." I sincerely doubted this as it was a hot day for October and there was not a sweat mark on him - clothing or skin. Whilst I was thinking this, he leant down and kissed me. I felt a little awkward standing in the station carpark on a Saturday morning being kissed by such a handsome boy. "Does that make you uncomfortable?" he asked, a little perplexed. "I'll give you more warning if you prefer," he said, "but I can't promise it won't happen again." His confident smile returned, playing the dimple, which was my greatest weakness. I blushed; I wasn't used to such a display of public affection. He laughed and took my hand, leading me to the stairs to take us to the other side of the platform.

"Wait, I need to tap my card," I stopped him.

"All taken care of Ash, today is on me." I smiled, excited at the gloriousness this day could become.

The train arrived on time and there were very few people in the carriages so we had our choice of where we could sit. "How about here," he suggested. He'd selected an area with only two three-seater pods, the middle level before ascending or descending to the other floors in the carriage. "More private," he said, letting me have the window seat. I argued that he should take it, being new to the region and all. "I have my landscape right here." I didn't know what to say to that so sat down and looked briefly out the window. The train started to move.

We chatted for fifteen minutes or so about nothing in particular - school, our friends, and things we liked to do. I found out he was a keen surfer and told him about the three wonderful beaches at Castlebrook. "I prefer South Castlebrook because of the rock pools and snorkelling. The two beaches further north are popular with surfers," I said.

"Do you surf?" he asked, slinging his arm across my shoulders and drawing me close. My barking laugh surprised him, so I explained about my levels of ability and therefore I'd never bothered to try. "Well you must come with me one weekend, and you *shall* try. You have to find out whether or not you can. Because if you can, it is the greatest thing on earth, well, one of the top two," he tipped me a wink. "I'm sorry," he'd picked up on my discomfort, not that I realised I'd emitted any. "I don't mean to be so vulgar; it's just my way when I'm unsure of myself." It was hard to believe he could ever harbour self-doubt, or that certainly *I* was capable of making him feel that way.

We sat in silence for a while, a comfortable silence. Eventually, he pulled me slightly closer and nestled his chin to my hair. "I really like you Ash," he confessed. "I want us to get to know each other better."

"I would like that too Elijah." Seriously, if there were a feather floating around the cabin, you *would* have knocked me over with it and if I'd been standing at the time, I think my legs would have buckled. Whilst going over these thoughts in my head, I felt his gaze on me. I looked up to see his blue eyes directed into mine. His face broke into a sunny smile, his eyes crinkling which I found infectious. As his smile slowly faded, he whispered,

"Can I kiss you Ash?"

"Do you usually ask?"

"Well, after last time…" he trailed off. "No, not usually, I go with my instincts as a rule," he answered, his voice lowered. He cleared his throat and angled toward me further, bringing his other arm up to complete the embrace. I sat there waiting; still not comprehending this was actually happening. Where did he come from? Would he disappear just as quickly?

He kissed me softly but lingeringly. It was a sweet kiss, a heart-thrumming kiss. I knew if he kept kissing me like that, I would literally ooze through the seats onto the floor like molten caramel. I wasn't sure how long he sat holding me, trading angelic kisses, but it was not long enough. He finally looked up and drew slightly away. "We're nearly there," he said. "Next stop I think."

"Huzza?" was all I could respond. *Nice one Ash! Pull yourself together girl.* He grinned at me and cupped my chin, pulling me in for one last kiss as the train started its slow stopping procedure.

I kept my eyes downcast for a few minutes, as I couldn't look into his without breaking into a jubilant grin. I pretended to go through the items in my pockets and bag to make sure I had everything. He seemed not to notice, or was too chivalrous to make point. As we stood to alight from the train, he casually took my hand. What a way for our day to start.

Even with the final light-rail ride to get to the centre of town, we were still about an hour too early for the matinee. It didn't start until 12.15 pm, so I took him for a walk to the beaches. We could see two beaches from a sole vantage point, with the other only needing to be pointed out around the hillside blocking our view. We leant over the railing watching the surf. "Whoa, awesome left-hander that guy just missed! Do you get many drop-ins here?" he asked.

"Ah, you're talking to me like I'm supposed to understand you, but I don't think it's English you're speaking," I said, pretending to frown.

"That's it," he chortled, "you're *definitely* coming with me one weekend." I sincerely hoped so.

We slowly made our way down the main drag, ambling closer to the cinema, but in no rush. Conversation once again came easily, as did the occasional silences. He really was an easy-going and comfortable person to be around, making me even more attracted to him. Perhaps it was *our* chemistry at work, but I sighed, knowing he was comfortable with everyone in his presence, as was his twin.

We arrived at the cinema with about ten minutes to spare. The lines were not long at the Candy Bar, so we had popcorn and drinks within a few minutes and were in our pre-selected seats before the ads even started to roll. I noticed Elijah had picked the far corner of the back row. It was funny in hindsight, realising how few people were actually in the cinema with us when the movie started. "So," he looked at me quizzically, "why do you locals call this the *cinema* instead of the theatre?" he asked.

"I would've thought a big-city boy like you would know the answer to that," I said, eyebrows raised.

"Nope, we called it 'the theatre', 'the flicks', or 'the movies' where I came from. As in we're going to the 'theatre' to see a 'flick' or a 'movie'. 'Cinema' sounds like it came from another century," he teased.

"I believe the subtle difference is that theatre encompasses live action, whereas the cinema is reel to reel. How's that for an answer?"

"Perfect," he said, and lowered his arm around my shoulders as the lights dimmed, signalling the start of the 'flick'.

"Is that *John Travolta*?" I whispered incredulously a few minutes later. Elijah smiled and nodded, although we could have spoken in normal tones, as there was no one in our immediate vicinity. It was just as well too, because when the 'ah, ahs' started in the chorus of the opening song, I laughed out loud, realising what Elijah had been alluding to that morning in the library. He obviously understood, as he laughed with me, squeezing my shoulders.

I got right into it, having had no idea that a *musical* could have such an interesting storyline. "When was this made?" I asked. The John Travolta from the movies I'd seen him in was a larger-faced, older man, although still with a ghosting of the good looks he held from his youth.

"Late 70s, around 77 – 78."

"How do you *know* this?"

"I told you," he laughed, "my time-warped parents. Speaking of which, have you seen 'Rocky Horror'?"

"Yes," I laughed quietly, I knew what the 'Time Warp' was and hence understood his connotation. I continued to watch, surrendering fully to this new movie genre. Well, new to me at least. I could get used to this, and smiled, thinking of what Michael and Bree's reaction would be to *that* little revelation.

Sometime later, I leant over to ask him when 'Grease' came out and his eyes were already fixed on me; my mouth snapped shut. He chuckled and pulled me closer. "Can I kiss you again?" he whispered in my ear, brushing his cheek against my hair, waiting on my reply.

"You can stop asking me that you know," I answered breathlessly.

"I do it for the reaction now," he smiled. He drew in and kissed me, as sweetly as on the train and I sighed contentedly and leant back into his shoulder. I was in heaven.

"What were you going to ask me in the theatre, before I caught you off guard?" he asked whilst we were waiting for our meals at the nearby restaurant. Even full of popcorn, I still found myself wanting lunch.

"Oh, ahhh…" I said thinking back, desperately trying to reclaim the moment. I didn't want him to think he had mind-altering powers over me. "'Grease'," I managed to spit out finally. "When was it made?" I sipped on the coke that had just arrived.

"About the same time," he said thoughtfully, "77 – 78, although I know 'Saturday Night Fever' was first." I was still sucking on my straw; I didn't realise how dry I was. "Thirsty?" he grinned, rubbing his lips, "I must admit I am too." Removing his straw, he lifted the glass to his mouth and drank deeply.

Our food arrived and we tucked in. I found I couldn't eat very much after all, but Elijah finished his plate and mine. "I love a man with a good appetite," I said, a little embarrassed at my bravado.

"I'm counting on it." He threw me a quick smile and went to pay the cashier.

So there we were again, walking casually down the main street, no particular destination in mind when he asked me what I wanted to do. "It's still only 3.30 pm. The party doesn't start until 8.00 so we have heaps of time."

"I don't know," I answered. I hadn't really given it much thought. Just *being* with him was enough to make me happy, not that I was about to tell *him* that. Actually, I could think of *many* things we could do, but I vanquished those thoughts back to where they came from. And, I wasn't talking sex. I could just stay lip-locked to him until our poor sore lips made us stop before they could fail us. I tried to hide my smile. I wasn't sure whether I was successful or not as he seemed to notice everything. If he did see and understand it, he didn't let on. I was starting to think he *was* that considerate. He chose when to make the 'unknowing' obvious, helping me avoid my discomfort. "We can go back and hang out at my place until it's time to go if you like," he suggested.

"That sounds great," and I was really enthused. I wanted a chance to see inside the school residence, find out what alterations had been made since the dimming memories I still possessed of pre-teen parties held there by previous owners.

We caught the light-rail back to the station and took the next train home. The good thing about Sommersett train station being a large interchange, it meant all the trains travelling from Castlebrook to Sydney stopped there, so it made no difference which one we caught.

This time he positioned himself opposite me, but still in the same area that we'd chosen before. He sat with my hands in his, and once again, conversation flowed easily. I pressed him about the twin thing; I had a genuine curiosity about them, as I'd never met any before. "What do you want to know?" he asked.

"Well, do you feel each other's pain?"

"Nope."

"Is there an evil twin and a good twin?" This made him laugh loudly.

"Yes, there is, and guess which one *I* am," he asked lecherously. I laughed with him.

"What about Lorien?"

"What about him?"

"I don't know him very well, are you alike at all? You certainly don't look very much alike."

"Hmmm," he considered, "that's a complicated one and in many varying ways... Let me see if I can get this out right so you can understand it." He thought a little longer. "Lorien and I don't think we're very much alike, although we do share common things and interests at times..."

"Such as?" I interrupted.

"Music, sports, pretty much standard sixteen year old stuff I guess."

"But that's because of your ages, not so much of a twin thing," I prompted.

"Yes and no, this is where it can get complicated. I love all sports, and can easily waste an afternoon watching cable TV, game, after game, after game. Lorien can't stand watching sports, but playing or discussing them is another thing. On the other hand we both also love music, all types of music, as you saw today," he stopped and smiled. "But I would never *dream* of going to the 'theatre' as you explained it, nor to an opera or the symphony, anything like that - whereas Lorien would be the first online buying tickets. I'll listen to it at home though. Am I making sense?"

"Yes," I drawled, "I *think* I'm getting you."

"It can be the same with girls sometimes too." I started to feel uncomfortable, thinking how Lorien had asked me to Bree's party when all I could say was no. Whether Elijah and I had planned on going or not, not that we'd even discussed the party at that stage, I still couldn't have gone with Lorien. I went to tell Elijah about this, feeling it should be out in the open. As I opened my mouth to speak, Elijah stopped me, obviously concerned about the worry on my face. "It's OK Ash, Lorien told me about asking you to Bree's party tonight."

"He *did*?" I asked.

"Of course, you know - the twin thing. There is very little we keep to ourselves. Pointless really. Not that we can read each other's minds or anything, but we're more attuned to how each other is feeling than your run-of-the-mill siblings."

"So what did you mean about it being that way with girls?" He'd lost me on that one.

"On occasion Lorien will end up with a girl that is meant to be with me, and vice versa. It usually sorts itself out though with all the pieces ending up back in the right box, for want of a better analogy," he grinned, which faltered as quickly as it hit his lips. "Oh hey Ash, that came out really dumb. I'm sorry." I didn't give him a chance to continue.

"So you're telling me you just *trade off* when you realise you have each other's property? Say in six months you could be handing me over to Lorien, apologising for getting in too quick. I was *always* his in the first place?" I couldn't believe the tone I was hearing come out of my mouth, but I wanted him to deny, deny, *deny.* The possibility was too much to bear.

Elijah moved over next to me and began rubbing my back, apologising again. "I'm so sorry Ash. I didn't mean for it to come out that way. It happens, but rarely, not every chance we get. And, it is fate; there's nothing either of us can do about it. One thing I can tell you for sure, I won't be passing *you* onto Lorien without a fight. In all honesty," he paused to turn my face to his, "I've never felt *this* strongly about a girl before." He stopped, smiled wanly and swallowed, waiting on my reaction.

"Oh Elijah," I cried and kissed him. He didn't even see it coming. After a few seconds, the urgency settled, and the kisses were sweet and searching. He pulled my face away and smiled at me.

"You didn't ask first." Before I had a chance to respond, we were locked as one again.

I could hear a lilting melody being played on either a keyboard or maybe a synthesizer before Elijah even opened his front door. It was something I didn't recognise. As if hearing *my* thoughts he said, "Lorien's latest composition." This is what Mr O'Dowd was obviously referring to when he made the comment *'we have one of the talented Standish twins in our presence'.*

"Wow, he's brilliant," I said, impressed. As we entered the lounge, I looked around with interest. "Your parents have made a lot of renovations since I was last here. It looks like a totally different house." I was also amazed at the many vases brimming with a variety of fresh flowers that filled the room.

"I never stopped to think you've already been here, but I suppose it was inevitable. Want something to drink?"

"Not just yet, take me on a tour of the house first." He took my hand and led me toward the opening of the kitchen.

"Not much to see down here that you can't see already," he started. He was right. They had managed to turn the main downstairs area into a massive, open-planned room. Rugs and screens separated the dining area from the lounge and the lounge from what appeared to be a family or rumpus room to the rear. I could see a pool table and stereo along the back wall and what must have been *thousands* of CDs. The kitchen still had a half wall and an island benchtop was at the centre, surrounded by high-backed stools. On the eastern wall, partly between the dining and kitchen, double sliding glass doors opened onto a massive Queenslander verandah, as was the style at the time when this house was built.

A barbeque and comfortable patio setting were positioned to make the most of the available space. The wooden floorboards had been covered in black slate pavers. Mrs Standish had evenly spaced large pots holding mature tree ferns and palms along its length, obscuring most of the lattice siding affixed to the railings. She had turned it into an outdoor conservatory, tropical and tranquil. This side of their house backed onto a buffer of bushland, so it was secluded and private from the residents living behind them.

We continued around the verandah to the northern side. This sunny spot opened onto the gardens below, understanding where the blossoms inside the house had come from. The garden would keep Mrs Standish's vases full for quite some time as many of the plants were only just budding. A pair of wicker sun lounges made their presence known by the fat colourful cushioned covers. They looked welcoming and I could imagine Mr Standish falling asleep on one with the Sunday paper strewn across his lap.

Elijah slid open another double glass door, taking us into the back of the house. "The bathroom," he said, pointing to his left, "and laundry," pointing to his right. We continued down the small hall that led us into the rumpus room I'd seen from the front door when we arrived.

"This is great, so spacious and homey," I told him. "Do you like living here?"

"We all love it although we miss the heart of a big city at times. We were in a two-bedroom villa before, this is the first time Lorien and I have had our own rooms. There is *nothing* better than that," he answered, a little mischievously. He then guided me toward a set of stairs on the western wall. "Floor two!"

"This storey was only added about five years ago," I told him. "It used to be several large rooms, all downstairs."

"I know. Dad ripped the guts out of the bottom floor when we bought it. Mum loves open spaces, and she can't get enough of them these days."

"At one stage of ownership back in the 1950s, the headmaster had so many kids the verandahs were shut in to accommodate their sleeping arrangements," I said. Elijah laughed saying,

"Now that's pushing the idea of wanting your own bedroom. If we'd tried that in our villa, we would've been lucky to get one single bed into the balcony space, let alone all the junk Lorien and I have accumulated."

He led me upstairs. "Mum and Dad's room," he pointed to the door on his left. As it seemed to be the only room on this side of the staircase, it must have taken up half of the floor.

"Room or suite?" I asked.

"Suite I suppose. They have a walk-in wardrobe and an ensuite. I'll show you." He opened the door on what I considered a five-star hotel room. A king-sized canopy bed took pride of place with a massive dresser, writing desk and bookcase. The curtains and bedding were a matching soft bronze, which worked wonderfully with the white carpet. The upholstery on the Louis XIV styled chairs sitting between the bookcase and desk tied the room in with their light shades of russet, picking up the subtle colours shared in the elaborate oil paintings adorning the walls. The woodwork in the bedframe and other furniture was a deep mahogany, continuing the warmth and feel of this century's old-styled room. It was odd to see a laptop on the desk and a plasma TV bracketed to the wall; they looked so out of place.

Elijah went to direct me into the room, and I hesitated, worrying that my shoes were dirty. "No, not today," I glanced down, and he took my meaning.

"You don't have to worry about that." But, there was no reason to enter *this* room. We turned around and continued. "Lori's room," he said, pointing to another door, "and..." he said, swinging open the door we stood in front of, "my room."

I stood there amazed at the size of the bedroom. Although less than half the size of his parents' room, it was still huge. His colour scheme was mostly shades of blue, whites and yellows with a little red thrown in for good measure. Centred against the far wall was a double bed, and another entire wall was cupboard space. He shoved a few things under the bed with his foot whilst I looked around. I checked out his desk, another laptop humming away. Magazines, textbooks and fiction books lined the bookcase, somewhat neatly. He pulled open the vertical blinds and opened the windows to let in some sun and air. "Have a seat," he offered. I looked at the bed and then at the comfortable looking pappadum chair in the corner. I chose the chair and tried to climb into it as gracefully as I could. He perched himself on the computer chair at the desk. Swinging himself lazily from side to side he asked, "What do you think?"

"Modelled on a beach theme?" I asked, noticing his board lying against the wall.

"Yep," he smiled. "Give Mum the idea and there's no stopping her. You should see Lori's room, all blacks, reds and whites. Typical muso," he scoffed, not unkindly. "Now just remember if you use this bathroom it's interconnecting between our two rooms. We never bother to lock each other's side when we use it, but you may want to remember that if you don't want Lorien bursting in on you unannounced," he laughed.

"Speaking of which," I sat up and struggled from the chair, "I'll put that knowledge to good use now."

I entered the bathroom and was careful to lock the door on Lorien's side, and Elijah's. As I used the facilities, I looked around; there was no greater tell-tale than a male's personal space. I wanted desperately to look through the cabinets that lined the walls under the huge, mirrored wall but restrained myself. I did check out the products and colognes on the bench as I washed my hands though. Good taste, *expensive* taste. I realised they were probably unaware that most sixteen year old schoolboys were not as upper class with their choice of scents and accessories. I took the lid off the closest bottle and sniffed. This must be Lorien's; it didn't smell like Elijah. I tried to wrap my tongue around the pronunciation - Issy me-yak. I laughed, thinking of cologne for yaks.

I remembered to unlock both doors as I went to leave the bathroom. I was tempted to peek through into Lorien's room as the beautiful melody I heard when we arrived was still playing. I once again restrained myself and slid the bathroom door shut behind me.

Elijah was sitting on the bed. He patted the space next to him. "Hmm, this is your parents' home; I think I'd better stand," I said. He joined me in the centre of the room, catching me by surprise when he lifted me off the ground and swung me around.

"You know, you're not the first girl I've had in here," he teased, putting me back on my feet.

"Oh, is that a fact."

"Yeah, Mum comes in here to clean now and then." He laughed, thinking himself hilarious. I rolled my eyes at him then took his hands, once again amazed at my own bravado. "Come here," he growled and dragged me to him, enveloping me in his arms and kissing me intensely. "You taste wonderful," he breathed into my ear when the fervour had passed.

We stood there cuddling, him tracing my outer ear with his lips, purring directly into my ear. He was driving me crazy, but it was a good crazy. Shrouded in our private bubble, I was remiss in drawing away from him in time when I realised there had been a slight knock at the door. Lorien was now standing in the doorway. I should have been keeping myself attuned to his music more carefully to avoid this unexpected encounter.

"Oops, sorry bro." He backed out guiltily, but not before adding, "Four out of five dentists say that's bad for your enamel." Elijah was not quick enough to hit him with the pillow he threw at his retreating brother.

I sat on the bed feeling nervous and guilty, not exactly sure why. Because I was in a boy's room alone? That we'd been busted kissing? Elijah turned and saw my face. "Don't worry about Lori," he said, "It's all OK, OK?" I nodded, still feeling weird. I heard an engine stop and two car doors thumping shut. "Mum and Dad are home." He came toward me again, and I could tell by the look on his face it was *not* to lead me back downstairs.

"Elijah! *What* are you doing?" I asked, pushing his hands from my waist. "Your *parents* are downstairs."

"Eli? Lori?" I heard their Mum call. "Are you home? Who owns the car in the driveway?" I heard Lorien's door open and close, and he trundled down the stairs. Elijah didn't make a move.

"Don't I get one more kiss before this sweet, sweet afternoon turns into night?" he asked, sidling towards me again, pouting.

"You must be kidding!" I said. He laughed again and took me by surprise once more by swinging me in his arms.

"You need to remember Ash, *my* parents only have sons. They aren't too stressed about us coming home pregnant," he chuckled. "Just one more quickie," he sighed, our lips forming a seal, not giving me a chance to argue.

That 'quickie' went on until his mother finally broke the cloud by calling up the stairs, "Eli, will you *please* show your guest the proper hospitality by bringing her down to meet the *rest* of the family." There was a hint of amusement in her voice.

"How embarrassing, this is my History teacher," I mumbled.

"How embarrassing," he mocked, "this is my mother." He smirked at me. "C'mon," he said, dropping his hand from my waist and taking my hand.

"Hang on one sec," I pulled him back. "I just need a minute, to ahhh, assess the damage." He laughed and leant against the door, waiting until I was composed.

Bree's Place

Music Selection: Wham, 'Wake Me Up Before You Go Go'
Diary Entry: You make all of my days full of sunshine, igniting me from a smoulder to a burning heat. My rapid heartbeat will never return to normal – I certainly can't imagine it.

IT WAS AROUND 7.30 pm when I suggested we should make a move. I had a great meal with the Standish family. You could see they were very close. Mr Standish was a wonderful man, full of news and jokes, obviously enjoying the additional moments he could now spend with his family. Unfortunately, he'd had to leave for work about an hour ago. Such was the life of an on-call Mine Manager in the Hunter Valley. "I assume you'll be going with Ashlyn and Eli too, Lori?" his Mum asked.

"Mum," Elijah reminded, "I'm supposed to be on a *date* here!" Lorien looked relieved.

"OK Eli, don't bust a gasket, it was just a suggestion," she apologised. I thought about it and it did seem a wasted trip for Mrs Standish to take Lorien separately when I *was* already taking Elijah there and home. I looked at Elijah, shrugged, and raised one eyebrow, asking him to think about it.

"Good one Mum," he said, "looks like we're taking little brother with us."

"I'm sure there's nothing you'd be doing alone in the car that you can't still do with your brother there, hmmm?" she questioned Elijah lightly.

"Come on then, let's go." He had resigned himself to the fact there would now be three of us.

I thanked Mrs Standish for a lovely evening and complimented her once again on her beautiful home and grounds. "Come around anytime Ashlyn," she smiled at me. "And I'm always here to help with your history." I waited for the boys at the front door whilst they gave their mother a peck on the cheek. I also happened to catch the grimace Lorien threw her. She grinned and gave his hair a quick tousle. "Have a great time kids. See you in the morning boys." She followed us to the door.

"Wow, she's not even worried about a curfew?" I asked as we all climbed into the car.

"She knows where we are," Elijah said, fastening his seatbelt, "but what about *your* curfew?"

"'Man-child', you are looking at an *older* woman. I haven't had a curfew since I was *sixteen*." I made sure I emphasised the age since they still were sixteen.

"So what are you then, thirty?" he laughed. Lorien chuckled in the background too.

"Funny, very funny." I realised they *knew* I was seventeen. I wouldn't be driving this car otherwise. "What is the date of the Wonder Twins' birthday, when *you* will be seventeen?" I asked as I gunned the engine, giving it a couple of revs before slowly reversing down the driveway. We raised our hands to wave back at Mrs Standish before she closed the front door.

"I'm not sure I can give you that information," Elijah said, "it's a little embarrassing."

"How can a birth date be embarrassing?" I asked.

"It's Valentine's Day," answered Lorien to save his brother the trouble.

"Aquarians then," I delighted.

"Does that make us compatible?" he asked, taking my left hand in his right. Luckily, the car was an automatic.

"Perhaps," I said. He raised and dropped his eyebrows several times,

"Wroof!"

If you believed in astrology, that made us very compatible actually. Leo was a fire sign and Aquarius, air. Air fanned fire – fire needed air to blossom whereas technically the earth and water signs extinguished it. This thought gave me a sudden gush of warmth; the stars were on our side.

It was hard to remember Lorien was still in the back. As if he read my mind, Elijah looked over his shoulder at his twin sitting directly behind me. "You don't have to pretend to be invisible Lori. It's OK," he said, before turning to me and adding in a lower voice, "if not a little inconvenient." Lorien obviously chose to ignore his brother's comment, as did I.

"Eli tells me you're not much of an 80s aficionado," he said.

"I have been *relatively* successful in my attempts to ignore the 80s, with no help in this endeavour from my friends," I threw across my shoulder.

"You know," started Elijah, "'Saturday Night Fever' is from the 70s and doesn't really count." He grinned at his brother on the back seat. "Think we'll try 'Flashdance' next time."

"Now *that's* more like it, hot-bodied hotties!" Lorien growled.

"Oh yeah!" added Elijah as he twisted in his seat to lightly knuckle-punch his brother's extended fist. The motion of their movements brought a further question from Lorien.

"You called us the 'Wonder Twins' before. I'm surprised you know the 'Superfriends' cartoon." I glanced into my rear-vision mirror to see him looking at me. I was once a kid too and we had so many American TV shows aired in Australia. It was impossible not to know of the Superfriends show with Wonder Woman, Aquaman, Batman, Robin, Superman and of course the Wonder Twins – one male and one female.

"Well *Zan*, or is it Jayna?" I ribbed him, naming the characters and showing I understood who they were.

"Jayna," Elijah quickly answered for him, laughing uproariously. Elijah had named his twin as the female. "She's got you covered on this one bro." Lorien was trying not to smile.

"I suggest you bump your own two fists together Lorien and 'activate' - let me drive." I said, also laughing.

I then sat thoughtful for a moment, pondering the twin thing a little further. I looked up and saw Lorien studying me in the rear-view mirror again. "Questions?" he asked, curiosity getting the better of him. I didn't have a chance to get any further comment out as Elijah interrupted me, laughing again.

"Lori, I didn't get a chance to tell you about our conversation on the train." He looked at me and I rolled my eyes, not stopping him, waiting for the teasing to start. He understood I didn't have a problem being ridiculed to his brother, so he continued. "She asked," he tried, still laughing, "asked me if…" but he was off in hilarity-land again.

"I *asked* him..." I said, frowning at Elijah as I addressed Lorien, "whether there was an evil twin and a good twin." Lorien laughed along with his brother. "I'm assuming that *is* what you were going to tell him Elijah?"

"He's the evil one," Lorien said, still laughing.

"That's what he alluded to, too." I was enjoying their amusement, albeit it at my expense.

"I assume you've not met twins before Ash?" asked Lorien.

"No, never. It's a little intriguing."

"So what else do you want to know?" they asked in unison. That set us all off laughing again. I was glad the atmosphere was relaxed and comfortable.

"Your names," I said.

"What about them?" again in chorus.

"You guys are a little weird, you know that?" I offered to them light-heartedly. They were both smiling at me, waiting for me to continue my point. "Well, you hear a lot of unusual names for twins, especially nick-names." I thought back to Michael's examples when he rang the evening after the first day back at school.

"Such as?" asked Elijah, his interest unwavering.

"Depending on gender of course; Bill and Ben, Bonnie and Clyde, Bob and Not Bob, Luke and Darth, Jesus and Judas, Thelma and Louise..." I trailed off.

"Those not being the nick-names, but the serious ones?" Elijah asked. Lorien laughed again. "Shush Thelma; the lady is still making her point."

"I think it's amazing she can rattle out so many off the top of her head, considering we're the first she's met," pointed out Lorien with a smile.

"Oh, I know plenty more labels," and I gave them Michael's examples. They both laughed hysterically, me along with them.

"Paper and plastic!" cried Elijah. "That's a new one to me!"

"Bag's I'm paper!" They both called together.

As our laughter subsided, Lorien brought me back to where I was going with this, prompting me to continue. They were both very engrossed. "I was wondering where your two names came from, I mean, why your parents called you Elijah and Lorien. I assume they're family names?"

"Take it Lori," Elijah directed from the front seat with a grandiose wave of his hand. I heard Lorien sigh, he'd obviously been asked this a lot.

"Mum was into her dark-ages period when we were born. Originally they'd planned to call us Jackson and Lachlan if you can imagine that." I looked at Elijah. He pointed to himself,

"Lachlan."

"Or even David and Jason before they got more creative," Lorien added.

"Jason," Elijah pointed to himself again.

"However, when it was time to name us, thanks to her history background, I got my name and Eli got his," Lorien finished.

"But what do they mean?" I asked. I heard Lorien sigh again.

"Elijah is Hebrew in origin and means 'the Lord is my God'."
Typical I thought, thinking of how I had labelled him God-like only a few
days ago. What a God!

"And?"

"Lorien..." he continued, shooting his brother a grimace, "is from J
R R Tolkien, he was the 'God of dreams'. In some instances it's referred
to in the Latin derivative of a laurel plant too, but Mum chose it because of
Tolkien."

"Where is it used in Tolkien?" I asked.

"Lorien is the name of one of the Valar in his lore of middle-earth."
I looked quizzically at him, not recognising the subject matter.

"'Lord of the Rings' to you and me," Elijah interjected.

"Impressive!" I *was* impressed.

"It could have been worse. Lorien is also more commonly known
as Irmo," he added. "I can *just* live with Lorien. I don't know what I
would've done with Irmo!" We had hysterics again.

"Two Gods hey?" I pointed out a few minutes later. "Lucky me."

"Come on then," incited Elijah, "give us *your* name's meaning,
Ashlyn."

"It simply means 'to dream'." Not much fun they could poke at
that one.

"So we have two Gods and two dreamers in the car," Elijah
recapped, "just don't fall asleep at the wheel OK?"

"Not a chance," I assured him, "we have the key with us."

"The key?" he asked.

"Lorien, the 'God of dreams'. Only he connects us all," I
surmised.

"Oh man," he muttered from the back seat.

"Not on your life, little brother! You aren't connecting with us two." We had stopped in Bree's driveway at this point, and I was in the process of unbuckling my seat belt. The two of them tore out of the car and the chase began. Eventually they walked back to the car with their arms slung casually around each other's shoulders, laughing. It had been an even tussle.

Bree, Michael and Keren were standing outside the front door watching with amusement. "Hey Ash," sang Michael. "What's going on?" Both he and Bree looked at me with an inflection in their eye, Keren only looked at Lorien.

"Hi," the twins chorused as they neared. Elijah trickled his arm around my waist.

"Lead us to the party people Breezy," Elijah said. Bree scowled at him. "Whoa, wrong words?" he looked at me.

"You don't want to be calling her that!" Michael answered, waggling his finger. "It's a *big* no-no."

"Noted," Elijah promised, smiling.

"Come in you boneheads," Bree said. "Simon, Cyndi and Frankie are downstairs." She started to lead the way.

"Hang on Bree, I'm just going to say hi to your folks."

"Sure, you know the way."

"I'll be back in a second," I told Elijah when I noticed they were both climbing the stairs with me.

"No, no, no," he corrected, "we *always* meet the parents. It's what keeps our pristine reputations untarnished." I looked at Lorien. He shrugged his shoulders and circled a halo a few centimetres above his head.

"We have good manners I guess," he explained, so I took the twins to meet Mr and Mrs Swain.

Keren was still standing at the front door. I felt terrible, as no one had really paid her any mind due to the merriment of our entrance. I know she would have been thinking that Lorien hadn't singled her out, even momentarily. She had all night to make her mark; there was no other unattached girl here, so she certainly had her chance laid out in front of her.

Bree's home was split-level. Her room, a spare bedroom, bathroom and the rumpus room was downstairs. The upstairs consisted of the rest of the family quarters. I led the boys upstairs and found Mr and Mrs Swain at the kitchen counter. Their twelve-year-old daughter Sara ran at me, throwing soapy arms around my waist. "Hi Ash, I haven't seen you since the holidays," she complained.

"What, last weekend wasn't it?" I rebuked her playfully, planting a kiss on the top of her head. She looked up to see whom I'd brought with me.

"Wow!" she exclaimed, her eyes huge. "What a pair of spunks!" Mr and Mrs Swain looked over at the twins, trying to hide their grins. The boys were also struggling to hold their composure. I guessed this was partially why they were both such confident and composed young men. They were used to the adoration of the female kind, taking it all in their nonchalant stride. "Are they *both* with you?" she asked in awe, still holding onto my waist.

"Back to the dishes," Mr Swain told her gruffly.

"But..." she stammered, not taking her eyes off the twins for a second. She stared at Elijah, and then at Lorien - back and forth, back and forth...

"Now!" her father commanded, pointing toward the sudsy sink.

"Wow," she muttered again softly as she resumed her position, plunging her hands back into the soapy water where she continued to watch them over her shoulder.

"This is Elijah and Lorien Standish," I introduced them to the Swains, pointing to each twin in turn. "These are Bree's parents, Mr and Mrs Swain." I pronounced Swain carefully, deliberately swallowing the 'n' on the end of their name, hoping Elijah would get the gist of Bree's mood outside. Poor Bree, she'd been called Breezy Breezeway all of her pre-teen life and was pretty much over it. Because of the embarrassment they knew it caused their eldest daughter, they usually reintroduced themselves to new company with their first names. They did not disappoint me.

"Al and Siobhan," Mr Swain extended his hand, and both of the boys shook it in turn.

"You know where everything is Ashlyn. Make sure you show the boys around - make yourselves at home," Siobhan instructed. The twins smiled at her. A hand slapped onto each of their outer shoulders, causing them to jump. It was Simon.

"Hi lads," he greeted the twins. To Siobhan he said, "Bree sent me up on reconnaissance, thought someone may have side-tracked the troops with their latest embroidered pillow." Siobhan smacked him with the tea towel as he patted her on top of her head. Simon was very comfortable with the Swains, as he'd been going out with Bree since Year

7 and often referred to Siobhan as his mother-in-law, and Bree as the old ball and chain. He also called them this to their faces, which did not always go down well with Bree.

"Go on Simon, get out of my hair," Siobhan pointed back to the stairs.

"Let's go," he snickered, avoiding her on the way past. I looked up toward the sink again, having forgotten Sara for the moment. She hadn't moved. The twins said goodbye to her as they left the room, and *I think I'm gonna die,* was written all over her face.

"About time," Bree said when we walked into the rumpus room. She was sitting on a barstool next to the alcohol-free bar. "Are you playing host Simon?" He opened the fridge and grabbed three random cans. Bree led me to the sofa where Michael was sitting with Keren. She looked distraught.

"What's wrong?" I asked quietly.

"He never even noticed me when you arrived," she complained.

I was not really a girly-girl when it came down to this kind of female interaction. Bree had always been taken and Michael quite the opposite - he was as single as they come. I wasn't much of a dater either, so was not well versed enough to sustain the high maintenance required here, and truthfully, it didn't interest me to do so. I could still see her sitting there at midnight, whinging that Lorien hadn't spoken to her. Would she have approached *him* to start a conversation? No, she wouldn't have budged all night. This kind of thing can ruin the person next to hers' evening. That namely being Michael, and he looked at me imploringly. "Listen Keren," I said frankly, "you are the *only* solo girl here tonight, so make the most of it. Go to him if necessary, he's just a person. What do you reckon?" I asked. She nodded; a few seconds later she smiled, knowing how ridiculous she was being, possibly unknowingly agreeing with what I'd also been secretly thinking. That was the thing with Keren; you had to snap her out of these remonstrations before they had a chance to take hold. "Go now," I advised, looking past her to the small group standing behind her, "join them at the bar. Simon and Elijah will come and sit with us eventually and that will leave you alone with Lorien."

"You're right!" she flustered, and leapt off the sofa immediately, quickly crossing the room.

"Where are Frankie and Cyndi?" I asked. Bree gestured over her shoulder. I hadn't looked far enough into the dimmer area of the rumpus room when we arrived. There were two sofas sitting opposite an empty space of floor. The dim lights slowly pulsed in the dark, barely lighting the area. Perfect for either dancing, *or* making out it seemed. "Did they choose the music?" I asked. Bree nodded. It was 'later in the night couples' stuff, not 'get the party started' type stuff.

"They'll move soon enough," Bree mused. "If not, they'll be infiltrated." I looked at Michael sitting next to her on the sofa hopping around on the spot, agitated.

"*What?*" I asked him.

"What is going *on?*" he stressed through clenched teeth. "*And* I want to know *all* about your day." He scurried over to sit next to me.

"I can't really get much out now, can I?" I reasoned.

"No… I guess not…" he drawled, a touch of Snagglepuss in his undertones. He glanced toward the bar. "Well!" he emphasised breathily, "check him out checking you out, and all the while you trying to *not* check him out right back." He thought my discomfort was so totally amusing.

Michael lowered his face to within centimetres from mine and threw out a quote from 'Grease' in a conspiratorial tone, alluding to me being watched. I knew this quote. I'd been made to sit through this movie over one hundred times, if not with Bree then with Michael, and then the possibility of with Bree *and* Michael. Why was everyone a retro nut? It was decades ago, let it go folks. I could hear this also in the ghosts of teenagers past, not involved with a kitsch anti-decade of their own. *Parents*, I realised. I thought I'd been lucky to have somewhat avoided it so far. Looks like two additional 80s lemmings had joined our pack however, and I was dating one of them.

"I'll meet you both here tomorrow afternoon OK?" I promised.

"OK with me, I'm staying over," answered Michael. "Make it early," he gasped, wide-eyed and touching my knee.

"Not *too* early." Bree liked to sleep in. I smiled back at her before responding.

"I need to do some more study tomorrow or I won't get out of Year 10. I'll be over after lunch." I rushed out that last thought, as Simon and Elijah were making their way over.

"Come on Bree, Michael." Simon took Bree's hand and pulled her onto her feet. "Let's go break up Cuddle Bunny and Monkey Buns!" They all whooped their way over, dancing into the darker side of the room - with intent to annoy…

"You left this on the bar." Elijah handed me my lemonade and sat down next to me.

"Thanks." He took my hand and smiled at me. I glanced up at the bar, seeing that Lorien was talking amiably with Keren. He said something that made her laugh. She was having a good time. "They're hitting it off?" I asked him.

"Well enough I suppose," Elijah said as he looked over his shoulder at them.

We sat there for a few minutes in comfortable silence, regardless of the background thumping - Simon had changed the music. I smiled at Elijah and he smiled right back. We sat there holding hands and looking at one another, smiling, getting lost in each other's eyes.

I didn't know how long we sat like that but the sound of the pack laughing it up in the background snapped me from my trance. All five of them were looking at us. Michael pointed animatedly at me and Elijah, and then at himself and Bree. He and Bree turned to face each other, and in a deliberate zombie-like fashion, goggled into each other's eyes, slack-jawed. Bree then pounced at Michael and they feigned passionate kisses. I was *so* embarrassed, but Elijah let out a bellow of laughter, putting his arm around me and pulling me tightly to him. Even Lorien and Keren were looking at us with amusement. "OK, go *back* to what you were doing," I waved them all off. I turned to nuzzle into Elijah's shoulder with a sigh. "Children, what do you do with them?" I felt his body move in what I assumed was a silent chuckle.

We sat like that for what seemed like hours. Occasionally, one of us would reach for our drink; he would play with my hair or entwine the fingers of his free hand in and out with mine. It was the every-now-and-then that mattered most to me, when he would lean down and brush his lips over mine; small, teasing kisses of two or three, the third one lingering a little longer. "You're well constrained tonight," I whispered after one of these intermittent moments. It was hard to believe we were still on our first date, after what seemed to have been our one hundredth kiss already. It had been a long day, a *brilliant* day, I corrected, and it was only 9.00 pm. This night was still young. He must have felt my mouth working into a smile against his chest as he looked down at me.

"What are you smiling about?" he asked light-heartedly, ignoring my prior comment.

"I was just thinking we're still on our first date, where technically it feels like about the third."

"It could certainly be factored that way," he said and folded my right hand out into an open palm. "The library," he bent one of my fingers down, counting off the dates.

"You can't count that," I reprimanded.

"OK," he folded my finger back out, "the movies," then bent the same finger down again. I smiled.

"Yes, that counts, that's a definite." He looked at me with mock impatience.

"*If* I may continue Miss Mercy," he lectured. "Dinner at my place," he bent another finger.

"That one's a bit of a push too don't you think?" I scoffed.

"No," he answered crisply. I laughed. "And... as we sit in the here and now." He bent a third and final finger. "Three dates, you were right. Now tell me," he said from the corner of his mouth, sidling even closer to me with one eyebrow raised. He pretended to look around surreptitiously, "because our readers would like to know if it's true..." I knew he was teasing by the tone of his voice, "that all girls put out on a third date?" He waggled his eyebrows at me. I thought I'd call his bluff so grabbed his hand eagerly and looked at him with wide-open eyes, saying breathlessly,

"Yes, let's go!" and made as if to stand and take him with me. He laughed and pulled me back to him, sharing more too-brief moments.

"You didn't answer my question before," I prompted.

"Hmmm?" he breathed, running his lips across my jaw. "Which one?" he murmured.

"Your constraint tonight," I reminded him. "Well, in comparison to what we went through today." I cleared my throat a little, feeling rather flushed. He sat up and pulled me onto his lap.

"You seem a little self-conscious in a crowd. I don't want to make you uncomfortable," he whispered in my ear. I didn't know what to say to that, and blurted out,

"I feel like a ventriloquist and his dummy."

"Hello dummy!" Michael had come up behind me. I laughed and climbed off Elijah's knee, knowing what was coming.

"OK newbies! That means you two," Michael said, pointing to Elijah and Lorien. "Because some of us have partners," he threw a look at Cyndi and Frankie on the sofa, but they were just sitting there calmly now, watching, "and some of us don't..." He looked to the ground forlornly, demurely, clasping his hands together in front of himself. The room snickered. "We always have a group session of something," he continued, looking up. "I believe it's Cyndi's turn to choose. Let's hear it for Cyndi." He took a dramatic step backward, starting the applause. Bree grabbed her on the way past and whispered into her ear. Cyndi looked at Bree and smiled knowingly, grabbing something from a bowl on the counter.

"This oughta be good," Simon murmured from the corner of his mouth toward me. Michael had moved to my side.

"What are you doing?" I asked him. "Nothing too hideous I hope."

"It's not about *you* Darling," he sing-songed to me," it's about Keren," he finished.

"Oh," I realised where this was going, or had a rough idea of the kind of carry-on to expect. Michael jumped slightly as if goosed, and moved to the other side of Keren. He must have been in the wrongly allocated pre-determined position. I wondered whether the three of them had cooked this up in advance just before we arrived. It certainly looked that way.

Cyndi pulled something from behind her back and held it in the air, moving her extended arm in a swinging motion for all to see. "Behold the orange of misfortune," she announced in a sombre tone, and then added more jovially, "one slip and you're screwed." I groaned. Elijah wrapped his arms around me from behind, laughing softly. Michael was watching my face like a hawk for any signs of protest, and when I opened my mouth to complain, he leered at me over one lowered eyebrow - telling me silently to be silent. I motioned a 'bring it down a notch' gesture. Michael looked back at me and tilted his head slightly to the side, drawing in one corner of his mouth. This was his patented 'well duh!' look. Cyndi threw him the orange and took her place in the scattered arc, between Simon and Frankie. At least it wasn't the full body-roll version tonight. Besides, Lorien and Keren may have dealt with it OK. I smiled to myself at the thought of having Elijah pressing against me and fell into a little daydream.

Shortly, Elijah nudged me, and I sighed resignedly, turning to take the orange from him. I was surprised to see nothing wedged under his chin. I looked to my left and saw Lorien standing there waiting for me, the orange under his. I hadn't stopped to think that although I was standing in front of Elijah, one of us had to get the orange first. It was naturally going to be me as I was technically the next girl in the chain. "Oh, right." I went to slip out from Elijah's embrace, but not before he could place a secret kiss behind my ear.

"I'll be watching," he cautioned cheekily. I rolled my eyes toward Michael before closing the gap with Lorien. Michael returned my look with a smirk. He *knew* how much I hated this sixth-grade mentality.

"If someone brings out a spinning bottle, I'm going home," I warned.

"Just get the orange," Michael said.

I realised I'd missed the set-up transaction between Lorien and Keren, wondering how *that* went. I faced Lorien and put my hands behind my back, as was customary. This was the hard thing about passing that damned orange; you basically had to be lying on top of each other on the floor to get the angle and pressure right. In a standing position, it was nearly impossible, especially with your hands behind your back.

I knew right away we had a problem. Lorien was about fifteen centimetres taller than I, so my forehead was at his chin height. *How did he and Keren manage this?* I wondered again. "Up on your tippee-toes lass," Michael recommended. I tried. In fact we tried for several unsuccessful minutes before I suggested we push together; he drop the orange onto my chest, and I roll it up my body to my chin by sliding down Lorien's.

"Let's give it a go," he agreed.

It was a good plan, but unfortunately, by the time I had rolled myself down his body enough to capture the orange under my chin, I was on my knees in front of him with the orange just below his belly button. It had turned out to be an only slighter rendition of the full body roll version after all. "Puts a whole new meaning to a *navel* orange hey Ash," Simon called. I was positively scarlet as I dropped the offending piece of fruit into my hands, getting up off the carpet.

"Yay," Michael led the applause, smiling at me apologetically. I glowered at him as I stuck the orange back under my chin and turned to face Elijah. What had his intake on all that been?

He stood there grinning at me as I walked up to him, ready to attempt it all over again. I pressed my body against his, already on tippee-toe, hands behind my back. I thought he was moving his head in sideways to have a go at the orange, but he whispered in my ear instead, "This is great, but I have another idea." With that, he hitched me up onto his waist in a reverse piggyback. In my surprise, I dropped the orange and it landed between our stomachs. "To hell with the orange," he growled and kissed me, still straddling his body. I was thankful it was meant as a crowd-pleasing venture and he didn't linger any longer than was required. He was right about my public affection anxiety.

"Put me down you idiot," I demanded as I tossed the orange to Bree. I was back on the ground and enfolded again in Elijah's embrace, his chest against my shoulder blades. He was chuckling in my ear and lightly swinging us from side to side.

"Hey, no hands!" ordered Keren as Simon physically grappled with Bree, pulling their bodies together with his arms. Simon looked up victorious however, the orange secured under his chin. He turned to pass it to Cyndi, and we all realised the final two had moved back to the darkened area of the room.

"And now back to Michael," Michael declared. His hands, with fingers splayed, pointed at his chest. Simon laughed and pegged the orange at Michael, which he caught deftly in one hand.

"Get yourself a woman, Lennox," Simon joked. Michael reached over and grabbed Bree, dipping her backwards.

"How about it Baby?" he offered.

As we were all so close, we sometimes forgot Michael was taller than the other boys in our group, had a more defined shape and was much better looking. He could hold his own on the sporting fields when he chose to. He didn't often choose to though. None of us were surprised he'd caught the orange so perfectly. "Let... me... up," demanded Bree. Michael returned her to a vertical position and twirled her back to Simon. "Come and help me bring some more food down Simon," she said when she'd recovered from her giddy spin. They trotted off up the stairs.

I surveyed the room and looked at my watch. It was 10.30 pm. "Getting late?" Elijah asked.

"Not really," I told him, "but I don't think I'll last much past midnight. I have a lot of studying to catch up on tomorrow," also remembering my promise to Michael and Bree. Lorien and Keren were sitting on one of the two sofas in the well-lit area of the room and Michael was digging around inside the coffee table that sat between the sofas.

"80s Trivial Pursuit!" he triumphed, with the box raised high. He started to set it up.

"Do you want to play?"

"Not tonight. Not yet anyway. Will Bree and Simon play when they come back?" Elijah asked.

"Who do you think owns the game?" I pointed out.

Bree and Simon trounced back down the stairs at that moment, Simon with a plate of sandwiches in one hand and a plate of cheese and deli meats in the other. Bree had some more chips and dips, nuts and whips. Simon offered the plate of sandwiches to everyone and all the boys took one except Elijah. Simon looked briefly in Frankie and Cyndi's direction and thought better of it, placing his plates on the bar. He flopped onto the sofa opposite Lorien and Keren, munching on his sandwich, three bites and gone. Michael pulled a bar stool over to the coffee table and started shuffling handfuls of the question cards. "What are the whips for?" Elijah asked, laughing when he saw them.

"It's one of Bree and Michael's games," I tried to explain. "When there are food items - or anything really, three things must rhyme when you present them." I saw Elijah making the connection. He laughed aloud, catching the eye of Simon who grinned knowingly with him.

"I thought Bree, Michael and you were pretty much a trio." Elijah stated. I nodded, looking at him curiously. "Well," he drawled, "doesn't it make it one of Bree, Michael and *your* games?" he smiled teasingly. I sniffed, putting my nose into the air, showing him I was above such things.

"Well done Bree!" exclaimed Michael.

"Bree, I will have the riding crops back up here now please," her dad called down the stairs. "Your allocated five minutes are up!" Bree laughed and disappeared back up the stairs. Her parents were also aware of the rules to this game.

I noticed Lorien and Keren chatting on the sofa. Lorien's arm draped over the back of it, behind where Keren sat. It was a good distance above her, so it appeared he had it there for comfort, not as a romantic ploy. Time would tell.

Elijah had moved us closer to the bar. Bree scuttled back down the stairs and sprawled out next to Simon. "Do you want to get another drink and go outside?" Elijah asked. I nodded, keeping my eyes averted from the 'dark side of the room'. I was glad he didn't think it overly appropriate to sit with Cyndi and Frankie, separate sofa or not. Elijah went into the fridge, turning and asking, "Anyone else?"

"Right here bro," answered Simon. Bree shook her head and turned back around to face the playing board. Elijah lightly tossed a can to Simon and then placed one into Michael's open hand. Michael didn't even look up from the cards.

"Ta," he said as the cold can hit his palm.

"Lori?" he asked his brother. Lorien spoke quietly to Keren and held up two fingers, but not before shooting his brother a scathing glare. I guessed 'Lori' and 'Eli' were for home use only. I smiled, knowing I had a little something about them that was semi-private. Elijah lightly lobbed the first can, as he did with Simon's. He waited for Lorien to open it and pass it to Keren. When he had his brother's full attention again, Elijah threw the next can, with more force than the first.

"Thanks big brother," Lorien growled, only slightly cracking the tab to let as much gas escape before opening it fully.

"Here, I'll take that one," Elijah offered graciously as he crossed the room to his brother and swapped the cans over.

"That's really big of you *Eli*," Lorien retorted, a smug smile on his face.

We had our drinks and were ready to go outside. As I turned to go, Elijah said to the crowd, "How's this one?" we all looked at him. "This bloke," he said pointing to himself, "with his coke," he raised the can, "is taking his chick out", he pointed to me, "for a...," he trailed off looking at me out of the corner of his eyes. Everyone was laughing. "Would you believe some night air?" he countered when I jabbed him in the ribs with my elbow.

"Not bad Elijah," Simon winked. Elijah laughed too and started to guide me toward the glass sliding doors at the rear of the room.

"Alright people!" Michael exclaimed in a ringmaster type cadence. He clapped his hands together once loudly and then rubbed them together briskly, warming up to the game. "Tonight I will *be* the quiz *master...* you will all *be* my quiz *minions.* There will be no *hair pulling*, no rubbing *dirt* into the opponent's faces; the throwing of faeces is *definitely out.* I make and break the rules and tonight I call... strip trivia!" Keren looked nauseous. She'd work out eventually that Michael was having a lend, unless he took pity on her and just told her so. As Michael continued with his spiel, it seemed Keren was left to work this out on her own. Lorien looked unworried, a slight smile on his lips.

I shook my head as we exited the room. Elijah slid the door closed behind me, muffling the sounds from inside. "I can't see a thing," he whispered. It was a dark night. "I assume these doors lead to something out here right?"

"Wait there." I ran my hand over the top of the brickwork to the right of the doors where I knew I would find a box of matches or a lighter stored. Bree sat out here a lot on summer nights, and there were always candles on the patio table waiting to be fired up. My fingers stumbled across a lighter. I edged forward a few metres to where the table was waiting in the dark. I leant across it and sure enough, in the centre of the table was a fresh candle set in a holder.

"And then there was light," Elijah said, making his way over to the table, holding the drinks in one hand. "Hang on one sec," he said, handing my drink to me before he disappeared back inside, sliding the door shut behind him. A roar of muffled laughter rang out a few moments later, and Elijah was back at the door, closing it against the noise once more with his foot. In his forearm was cradled the deli plate.

"What was *that* all about?" I asked.

"You don't want to know," he responded as he set the plate on the table and jiggled his coke at me.

"Oh," I answered a little coyly. He grabbed the closest chair and dragged it over next to mine, not in the least bit fazed. He took a swig and put the can down before taking my right hand in his left.

"That's a lot to process for one night," he said, reaching for some ham. "So what's Michael's story?" he asked and popped the ham into his mouth.

"Well, so far there is no story. We're not one hundred percent sure, but he'll let us know when he's ready, if there is anything to tell," I shrugged. Elijah placed my hand on his leg, massaging his over mine.

"Good guy, funny." He remarked, going for some cheese.

"I'm glad you don't have an issue with it."

"I think it comes down to who anyone chooses to sleep with is no one else's business but their own. There is no more private a subject to two people than that right there."

"I'm impressed with your insight and acceptance," I told him. In fact, I was completely shocked with his insight and acceptance. Not *that* many guys were so cool about what some held as a contentious issue, especially our age group. The current term of 'that is so gay' being used as a derogatory statement of dislike expounded this fact.

"Simon and Frankie seem to be OK with it." This was not really a question or a statement.

"We all grew up together; it's just part of our life with Michael. What you may not realise though is most of the school has no idea Michael would be anything *but* straight. He's more relaxed around us so has a lower guard but you watch on Monday, he has a faithful harem following between classrooms. He may lose a few loyal subjects to the new dashing twins however and that may even hurt him a little," I laughed quietly. "He does like an audience."

"I've noticed," he said, looking amused. He finished his snack and took a napkin from his pocket, wiping his mouth and fingers.

"When did you become so worldly," I asked teasingly.

"When Lorien and I were hit on in the past…" I interrupted him, "Really?!"

"Our family liked to have Sunday breakfast in one particular inner-city suburb about once a month when we could," he explained. "Lorien and I would take off when we'd eaten, leaving Mum and Dad to sift through the kilo of Sunday papers for an hour or so. Great shopping there, with one or two gay men also living in the vicinity," he laughed at his own joke. I didn't get it.

"So tell me about it." He had my undivided attention. When I'd called him worldly, I was joking. Another roar of muffled laughter came from inside. We both looked around to see Lorien taking off his shirt. It looked as if they were playing for 'sheep stations' after all. I considered Lorien's naked upper body - he was brown and muscular, quite tasty.

"Excuse me, back to me please," he tilted my face in his direction and pulled my hand to *his* chest. "You can have mine." He looked at me, his eyes liquid and dancing in the candlelight. "What was the orange thing about anyway?" he asked curiously.

"Finish your story first and then we'll discuss the orange game," I grimaced, ruefully. "Now, what kind of 'offers', for want of a better word, did you get and how did you handle it?" I asked, bringing him back to his previous comments.

"How we handled it depended on the circumstance. If it was a look, you ignored it. If it was a touch, which never happened to me and only to Lorien once…" he started to snicker, obviously at his brother's expense. Seeing me about to question him, he continued. "We were flicking through a CD bin in a music shop and this old guy pinched Lori on the bum." He laughed again at the memory.

"How old is 'old'? What did Lorien do?" I was looking at him in amazement.

"Oh, about forty I guess. Lori's face…" he interrupted himself with another chuckle. "When he turned around and saw him, he said the first thing that popped into his head, so he told me. *'Don't touch what you can't afford grandpa'*. Lori said to me after the old guy had left the shop he didn't know why he'd even bothered. *'Like I would be interested in a woman that age either, old enough to be our parent, erck!'* he'd said." He laughed again, "But you can't tell Lori I told you, he will *castrate* me... we found some great music that day too," he finished.

"And the actual *offers*?" I wanted the entire story. It wasn't the kind of conversation that would easily be brought up again.

He shrugged, "Only once each, a simple 'no thanks, not gay' sufficed. We also had our youthful faces on our side. Legally we were 'jail-bait', and gay doesn't mean stupid." He smiled at me, "Satisfactorily answered Babe?"

"I'm just so impressed. You are so *wonderful*." I was gushing. "I'm not sure how I would feel if a woman was checking me out." I'd never really thought about it.

"Just because you're on a diet doesn't mean you can't look at the menu, right?"

"I guess so... I don't know..." He interrupted my stammering with,

"I'm an 'a lá carte' kind of guy, not really into the smorgasbord scenario; one menu, no diets." He was starting to lose me. He looked at me and smiled, leaning over to kiss me. I moved in closer, kissing him back. When he drew slowly away from me, he said, "I'll take you to breakfast one weekend at the inner-city sister suburb, and *you* can then tell *me* all about the menu/diet thing OK? It could make for a fairly arousing story if you tell it right and embellished a little." He grinned at me. I had no idea what he was talking about. Sister suburb, menu... oh, the penny dropped.

"Now you owe me a story," he said, taking another swig on his coke and capturing my hand again. He went to place it back on his leg and obviously having second thoughts, held it back to his chest, palm side facing out. He traced his fingers along the underside of my forearm, from elbow to fingertips and back. It was electric.

Another peal of laughter came from inside. I didn't want to know. I looked at my watch; it was 12.15 am. "I hear you," he said before I could speak, obviously noticing my glance, "but the orange story first, then we can take off."

"It's not that much of a story really," I told him truthfully. "I missed the manoeuvre from Keren to Lorien. What happened there?"

"After a few seconds of trying, they dropped the orange. Keren bent down to get it and handed it to Lorien."

"Poor Keren," I sympathised. Elijah looked at me thoughtfully.

"Why?" he asked.

"It was an icebreaker for Keren." Elijah looked confused and then his face showed understanding.

"Fancies Lorien that much hey?" he grinned. "Poor Keren," he agreed. Now his fingers were circling my palm.

"Why do you say that?"

"Well, I could be wrong, but she really isn't his type. He likes them a little sassier than that."

"Lorien was her second choice actually," I confided.

"Oh *really*?" he said, getting my drift and pretending to look around for her, but I didn't bite. He took me into his arms, initiating a deeper kiss than the slight lip caresses we'd traded inside. This was more akin to the ones we'd shared earlier in the day. "Come on Cinderella," he prompted eventually, starting to rise, "we'd better get you home before your chariot turns into a pumpkin."

"So brother, tell me why you were the *only* one to be shirtless when we came in to collect you?" Elijah asked when driving home, and Lorien laughed, now fully clothed again.

"The quiz *master* reserves the right to *change* the rules 'at any given time'. The quiz *minion* will do as *instructed* by the quiz *master* 'at any given time', for fear of a public lashing. The quiz…"

"OK, I get it," snickered Elijah.

"Poor Lorien," I consoled, "Michael really does like to play the fool. Who ended up winning?" I'd just pulled into their driveway.

"We did," he replied, getting out of the car. "Thanks for the lift Ash," Lorien said, "see you Monday." I smiled and said goodnight. "Don't be *too* long Eli," he advised with a hint of sarcasm as he shut the car door.

Elijah watched his brother enter the house and took my hand again, moving in closer to me. "I've had one of the best days of my life today, thanks to you Ash," he professed to me.

"Me too," I whispered.

"Can I see you tomorrow?" he asked casually as he moved in and started to graze his lips up and down my neck. He paused to savour my lobe, pulling it between his lips gently, his breath tickling at my ear. "Hmmm?" he mumbled when I didn't answer. I didn't get a further chance to make my reply.

He was such a great kisser, and I could die happy right there in his arms. The thought of that so *not* romantic outcome made me smile, which he could sense through our kiss. He slowly drew back, cupping my jaw with his hand. "You're a funny one Ashlyn Mercy." He smiled the smile I'd seen hundreds of times over the course of the day. "Tomorrow?"

"I can't Elijah. I've *got* to get some preparation work done in the morning and I promised Bree and Michael I'd come over in the afternoon." I looked at him with sorry eyes.

"Will I be on the 'topic of conversation' list," he asked playfully, lazily brushing his thumb over my cheekbone.

"Most assuredly," I guaranteed. He laughed.

"If you're feeling up to it when you get home, come over after dinner. We can do some more studying together if you like. We'll tell Mum it's History - she'll love that. Actually, no," he stopped to correct himself, his brow furrowed, "I don't think so, she'll have all three of us at the island bench doing trial tests," he laughed. "Goodnight Ash," he kissed me once more.

"Goodnight Elijah, and thanks again for an amazing day," I kissed him back.

It was another ten minutes before I finally waved goodbye as he reached the front door. He blew me a kiss and was gone. I backed out of their driveway with the headlights off. It was well after 1.00 am and I was exhausted, I'd just been on a fifteen hour date. *No*, I corrected, *I'd been on three dates over fifteen hours.* I drove home smiling, knowing there would be a lot to think about before I fell asleep; assuming my weary body and mind would allow it. As a precaution, I rolled down my window as far as it would go, letting cool, fresh air into the car to perk me up for the drive home. I hummed all the way, and only realised as I locked the car it was Lorien's melody. I wondered whether Elijah played an instrument too.

FAREWELL YEAR 10

End of school

Music Selection: Michael Jackson, 'Billie Jean'
Diary Entry: Listen to me – always recheck your evaluations.

WHEN THE BELL RANG, signalling the end of Music and the start of lunch, I told Keren and Lorien to go on without me, as I needed to speak to Mr O'Dowd. "To what do I owe this pleasure Miss Mercy?" he asked.

"I wanted to ask you a favour, Sir." He lifted his eyebrows in curiosity. "You're fairly familiar with the composition Lorien is going to play for his final practical exam?" Mr O'Dowd nodded, watching me take my violin from its case. "I wanted to get your opinion on the descant I've written to accompany it."

"Go ahead," he encouraged.

A few minutes later, I drew the bow slowly across the strings in the final movement and looked at Mr O'Dowd hopefully. He clapped lightly, "Wonderful Ashlyn, truly excellent. And you have played this for me...?" his statement a question.

"I was hoping to accompany Lorien as my practical exam, but I want to keep it a secret from him, a surprise."

"I see," he mused, "this puts me in a rather excellent position." He smiled at me and I knew what was coming. "I'm prepared to keep your secret and let you accompany Lorien. However, as a trade for my deception you will *also* accompany him when he plays at the awards day ceremony."

"Sir, I…"

"That is the deal. Take it or leave it Miss Mercy," he concluded. I took it.

Our school exams were spaced out over the next two weeks, with this Friday being the day of the practical Music exam.

I was a little nervous opening my case on Friday, plucking the strings on my violin to see if they needed tuning. I felt edgy, even though I'd played hundreds of times in front of my Music class. I was aware it was due to the surprise no one but Mr O'Dowd and I knew was coming.

Lorien entered the classroom and made his way over to the keyboard. "Hi Lorien, can you give me a middle C so I can make sure my violin is in tune." He hit the note and ran it into a chord. I bowed along with him.

"Since the two of you are in position, you may go first," Mr O'Dowd instructed as he entered the room. If Lorien noted the 'two of you' mentioned, he didn't react, not that it mattered now as he was about to strike out the first note. I was ready. Mr O'Dowd smiled at me.

When Lorien realised I was accompanying him he couldn't hide his surprise. He performed skilfully and we ended up playing off each other with the practice of an experienced duo. Not having heard the melody played against my descant or with both of our instruments at the same time, I had to admit we'd done very well. The class burst into applause the moment we'd finished, stomping their feet and clapping loudly. "OK people, tone it down please," called Mr O'Dowd over the din. "I must congratulate you Lorien for a beautiful and original piece. It was excellent. Well-constructed and full of vision. And Ashlyn", he turned to face me, "for not having been able to accompany Lorien up until today, you also turned in a master effort for your practical. Congratulations to both of you." The class cheered again. "Miss Mercy has also kindly agreed to accompany you at the awards day ceremony in a few weeks," Mr O'Dowd said to Lorien, but smiled at me. I sighed. "I suggest the two of you get some practise in between now and then." We both nodded and took our seats. "Now, who will be next?" Mr O'Dowd mused.

Sitting at the bench during lunch, Lorien mentioned the recital. "Do you want to come over this afternoon and practise? You could stay for dinner if you like, Mum won't mind."

"Are you asking my girl out little brother?" Elijah smiled as he joined us, and Lorien explained the situation. "Excellent, I'll be able to finally hear you play Babe," he said. I hadn't thought about that and wished we'd arranged for Lorien to come to my place instead.

"Great, just great," I mumbled. He wrapped his arm around me and gave me a squeeze.

"It won't be that bad will it?" he asked. I gave him a little smile and didn't answer. He laughed and planted a kiss on my forehead.

When I arrived at the Standish's, Elijah was waiting at the front door. I could hear Lorien already playing his composition upstairs. "Want a drink before you start?" he offered.

"Coffee please." I followed him into the kitchen.

We sat on the side verandah to drink them. Draining his cup, he motioned for me to come over to where he was sitting. He pulled me onto his lap, saying, "Before I release you to your practise, a little afternoon delight!"

Our kiss was slow and tender, not mounting with the heat they had erupted into in the past. I supposed he didn't want me all fired up and then spending the afternoon in his brother's room with the door closed. I couldn't help but smile, which Elijah felt once again through our kiss. I explained my speculations, which made him laugh, and he kissed me again, more intensely than before.

The noise of the sliding door in its tract brought us back to reality. "Give her up bro," Lorien told Elijah. "She's supposed to be *my* date this afternoon."

"In your dreams pal," Elijah said as I stood to let him out of the chair. "Come on Ash, I'll escort you." With that, he hooked one arm under the back of my knees, the other behind my back.

"You're not going to *carry* me, are you?" I asked a little frantically. He paused next to the kitchen island long enough for me to grab my violin case.

"Nearly there already." He took the stairs two by two.

Lorien's room was the same size as Elijah's but decorated in a completely different style. As Elijah had said, the room was red, white and black. The ceiling was painted in alternate squares of black and white, like a chessboard. The wall that contained the bathroom door was the same pattern, but in red and black. The other three walls were a single solid colour on each, one black, one red, one white, and the carpet was thick black shag. It was very dramatic. Instead of a surfboard, a black bass guitar was leaning against a wall. "Is there any instrument you don't play?" I asked.

"Yes, André Rieu," he said addressing me, "the violin."

We played for about half an hour before we heard a light knock at the door. It was Mrs Standish. "How are you two doing?" she asked, walking into the room, two bottles of water in her hands. "I thought you might be ready for a break."

"Thanks Mum, great timing," Lorien answered, taking the bottles. He opened both and passed one to me.

"Has your brother been making a nuisance of himself?"

"Not so far, but I'm waiting on it," he speculated.

"What time are you expected at Keren's tonight?" she asked him. That took me by surprise, Keren had been holding out on me.

"Not until after dinner," he replied, "we have plenty of time."

"OK," said his mum, "I'll see you both later."

"Keren huh?" I asked when his mother had left.

"Yeah, we're going to do some homework together. I've seen her a few times now."

"Why the big secret?" I took a swig from my water.

"No secret, we get on, she's a nice person..." he trailed off and I waited for him to continue. "It's nice to have someone to hang out with."

"Are you taking her to the end of year dance?" I asked, and realised it was none of my business.

"Uh huh," he nodded, retaking his seat at the keyboard. He looked a little embarrassed and it appeared the conversation was over.

About fifteen minutes later, there was another knock at the door. This time it was Elijah. "Come on Lorien," he complained. "You've been at it for nearly an hour, isn't that enough?"

"I suppose so. Are you OK with it Ash?" Lorien asked.

"My fingers are starting to hurt anyway," I said, shaking out my left hand. I loosened the strings on my bow before putting it and my violin into their case, and snapped the lock shut. Elijah took my hand and led me to the bathroom door. "Thanks Lorien," I called back over my shoulder. "We'll do it again next week OK?"

"Sure," he answered as Elijah pulled me through the door.

He didn't even wait to get to his room, he kissed me right there in the bathroom, backing me up to the vanity and placing his hands on either side of me, holding the countertop.

"I missed you," he whispered into my ear. A delicious silence followed.

Whilst eating dinner, Mrs Standish brought up the end of year dance. "I'm assuming you're going together?" she addressed Elijah and me. Elijah nodded, forking food into his mouth. "What about you Lori?" she asked.

"I'm taking Keren," he told her. "Well, I'm asking her tonight actually." He smiled and blushed slightly.

"Pretty sure of yourself bro," Elijah jeered. "What makes you think she wants to go with you?"

"She's hinted..." was Lorien's short reply.

"If you want me to drive you there, you'd better hurry up and finish," Mrs Standish told him, starting to clear the plates. I got up to help.

"No need for that Ashlyn. Take your guest outside Elijah, Lorien can help me tonight." Elijah shot his brother a mocking glance, Lorien grimaced back. "Assuming you *want* a ride young man?" his mother asked humorously.

"Make him walk Mum, it's only ten minutes!" Elijah taunted before closing the sliding door behind us.

He went to switch on the outside lights and thought better of it. "The moon is bright enough don't you think?" he winked at me and took my hand. "I got the tickets for the dance today," he told me, sitting down.

"Great, I'm going shopping for my dress this weekend with Bree and Michael. What are you wearing? I'll try to work your colour scheme in with mine."

"You tell me what colour *your* dress is when you've bought it, and I'll work with you. Not too hard to buy a matching tie and handkerchief."

"You're wearing a black suit?" I asked him, assuming from his comment that he was.

"You could say that," he smiled, and would not give me any more information. "Do you want to come here and get dressed, maybe stay the night?" he asked.

"Won't your parents mind?"

"It's not like we'll be sharing a bed or anything," he laughed. "I'll crash with Lori and you can have my room. Mum and Dad are cool about this sort of thing, especially when we're under their roof."

"Will I be able to trust you?" I asked a little flirtatiously.

"Will you be able to trust yourself?" he threw back.

On Saturday morning, I picked up Keren who had also decided to come with us, and then Michael and Bree. We chatted excitedly in the car all the way to Castlebrook, discussing styles, lengths and colours.

The third dress shop we stopped at had the best selections and we all decided this was our last stop. If we couldn't find anything here, we weren't going to anywhere else.

A deep cherry-red, full-length dress caught my eye. I fingered the silky fabric as I pulled it off the rack and held it up against me. "What do you think?" I asked them.

"Woo hoo!" replied Michael. "That will get your twin pumping… his heart of course." I poked my tongue out at him and went to find a vacant change-room.

I stood up on tippee-toe to get the full effect of the gown. The halter style plunged all the way to just below my navel. The skirt was slightly A-line, with a burst of flouncy ruffles starting from roughly twenty-five centimetres lower than where the plunge finished, lining either side of a full-length centre split. It was breathtaking. "Come on, show us then!" ordered Bree from outside the door.

"Wow! That's brilliant Ash," chimed Keren, "you look amazing!" Keren was excited and had been in an upbeat mood all morning. Lorien *had* asked her to the dance; naturally, she'd said yes.

"You don't think it's too much do you?" I asked a little worried as it was rather provocative. "I don't look like a hooker or anything?" I turned around so they could see it from the other side. My back was completely exposed from neck to just above my butt cleft.

"They should be so lucky," scoffed Michael. I did agree with him, I looked great. I sat down to get a better idea of the amount of movement I had, and when I crossed my legs, the flounces parted in a flattering way to reveal my legs.

"Get it!" Michael said.

"I might try on a few more, just in case." I wasn't sure I'd be able to wear it when the time came. It scared me a little.

Bree chose a strapless dark blue cocktail dress with a full skirt and cinched waist, a nestling of diamantes glinting at the waistline. She twirled in it, making the skirt spin out. Keren decided on a soft rose gown with a princess neckline and straps that crossed over her back. The skirt was shorter in front, fishtailing around to the back where it became full length. I was standing there with another dress draped over my arm. When I tried it on it looked fine, but it wasn't as dramatic as the cherry-red number I'd had on earlier. The light blue colour accentuated my eyes, and I thought its style was more appropriate. "You aren't seriously going to get *that* one?" asked Michael. "Are you crazy?"

"Well if you aren't getting the red one, I am," Keren said. All three of them just looked at me, waiting for me to decide. I couldn't bear the thought of someone *else* wearing that dress, so the decision was made for me.

We grabbed our accessories from the same shop. I bought a small black satin bag with a drawstring so I could have it over my arm without it being a nuisance. My shoes were strappy four-inch stilettos, also in black. On impulse I bought a long gold chain I spotted as we were about to leave the shop. *At least I will be closer to his height in these shoes*, I mused. I admitted to myself that I was very happy with all of my purchases. I was excited thinking about the wonderful time we would all have.

Awards Day

Music Selection: Madonna, 'Lucky Star'
Diary Entry: I wish I may I wish I might, have the wish I wish tonight...

WE'D BEEN KILLING TIME until school holidays, and here we sat at lunchtime on Wednesday, the final day before we had our end of year ceremony. Friday night was the big dance, and Michael had arranged an all-weekend party at his place. Mrs Lennox and all of Michael's guests agreed that it was *most* suitable his mother was leaving after our awards day ceremony for a long weekend away. The next few days were going to be wonderful. "Anyone heard anything about the yearbook?" asked Cyndi. None of us had been on the committee.

"Irene will have all the info, I'm sure," Keren said. "She's been organising it from the beginning of the year." Irene was the dux of the school and we were all expecting her name to be read out last in the 'top five students' list tomorrow. She'd been snapping countless photos over the past few weeks, capturing our year in candid and planned poses.

"When are we getting them, does anyone know?" I asked.

"They're giving them out at the dance on Friday night," answered Michael. "If you like, I can take our copies home with me and you can go through them over the weekend at my party." We all agreed this was a good idea.

"Still no hint what your dress looks like?" Elijah teased me, curling my hair through his fingers.

"I told you the colour, but the rest will have to wait until Friday night." Elijah sighed and looked at Michael.

"Don't look at me twin," Michael told him. "She would *kill* me if I divulged anything about the plunging neckline and full-frontal skirt split," he laughed as he dodged out of my way. Elijah purred in my ear saying,

"I can't wait to see *that!*" Michael smiled at me, knowing the reaction this dress was going to have. "Are you coming over straight from school?" Elijah asked, reminding me we'd planned for me to get dressed at his place. "You can have my room all to yourself. I promise I won't be hiding under the bed watching you dress." He grinned and the others laughed.

"I can't. Mum and Dad want to do the whole 'photo thing' before I go, otherwise they won't get a chance to see me dressed up." I was still planning to stay the night. "I'll be there in plenty of time." I promised.

"Well… OK then," Elijah conceded. The bell rang and we were off to our last classes of the day, the last formal classes of the year.

I awoke early on awards day, feeling a little flutter of butterflies ascending in my stomach. I changed out of my pyjamas into my uniform and grabbed a quick bite to eat before I started a final rehearsal for the recital Lorien and I were to give later that day. I was thinking to myself I could 'just say no' to Mr O'Dowd, but knew I couldn't disappoint him or Lorien. I had to keep my end of the bargain.

I had quite a lot of time this morning, as we weren't due at school until 10.00 am when the ceremony started. The parent's invitations included the opportunity for them to arrive earlier if they wanted to speak to any of the teachers in advance. Thankfully, neither Mum nor Dad could think of anything they needed to discuss. "Ashlyn, you're driving me crazy," said Mum. "Will you stop pacing around the house? Why don't you go in early and read in the library or practise your piece in the Music room? Maybe Lorien will be there too," she suggested.

"I suppose so," I sighed, glad to have something to do. "See you there around 10.00 am OK?"

"Alright Darling," Mum kissed me on the cheek. "Good luck!"

I couldn't believe the amount of people already at school when I pulled into the driveway. Nearly all of my year appeared to be here, and it was only 9.10 am. On occasion, a teacher would stick their head out of a window or doorway to yell at nearby rabblers to shut up; the other years had gone into class fifteen minutes before.

Elijah ran to greet me as I crossed quad two. All of our group were there, sitting in our usual position. "Last day of school!" he called as he swung me around in his arms. Technically, school didn't finish until the following Friday, but parents and students didn't really care about the last week of school. "Nervous much?" Elijah asked, putting me back on my feet. He took my hand and led me to the benches.

"Sort of," I admitted. I looked at Lorien and asked him how he was feeling.

"Fine." He shrugged his shoulders and smiled.

"My brother has never suffered a nervous moment in his entire life," Elijah told us.

"Lucky you!" I retorted.

At 9.50 am, we made our way to the MPC before the teachers started the round-up. There were only about two hundred students in our year, and the front several rows had been reserved for us. A vacant aisle was behind the Year 10 seats, and then the rest of the chairs were set out for the parents and teachers.

We were nearly the first ones there, so we all took a seat in the front row. As the MPC started to fill, kids stood up and looked around, trying to find their parents. I caught Mum and Dad's eye and waved. They waved back and sat down. I was glad to know they were here - it eased me a little.

Mrs Lawper, the headmistress, stood at the microphone, and the handing out of the individual year awards commenced after her brief introductory spiel. They were read out alphabetically, so when I received mine, I knew we were roughly halfway through. It was taking longer than I expected, which was making me nervous all over again.

I got first in French, which was at least something. Elijah squeezed my hand. When I met his gaze, he gave me a small smile and whispered, "You'll be OK." My nerves must have been obvious.

Finally, Troi Zeta was called, signalling the final hand out. Mrs Lawper shook his hand and then returned to the microphone. "We'll be having a special presentation from two of our advanced Music students shortly, and we then invite the parents to stay for lunch outside if they have time. But now, I would like to read to you the list of the top five students for the year." She unfolded a paper and commenced. "At number five, we have Joel Naismith." The assembly clapped as Joel got to his feet and approached the podium. He stood next to Mrs Lawper, grinning, always the clown. "Number four goes to Ashlyn Mercy." Mum and Dad jumped to their feet, clapping and cheering loudly, as did the rest of my group.

"Yeah, thanks guys," I hissed as I walked past them to the podium, where I stood to the right of Joel.

"Number three goes to one of our newest arrivals to the school, Elijah Standish." This time it was Mr Standish that jumped to his feet applauding. Elijah raised his hands in dual peace signs, waving them around as he reached the podium. He leant in and gave Mrs Lawper a quick kiss on the cheek before standing next to me in line. The crowd laughed. "Thank you, Mr Standish," she commented before continuing. "At number two, we have Irene LaPier." Irene looked a little shocked as she was obviously expecting to be first, not second. She composed herself and beamed at the assembly, waving to her parents. I knew then who had topped the year. "It is with great pleasure I now introduce your dux for Year 10 – Mr Lorien Standish." Lorien rose and walked over to join us, smiling a little bemusedly. Mrs Lawper shook his hand and presented him with a plaque. He glanced at it briefly before holding his hands behind his back. His father was on his feet again and his mother stood beside him, both applauding their two sons with pride.

Lorien had also won first in History, Music *and* English. Irene had come first in Maths, and Elijah first in Science. "Congratulations to you all." Mrs Lawper commented, starting the applause again, for all of us. "Now, if you would be so kind as to retake your seats," Mrs Lawper gestured to Joel, Elijah and Irene, "two of our talented students will perform a piece they have written themselves - Miss Ashlyn Mercy on the violin and Mr Lorien Standish on the piano." She applauded as she took her seat. We took our positions and Lorien played a middle C to make sure I was in tune. Simon started clapping and Mrs Lawper shot him a silencing glance. Lorien grinned at me and softly counted me in,

"Two, three, four…"

The melody sounded wonderful when played on a keyboard, but the piano gave it a much richer and resonant sound. It was as if I was hearing it again for the first time. The MPC had great acoustics too, and we filled every crevasse in the hall. We played without a hitch, and as the last note still hung in the air, the assembly stormed. We were both beaming. Lorien stood and we bowed together. He then turned to me and gave me a quick hug. Someone wolf-whistled and we both blushed.

We grouped together outside the MPC eating sausage sandwiches. Mr O'Dowd tended the barbeque, red-faced and perspiring. Our parents sought us out from time to time but were more or less busy catching up with the other parents. I realised when I saw Mum and Dad standing with Mr and Mrs Standish that they had not met before. "Looks like the in-laws are becoming acquainted," Elijah poked at me. It had been a perfect day leading up to what I hoped would be as perfect an evening, tomorrow at the dance. I leant back into Elijah's arms, at peace.

End Of Year Formal

Music Selection: Whitney Houston, 'I Wanna Dance With Somebody'
Diary Entry: Tripping the light fantastic with someone who cares for you is the most exceptional feeling in the world.

I WAS PACKING AN OVERNIGHT BAG, making sure I had all the essentials for staying the night at Elijah's and then Michael's. I'd been a little worried running it by my parents about staying at Elijah's, but it turned out to be in vain. Mrs Standish mentioned it to Mum at the barbeque after our awards day ceremony and she had assured her everything would be fine. "Worked better than a charm," I told George, lifting him from my bed and putting him on a chair; I was about to spread my dress out and I didn't want him pawing at it.

Bree had been over earlier to do my hair. She had piled it up at the back of my head, leaving only a few pieces dangling to soften the look. I applied my makeup after she'd left, so the only thing I still had to do was actually get dressed. I had no underwear on due to the style of the dress. I'd been wearing briefs before, but ended up discarding them, as they were too obvious through the clinging fabric. There was no way I could have worn a bra. I didn't see how it mattered anyway. I was fully covered. It was the cut of the gown that was provocative, not my lack of underwear.

I strapped my shoes on and wound the gold chain around my waist, clasping it securely so it would sit just above my hips. It winked playfully under the vertical straps of the halter, completely exposed across my lower back. I lifted the gown over my head, dropping it into place. I looked at myself in the mirror and couldn't believe the gorgeous creature standing there was me. I worried again, but only slightly, that I'd picked a too-mature dress. *Too late now*, I smiled as I grabbed my bags and car keys. I made my way to the living room where I knew my parents were eagerly waiting for me. "Wow," Dad whistled as I walked into the room. "You look beautiful Honey. I can't believe my little girl has grown into such a lovely woman."

"Oh Dad," I complained, feeling self-conscious.

"A little briefer than it looked on the hanger though," Mum said as she tried to yank the halter further across my bosom. By moving it one way she realised she was exposing too much breast on the opposite side. She finally sighed and left me alone. "You do look beautiful Ashlyn."

Many, *many* photos later I was finally dismissed and climbed carefully into the car. It was 6.00 pm. I drove to Elijah's at a slower pace than my racing pulse insisted. I could almost hear my heart thrumping along; I was so excited to see him. "Hello Ashlyn," Mrs Standish greeted me at the door. "Don't you look captivating." I heard thunder on the stairs, and then Elijah was there.

"Man!" he said, standing there gazing at me. Mrs Standish disappeared. "Oh man!" he said again. He took my hands and held them out from my body, scanning me from head to toe. He twirled me once under his arm and pulled me to him.

"Hmmm," he whispered, "you look *so* sexy." His hands ran down my bare back, not stopping once they met the border of my gown.

"Audience!" Lorien said as he came down the stairs.

"Great timing bro!" Elijah groaned. He lightly squeezed his moulded hands to me once more before coming to stand behind me and placing them around my waist, capturing me from behind. "That better, prude?" he asked, leaning me into him.

"Wow, you guys look great!" I told them, and they did.

They both had identical black tails on, not unlike what the symphony pianists wore - a bolero-type waisted jacket, which graduated into knee length tails at the back. Elijah had on a deep red bow tie and handkerchief in his breast pocket. He had also rolled the pants up enough at the cuff to expose the matching socks – Michael Jackson style. Lorien was dressed the same, including the cuff roll, but his accent colour was a soft pink which would match Keren's dress perfectly. There was a knock at the door and Lorien went to answer it. "Come with me," Elijah said, leading me out onto the verandah. "I need some more of you – private you."

I drew my face back from his several minutes later. "What?" he asked. His hands had been busy during this kiss - playing light caresses to all the exposed areas, once or twice sneaking under the fabric; purring in my ear. This had taken a toll on him as I could feel him hard against my stomach. I looked down pointedly and then into his grinning face. "I think I'm going to explode," he complained.

"We'd better get back inside," I suggested, and he followed behind me, *closely* behind me, using me as his shield.

It was with great surprise that we encountered Lorien and Keren in the lounge room; they were also kissing. "They've moved it up a notch," I whispered to Elijah. He just shrugged. Keren moved awkwardly away from Lorien, looking uncomfortable. Lorien just smiled and draped his arm around her shoulders, whispering something in her ear. "Come on Keren," I said, "let's use the bathroom and drop my bag off. Am I still in your room Elijah?" I asked over my shoulder as I paused before climbing the stairs.

"Uh huh," he mumbled, his eyes were *not* on mine. He was running them over my body again, obsessively. "Every question you ask me tonight, the answer will be yes," he confided. We all laughed, and Keren and I went to freshen up.

At 8.00 pm, we said our goodbyes to Mr and Mrs Standish, but not before we posed for more photos. As we crossed the road to the high school, Elijah took my arm and formally escorted me the rest of the way. I noticed Lorien had done the same thing with Keren and assumed the twins had no doubt attended 'little gentlemen' classes at some stage over their youth; possibly had partnered a few girls to their debutante ball.

The MPC looked great. Disco balls hung from the ceiling, which captured and returned the coloured flashes of light. A fast number was playing as we stood on the top step looking over the crowd. We finally spotted Michael dancing with Bree and Simon - Cyndi and Frankie were nowhere to be seen. Michael looked up and waved us over and we joined them on the dancefloor.

About twenty minutes later Elijah mimed having a drink to me and I nodded, following him from the floor. Tables and chairs had been set up around the fringe of the dancefloor allowing couples or groups to take a break. We got our drinks and sat down at a vacant table. "Whoa, it's hot in here," Elijah said, fanning himself with his hand. I sipped on my drink, crossing my legs; it had the reaction I was hoping for. My gown separated and flowed down either side of my thighs. "Sure *is* hot in here," he repeated, staring. "Hmmm," he said, sidling closer to me. He leant forward and ran his hand slowly up and down my exposed leg, smiling at me.

A slow song started to play, and we watched the dancers for a few minutes, noticing Lorien and Keren drawing in for another kiss. "Let's dance hottie," Elijah said, pulling me to my feet. We slid onto the dancefloor and ground ourselves together for the remainder of the song, kisses and caresses all playing their vital role.

We eventually went looking for our friends, finding Michael, Bree and Simon seated at a table. Not long after, Frankie and Cyndi joined us. "Where have you two been?" asked Michael suggestively. Frankie just grinned and Cyndi swatted him with her purse.

"We had a flat tyre!" she explained. "Where's Keren?" she asked no one in particular, looking around the room.

"She's still dancing with my brother," Elijah smirked, pointing. Just as he was about to continue, the music stopped, and Irene was standing on the stage with the microphone.

"Hello Year 10 Graduates!" she called. Whistles and cheers were her response. Everyone was in an elated mood. "I just want to get a few of the formalities aside so we can go back to dancing." The crowd quietened a little. "The yearbooks are at the entrance door for those of you who are interested in a copy, one per person please," she instructed. We looked at Michael, who nodded, noting that he was taking nine copies home with him tonight. "We had the formal awards given out yesterday," she reminded, "and we will now be presenting the parody awards to those, who we on the yearbook committee, deemed worthy." The crowd laughed. "With no further delay, I have our first award – the most popular boy. It was a close race this year, but it will still come as no surprise that *Michael Lennox!*" she cried, "has taken it out again." The crowd clapped as Michael jigged his way to the front of the room to accept the award. He bowed deeply and then winked, shooting his index finger at the crowd. He grabbed the microphone off Irene and said,

"Thanks to all my loyal voters, there will be something extra special in your Christmas stockings this year...my feet!" The crowd urged him on with their laughter. He handed the microphone back to Irene and grabbed her, bending her backwards and planting a big wet one on her. When he straightened up, she looked a little exasperated. Michael gave her another quick peck on the cheek and made his way back to our table, high fives slapped along the way.

"Thank you, Michael," she stammered, and continued. "Most popular girl will come as no surprise to any of you either since the winner has held this esteemed title for the past three years." I looked at Bree, smiling, she poked her tongue out at me. "*Breezeway!*" Irene called, laughing. Bree wasn't going to go up and receive her award, so Simon hoisted her over his shoulder, carrying her through the crowd like a sack of potatoes with Bree protesting the entire way. Lorien and Elijah broke into peals of laughter.

"*Now* I get why she was so irritated with me when I called her Breezy," Elijah choked. I was surprised he didn't already make that connection on the night of Bree's party; it wasn't mentioned again, so I hadn't thought of it since. Bree made her way back to the table on her own two feet, Simon following with a massive grin on his face. They sat down and Bree scowled. Simon tickled at her until she gave up the act and laughed, leaning over to kiss him.

"Now we all know teens do bizarre and dangerous things," continued Irene. "Smoke, drink, take drugs, have unprotected sex and ride in cars with people who have been drinking..." She paused for effect and the crowd tittered. It was actually a little-known fact that teens deliberated outcomes more effectively than most adults did. "Our next award is called 'Stupid things that teens do' and it is being presented for turning Mr O'Dowd's Ute-tray into a swimming pool - to *Alex Steele!*" Everyone roared with laughter. When we found Alex in the 'faux' pool during classroom shuffles, it was hard not to join him. It *had* been a sweltering day.

The awards went on for several more minutes. Some were just hilarious, some hilarious *and* embarrassing for the receiver. Fortunately, I'd not received one and I was glad. "We now come to the final two awards," mourned Irene, she'd done a great job in presenting them, "the luckiest girl and the luckiest guy awards. Tonight the luckiest girl is a tie... The female student body is pretty jealous of *Ashlyn Mercy* and *Keren Kelly* tonight!" she called, "the dates of the two newcomers – the Standish twins!"

"Great," I mumbled as Elijah leant over laughing and kissed me.

"Go on, get your prize," he said. "Or do I have to drag you up there like Bree?"

"No, I can make it on my own!" I reprimanded, getting to my feet. Keren looked at Lorien as she stood, smiling dejectedly; she did not like public attention *at all*.

We made our way to the other end of the hall amid wolf-whistles and catcalls, both nearly purple with embarrassment by the time we reached Irene. She leant down and gave us both a kiss on the cheek, handing us our awards. As we went to return to our seats, Irene grabbed my arm and told me to wait a second. I knew in that instant who'd won the luckiest guy award and inwardly groaned. "You will note how wonderful Ash is looking tonight," more wolf-whistles resounded. "Many a young man is sitting here wishing they had asked her out years ago. Instead, it took a newcomer to bring our Ash to full fruition. I now proudly present the final award of the evening – 'the luckiest guy award' – to *Elijah Standish*!"

Elijah trotted through the crowd, receiving slaps on his back as he passed. His pace didn't slow as he neared; instead, he wrapped himself around me, kissing me fervently in front of our peers. They loved it. "Sorry," he said to me after a few seconds, breaking the kiss, "it had to be done." I just smiled at him. He swept me back into his arms for the next dance as Michael approached us.

"My turn?" he asked. Elijah bowed graciously and passed my hand to Michael, winking at me and disappearing into the crowd. Michael was a great dancer, and it was wonderful being led by the most talented man on the floor; he made all his dance-partners look fabulous.

The next song was a slow one. I felt him twirl me out and I assumed I would have Elijah waiting in front of me to continue where Michael had left off. I was very surprised to find it was Lorien. "Hi!"

"Hi yourself," he said, taking me in his arms. "I didn't think I would get a chance to dance with the belle of the ball tonight."

"I wouldn't let Keren hear you say that," I said, laughing. "Where is she anyway?" Lorien gestured over my shoulder. Michael had her in a traditional tango pose, moving her rapidly across the floor and back. I couldn't help but laugh. Lorien laughed with me then moved his right hand down to the small of my back, which drew me slightly closer. I felt him finger the chain around my waist briefly and he gave me a coy smile.

I breathed deeply, noticing the fragrance was the same as the cologne I'd examined on the twins' vanity. "You and Elijah don't have the same signature scent?" I asked jokingly.

"Eli's more of a Giorgio Armani type..." he replied.

"And you?" I raised my eyebrows.

"I delight in the rugged manly smells that only Issey Miyake can craft," he chuckled. "Eli likes the western *aromas* and I like the eastern *bouquets* ..." he rolled his Rs and laughed at his own joke. "More of the ying versus yang of the twin topic that amazes you so."

"I was wondering how you pronounced that," and repeated it – "*Izzy Me-yar-key.*"

"Oh, been snooping through the bathroom have we?" he asked with raised eyebrows but accompanied by a smile. The song had ended, and Keren was standing at his elbow. He dropped his arms and took her by the hand, walking off before I could answer.

It was customary for Donna Summer's 'Last Dance' to be played as literally *the* last dance at all of our school's social functions. When I heard the opening intro' I asked Elijah the time and was surprised to find it was nearly midnight, the evening had sped by. It was a great song to finish on I had to admit. It opened slowly and romantically and then sped up to become a crescendo disco tune, easy to dance to. Elijah was familiar with the song of course.

To avoid the rush, we decided to leave halfway through so we could find the rest of our group and tell them goodbye. Michael already had a stack of yearbooks under his arm, cleared of course by Irene. He was waiting on Bree. Simon, Michael and Bree had come in Mr Nobel's car and Mr Ashton was picking up all five of them, hopefully on four inflated tyres. Lorien leant over and said something to his brother and left, Keren on his arm. "We can go," Elijah told me, "Lorien is walking Keren home."

When we got home, Mrs Standish was sitting at the kitchen island looking sleepy. I noticed their car was not in the driveway. Mr Standish must have been at work. "Did you have a good time kids?" she asked, turning her cheek for Elijah to kiss. He waved our awards at her, laughing. She grinned. "Where's Lori?"

"Walking Keren home, he won't be long," Elijah told her.

"Well I'm off to bed," yawned Mrs Standish. "Have a sleep-in tomorrow. Your father and I are going to your Nanna's as soon as he gets home in the morning, so we won't be around to disturb you. "Oh," she said, "I forgot about the party at Michael's this weekend. Is it OK for you to take the twins Ashlyn?"

"Not a problem," I told her, and with that, she wished us goodnight, telling Elijah she would pick them up around 5.00 pm on Sunday.

Elijah waited until he heard her bedroom door snick shut and moved to subdue some of the lights. He knelt at the stereo and pulled out a few CDs at random. "Perfect," he crooned, showing me the jewel case. 'Lionel Richie: The Ballads'. I didn't really know who he was although I was sure his daughter had an on-again, off-again friendship with Paris Hilton. As the CD started to play, the first song sounded somewhat familiar. Nervous, I mumbled some comment about new technology versus old, and asked where his docking station was. "We have vinyl, cassettes and CDs, as well as new-tech," was his simple reply, adding, "and newer than a docking station!"

Elijah crossed the room to where I stood, waiting for him. He ran his hands down the length of my arms, taking mine in his. Leaning toward me, he feathered a kiss over my lips, the only part of our bodies touching other than our stabilising hands. He drew me closer, his hands pressing firmly between my shoulder blades. Maintaining this pressure, he started to glide them down my naked back, his fingers sliding under the material as they traced the curve of my body, continuing around my hips and coming to rest on my stomach. He toyed with the chain around my waist before slowly marching his searching hands upwards. He cupped my breasts, lingering only momentarily, teasingly, before he continued his journey north. Up over my chest, forming his hands to the sides of my throat, my jaw and finally to the nape of my neck, twining into my hair. He commenced the circuit again...

My breathing had become short and erratic and with blatant hunger, we stared into each other's eyes. He pulled my face to his, not slowly this time, our mouths starving for each other as we locked together, my arms wrapping themselves around his neck to complete the formation. He held me even tighter, his arms around my waist, and I groaned as I moved my upper body against his rough coat lapel, absorbing his electricity through the thin layer of my halter. I could feel him hard against me again, a granite pestle wanting the secreted mortar I held within my confines.

His hands were again on the move, finally stopping on the clasp at the back of my halter. I calculated the risk of his brother or possibly mother walking into the room to find me naked from the waist up, in less than a second. The thought of this did *not* thrill me. "I think I should get changed," I rasped in his ear as I brought my hands up to meet his, stopping them from following what was both of our natural desires. He looked at me through half-closed eyes, cupping my face in his hands; his breath still racing, critical. He nodded, continuing to hold me for a few more minutes. When his urgency started to abate, he led me upstairs to his room so I could change.

I sorted through the few items I'd packed: three changes of underwear, swimmers, and a sheer overshirt. I pulled my vanity bag out of the way to reveal the actual clothing I'd brought – my shortie PJs and three changes of casual clothes. I weighed the options of whether to put on my pyjamas or actual clothes. Considering the recent circumstances, I thought clothes would be less tempting.

Whilst I changed, I tried to address the decidedly weird feelings I was experiencing and could not place the reason. I had ruled out two possibilities - his mother being home, and staying in his room. I sat on his bed, mulling this over in my head. The more I thought about it, the more uneasy I became. Then it hit me – today was the first time Elijah had done anything other than kiss me. We'd moved from teen innocence to a new level of intent.

I felt better when my body started to relax, realising this had been the problem. *Problem*? I thought. I hardly considered it a problem. It was *realisation* possibly, but definitely not a problem. I was eighteen in just over six months and was more than old enough to be sharing a physical relationship with someone I cared for. *Do I love him?* I asked myself. I loved being with him and sharing our times together - we had a lot of fun. I was also seriously attracted to him. Our chemistry was relentless and the passion I felt when we kissed was *very* real. The *problem* was, I had nothing to compare it to and was confounded whether this *was* love, or something at least bordering it. I appreciated it didn't really matter at the moment, as long as we were doing what we wanted to do and were happy doing it. I accepted in a blinding flash of maturity that if I had to question whether this was love, it probably wasn't. Nevertheless, it *was* growing, every day, every moment spent together, and every second on the clock.

I was fully dressed when I heard a slight knock at Elijah's bedroom door. "You decent?" he whispered. It was amusing to hear him ask me this within ten minutes of the furore downstairs. He carefully closed his bedroom door behind us and tiptoed back down the stairs.

He was dressed in a pair of silk boxer shorts, no doubt designed specifically for sleeping. "No cute matching top?" I asked, following him into the kitchen.

"No," he responded with a smile, reaching into the fridge to get us something to drink. I watched the muscles rippling in his back as he moved, finding myself hungry again. He reached upwards, opening a cupboard to get some glasses, and the muscles moved in a whole new appealing way. I found myself staring at him, realising I hadn't seen *him* with his shirt off before. Boy, had I been missing out. He noticed my penetrating gaze and smiled.

"What a pair hey?" he laughed, coming over to me, hugging me briefly. "We could just eat each other alive." Fortunately, before we had a chance to get lost in another moment, a key rattled in the front door. Lorien was home.

"You took your time little bro!" Lorien just grinned at him and headed for the stairs, his jacket slung over his shoulder.

"'Night Ash, 'night Eli." He would not give his twin anything more than that.

Elijah positioned himself on the sofa, motioning for me to join him. I lay in his arms, drifting in and out of the night's memories and future dreams.

It was with great disorientation I woke to the sound of Mrs Standish's voice. "Go up to bed Honey, you've fallen asleep on the sofa." I blinked my eyes as Elijah and I sat up, realising where we were.

"Obviously nothing out of sorts happened here," Mr Standish said, smiling at his first-born. As I was fully clothed and Elijah had bottoms on, we got his meaning.

"What time is it?" Elijah asked his father.

"Just after 6.00 am. Go back to bed; it's too early for sane people to be up yet." He winked at his wife. Elijah led me up the stairs after we said goodbye to his parents. I changed into my pyjamas in the bathroom and when I re-entered his room, was surprised to see him climbing into the other side of his bed, apparently joining me.

"What about your parents?" I asked, concerned.

"They won't come back upstairs, and even if they do, they won't stick their heads in here... Besides, *you* have nothing to worry about, well not until I wake up again." He positioned me slightly onto my side and moved in behind me, spooning. He played a few soft kisses to the back of my neck, wrapping his arms around me tightly. "I'm never going to let you go you know," he whispered. I fell asleep for the second time, held in his wonderful arms.

The Party

Music Selection: Charlene, 'I've Never Been to Me'
Diary Entry: Eden is not real, it's something we hope for, and want to exist, but it doesn't.

"GOOD MORNING SLEEPYHEAD," Elijah whispered into my ear as my eyes fluttered slowly open. Leaning on one elbow, he looked down at me.

"Morning." I stretched and yawned, smiling up at him. "What time is it?"

"Just after 9.30 am," he answered absentmindedly, playing a strand of my hair through his fingers. He leant down and kissed me softly. "I'm glad I didn't take your pyjamas in *too* closely this morning, you are one sexy lady Ash."

"And just how long have you been lying there watching me sleep?"

"Fifteen minutes or so," he smiled and jumped out of bed. "Be right back…" I took this opportunity to use the bathroom and give my teeth a quick brush. It was a fresh morning, so I climbed back into bed, sitting up with the covers pulled to me.

The door opened and Elijah had a tray balanced in one hand, with the other, he closed the door behind him. "Hungry?" I was.

"You don't expect me to eat all this do you?" I assumed it was all for me as there was only one glass of juice. Accompanying it though was a bowl of cereal, two pieces of toast with vegemite and some sliced fruit drizzled with yoghurt.

"You eat what you can," he said, kissing me on the nose. He helped me.

When we were finished, he put the tray on the floor and sidled up to me. I rolled over into the crook of his arm, toying with the hair on his chest; he had quite a lot. I heard the stereo go on downstairs; Lorien was up and active. "What time do we need to be at Michael's?" he asked, tracing his fingers lightly over my back.

"Whenever we want, I was thinking early afternoon, around one-ish."

"Great, we have plenty of time."

I lay there listening to Snow Patrol chasing their cars. It was such an appropriate song; we both lay quietly taking it in. Eventually I laughed, realising it was the first 'current' music I'd heard from either of them. "Snow Patrol not one of your top ten?"

"No, it's *modern* music. Unheard of in this household isn't it?" I replied teasingly. "You know, from this century."

"We *know* a lot of the older stuff, that doesn't mean we haven't got *real* music too." I knew this as I'd seen the CD collection downstairs, and his digital music access.

I found myself caught in his gaze. My heart thrummed in my chest as his lips moved to mine. The kiss grew deeper. He rolled so I was lying on top of him, his hands slowly sampling from my waist to my thighs. I moaned, surprising myself and slowly drew back. "Don't you think we should get up? I don't want Lorien thinking anything untoward is going on up here." We'd been lying there for quite a while as a new selection was playing, something I didn't recognise.

"Like it has been?" he said, his eyes flashing. "I guess so," he sighed. "Let's get this day underway." He ripped the bedclothes off in one fluid motion.

"Hey!" He swept me up and carried me to the bathroom. "Thanks, I'll be fine on my own." A few moments later, there was a knock at the door. I wrapped the towel around me before opening it.

"I thought you might want this." He handed me my vanity bag. "Thought I may also have caught you in a more compromising position," he grinned, looking down at the towel. "I'm going!" he laughed and backed away as I feigned slamming the door.

I debated whether to put my swimmers on under my clothes, saving time at Michael's. I checked my watch; it was nearly noon anyway so decided for it. I had a black tankini, fairly basic but flattering. The best thing about a tankini was it held everything south of the border in place. I put on my denim cut-offs and pulled on my overshirt, no real need for a proper shirt as I'd have this on for most of the day anyway. The only reason I'd packed so many clothes was that Bree and I were staying at Michael's on the Sunday night too. We thought he'd need some help getting the house back into shape before his mother came home on Monday.

I made sure I had all of my belongings back in the bag. My shoes and accessories from last night were in a separate bag, my dress draped over the pappadum chair. I slid it over my arm and carried everything down the stairs. "Want a hand?" asked Lorien, Elijah was nowhere to be seen. I nodded and he slid the overnight bag off my shoulder and took the car keys from between my teeth.

I opened the boot first, gently laying my dress inside. There was room for everything else on the back seat. "You looked beautiful last night," Lorien said, eyeing the dress. "The waist jewellery was exceptional, very sexy." He looked at me and waggled his eyebrows. I laughed as I opened the back door and put everything else onto one side of the seat.

"You won't be too crowded?" I asked him.

"No, I'll be fine. I suppose we should pack too."

When we went back inside Elijah was standing at the island making coffee. He was fresh and dressed, having used the lower floor bathroom when I'd finished, or possibly his parent's ensuite. "Have you packed anything Eli?" Lorien asked him.

"Not yet, but I have everything pulled out ready to go."

"I should get my stuff together," he said and took to the stairs. "I'll have one too please," he called back to his brother as he reached the top.

"Put my gear that's on the bed in too!" Elijah yelled back.

He was dressed in board-shorts and a T-shirt with some surf logo on it. He grabbed two of the mugs and moved to the sliding door, opening it with his foot. I followed him outside. "What a great day," he enthused, taking my hand. We chatted for a while; flirting, enjoying each other's company. It was going to be a great weekend. Lorien dumped a bag in the lounge room and grabbed his coffee, joining us. "How much have you packed?" Elijah asked, checking out the size of the bag.

"There are two of us you know." He also had on a pair of boardies, teamed with a tank. "Two sets of everything from toothbrushes to undies," he pointed out. We finished our coffees and decided to go.

We could hear the music already playing as we pulled up out the front of Michael's. There were no other cars parked there, but this didn't surprise me as most of the guests would be dropped off or walk. "Nice place," Elijah said.

"Wait until you see the pool," I said. Michael came bounding down the drive.

"Mwuah," he kissed me on the cheek. "Hi twins." He was in an elated mood, already into the swing of the day. "You guys are the first ones here except for Bree and Simon. Come in and choose your spot on the floor." We grabbed the bags from the back seat and followed him inside.

He had the entire downstairs living room area littered with mattresses. A pile of pillows and covers were in the corner. "Pick what you want and stake your claim, I'm not sure how many will be crashing, so first in best dressed." Lorien waited for his brother to grab some bedclothes and pick a position before he chose a spot on the other side of the room. He obviously didn't want to be sleeping too close to us. Elijah headed for the corner nearest the kitchen and kicked two mattresses together. He spread the cover over them both and placed the pillows at the wall end.

"I wish it was *much* later," he crooned into my ear, pulling me to him.

"Enough of that you two," Michael told us. "You can get jiggy wit it later, when the rest of us are asleep!" Elijah pulled back, smiling at me.

He took my hand and we all followed Michael through the patio door onto the lower level of the backyard, past the barbeque and some seating.

He had a perfect place for parties, as the yard was three levels. We followed the curve of the grounds up to the middle level - the pool and more seating. The driveway continued past us, ending at the garage. Michael had hung fairy lights, which wouldn't make a difference until about 8.00 pm when it started to get dark. Not that it mattered - the grounds were spectacular without them. The pool was a huge in-ground concrete one, complete with a spa seat at one end and a three metre wide rocked waterfall that cascaded over the arc of the deep end. The main entry steps were centred on the right-hand side of the pool. The spa seat already had its frothy bubbles bursting in from the side walls, the waterfall was still silent. "Wow, this is something Michael," Elijah told him. "Do you have any brothers or sisters?"

"Nope, it's just Mum and me," he said.

Mrs Lennox had done very well out of her divorce a few years ago. Michael had been crushed. No one expects nor wants to see their parents split up, but he'd grown used to it over time. In fact, he said things were better now than they'd ever been. When he spent time with either parent, it was now quality time, not simply going through the motions. He loved his parents very much and I was glad it had worked out for him.

We continued past the pool to a set of wooden stairs, taking us up to another level that overlooked the pool. Here we found Bree and Simon. "Hi guys," they chorused.

"Good timing," Bree said, "we just finished hanging all the lights." She pulled a face, something she had not enjoyed.

"We?" asked Simon and she mushed her face up at him. We were on a decked area, about five metres square, complete with side and handrails. I took the twins to the sliding door at the rear of the deck.

"We'll be back in a second," I said and led the boys into the house, pointing out the bathroom before taking them back down the staircase through the mattress-littered living room, which joined the kitchen in a semi-open arrangement. I directed them through the kitchen and out towards the rear door off the laundry, which held another toilet. That was the great thing about this place, depending on where you were in the yard, you had a toilet close to wherever you were sitting. Michael was back in the kitchen putting together some food.

"I'll see you soon," I told Elijah. "I'm going to give Michael a hand."

"OK." He kissed me briefly and they went to walk out.

"Send Bree down!" Michael called as they left, then turned to face me. "So, 'Mrs I'm so in love I can't keep it off my face', how are you?"

"Fine," I laughed, "but you're being a little premature." He smiled at me as Bree entered the kitchen.

"Alright wenches, I want cheese, deli meats and dips on each of the platters, nicely placed please!" He motioned to the four massive platters sitting on the counter. He had already broken mandarin wedges and grapes into one section of them. I opened the fridge to get the food.

"My God, how many are you expecting Michael?" His double-door fridge had never had so much in it. There were bowls of made up salads, buttered rolls, raw steak and sausages, sliced onions in a covered dish, and more pre-prepared food platters matching the ones we were about to create. We heard a splash; the boys were in the pool.

"We have to eat Ash and I don't want to be in here all day." He must have been at this most of the morning; he was a wonderful host. Michael pointed to the half dozen cartons of various soft drinks sitting on top of the fridge. "The other six are already on ice in the eskies." I noticed that a few games were also on the top of the fridge, including his favourite of course, 80s Trivial Pursuit.

"Where are the cheese, meat and dips?" I laughed, not being able to see anything through the crowd of food.

"Try the crisper." They were in there.

I handed the meat to Bree, which she started to divide onto the platters. Michael handed me a cutting board and a knife, and I started on cubing the larger blocks of cheese. He separated some bowls, opening several of the hundred or so packets of chips, pretzels and corn chips sitting on the bench. We could hear laughing from outside then another splash. People began to arrive in dribs and drabs. Michael tapped on the kitchen window that overlooked the driveway and waved, directing them to the backyard. The party had started.

I placed the dips into each of the centre areas of the platters and we were done. Keren arrived, coming through the front door. "Hi!" she was excited. "Need a hand?" We passed her a platter and some bowls of chips and they started carting it outside. I grabbed my sunglasses and sunblock out of my bag before taking my allotment up the staircase and out onto the top deck. I put the food down on the table and leant over the railing, watching the boys fooling around in the pool.

The water sparkled and moved in slow undulations in response to the activity of the swimmers. Lorien's hair hung halfway down his back, pulling all hint of curl from it. Elijah had hooked his elbows along the side and was wallowing in the deep end, slightly kicking his feet. His broad chest was prominently on display to me, unbeknownst to him. He looked up and saw me watching him. He ducked under the water, resurfacing at the other side and climbed out. "Hi." He grabbed me and kissed me, pressing me to him. I was soaked! He grinned; how could I be angry?

"Dangerous when wet?" I asked.

"To say the least." He grabbed his towel and quickly dried off, hanging it over the rail to air. Lorien, Keren and Michael joined us. Elijah tossed another towel to Lorien, who also dried off, rubbing his wet hair thoroughly and putting his towel alongside Elijah's on the railing. It had sprung back to the nape of his neck. I hadn't realised how curly it actually was until he was in the pool.

"Where are Simon and Bree?" I asked.

"I put them on music detail for the moment, you'll get your chance later too missy," Michael said. He stripped off his shirt and threw it inside the sliding door onto the bed.

"Anyone want sunblock?" I offered. I passed it to Keren. Lorien took it from her and started to apply it to her back and shoulders. When he was done, he handed it back to me. "Michael?"

"Yes please." I squirted some into his hand so he could get his front as I rubbed it into his back. I then felt the bottle taken from me.

Elijah stood there with white hands, waiting for me to turn back around. As I took off the overshirt and shorts, he pulled his chair in behind me. He began to rub it in slowly, but methodically, not missing a spot. I was glad, as I did tend to burn. He went to slip my shoulder straps down. "Hey!" I said, turning and laughing.

"I'm just moving them to make sure you're totally covered." Instead, he slipped his hands underneath the straps, which brought back memories of last night, standing in the lounge room. I shuddered in delight, remembering the moment. He moved in close to my ear, purring softly. I don't think anyone else noticed. "OK, turn around," he instructed. I swung my head to look at him and he grinned at me. Michael laughed.

"I think I can take it from here."

He watched as I applied it to my legs, neck, chest and face, avoiding my lips. I could feel myself blush as I rubbed it slightly within the confines of the bra section. I looked at him and he winked salaciously. *Stop it*, I mouthed, smiling. He winked again. Cyndi's head popped up over the top of the stairs, Frankie right behind her.

"Hi kids!" she chimed, dumping their bags in the corner near the esky.

"Not staying?" Michael asked.

"Well, technically yes, if anyone asks..." she trailed off. We knew what she was getting at. They obviously were staying somewhere if not here.

"Ready for a swim?" Elijah asked me.

"OK, just let me get my boardies on and I'll be right back."

"What do you need them for? You're all sun-screened up." I realised he was right. I was sitting here in just my swimmers now, so no real need to feel I had to cover up for swimming. He led me down the stairs.

"No sperm in the gene pool!" Michael called out. I could have killed him. The table roared with laughter and Elijah tried to hide his smile, unsuccessfully.

He jumped straight in whilst I sat on the edge. He surfaced, flicking his hair back from his forehead. "Well come on, what are you waiting for?"

"I just need a minute to get used to it."

"No chance." He took my legs and looked at me, testing.

"Elijah! No!" I warned him. He smiled and yanked me into the pool. I was on his hip with his arm around my waist when I surfaced, spluttering and laughing. His extra height was great as I could normally only touch the bottom on my tippee toes when I stood in the deep end. He however was a full head above the water.

"I feel like a baby," I laughed, still on his hip.

"Ooh Baby," he groaned, pulling me around to face him, his hand at the back of my head lowering me down, kissing me deeply.

He carted me around the pool like that for several minutes, still locked in the kiss. We eventually ended up with my back against one of the edges, his hands holding us to the side. "Oh!" I suddenly screamed out. Someone had dumped a bucket of water over our heads, water obviously drained from the bottom of one of the eskies as it was freezing. "Billy!" I yelled at him in disgust. Elijah laughed and pulled me under the water, which was much warmer. I'd never been kissed underwater before.

As we got out of the pool, I looked around the yard, waving at Irene. I pulled a face at Joel and Billy who were sitting with her among a few others. "I was getting too turned on watching," he implored, trying to turn that into some form of excuse.

"Well you should have dumped it over yourself then!" His crowd laughed with him.

We went back up the stairs and our group was cracking up, flicking through the yearbooks. We towelled off and I put my overshirt back on before sitting down. It was more shaded up here, and although not cold at all, was protected from the sun. Keren was sitting on Lorien's lap, turning the pages together. "There's a great one here of you and Lorien," she said, holding the book for me to see; I was still slightly wet. It was a photo from our recital on awards day. There were two shots, one of us playing and one after our bow. In both photos, we were looking at each other smiling, once in encouragement, once with pride. The yearbook committee didn't muck around getting the draft to the printers, a twenty-four hour turn around must have been organised in advance.

"Where are the ones you were laughing at?" I asked.

"There's a whole section on candid shots and some of them are priceless," Bree giggled. She flipped to a page and turned it around to show us. It was Alex in the back of Mr O'Dowd's Ute, lying in the makeshift swimming pool. I laughed.

"I have some more awards tomorrow," Michael told us conspiratorially.

"No more orange games?" Elijah asked. I elbowed him, as he wasn't supposed to be talking about that. I wasn't sure if Lorien knew or not - that it had been a set up. Possibly he did, as neither Keren nor Lorien seemed uncomfortable about it. I saw Keren look at him and smile. He moved her hair to the side of her face and leant in to kiss her. Bree looked at me and raised her eyebrows with a smirk. I smirked back at her. I supposed that the same expressions were made towards me and Elijah at times too.

The afternoon passed in a glorious movement of fun and activity, everyone was having a great time; people came and went. About 6.00 pm someone lit the barbecue and I realised I was famished. Michael disappeared, so I excused myself to follow him, he would no doubt need some help. When I got to the kitchen, Irene was already in there bustling about. "Need a hand?" I asked him. Irene turned to me,

"It's all under control Ash," she smiled broadly. Across her shoulder, Michael raised his eyebrows at me and shrugged. He wasn't sure what was going on either.

"OK, yell if you need me."

"I will." She continued her bustling, chatting and smiling all the while at Michael.

My swimmers were fully dry, so I grabbed my bag and pulled on a clean shirt and another pair of shorts. I ran my brush through my hair and drew it back with an elastic. My face felt a little dry from the salt, so I put on a quick application of moisturiser, finishing with some deodorant. I felt a lot fresher. I grabbed some lip balm and tucked it into my pocket, glancing into the kitchen as I passed through to the patio door. Michael was sitting on the counter watching Irene with a quizzical look on his face. Perhaps his harmless kiss at the dance was more than he had bargained for.

Elijah and Alex had found the pool ponies during my absence, currently in mid battle. "Hey, you're dressed!" Elijah cried. "We were going to do 'double-storey' fights." Alex took this moment of distraction to knock him off the float. He surfaced laughing. "Game to you," Elijah said, climbing out of the pool. Joel grabbed the pony and readied himself for the onslaught.

The mood on the top level had changed dramatically from when I left. All three couples now cinched together; no one paid us any mind. Elijah pulled me onto his lap, slowly rubbing his hand over my back. "If you can't beat them…?" he whispered, tracing a finger over my lips. He kissed me softly. When I sat up, we found ourselves looking into each other's eyes again, lost in a moment. It was quiet up here, only the sound of breathing could be heard, different tones and escalations. Ours rejoined the rhythm.

Suddenly Cyndi yipped. "Something bit me!" Elijah and I looked at Frankie. He put his hands up, laughing,

"It wasn't me!" This broke the reverie on the top floor and the couples became a group again. Bree had her head laid on Simon's shoulder looking sleepy. Frankie got up and went inside for a moment, returning with some of the citronella candles Michael had set out on the bathroom counter. "This should help."

"I don't think it was a mosquito." She pulled her arm around, and sure enough, a welt was rising.

"Come with me and we'll play doctor and patient." Frankie took her inside.

The smell of the onions and meat cooking was making my mouth water. I went to get up to give Michael a hand then remembered Irene. Not sure what to do, I told everyone what had been happening downstairs. Should one of us save Michael? "Let him work it out," Simon muttered. "We might get a decision out of him one way or the other." He was stroking Bree's hair, nonplussed. A few minutes later Michael called out,

"Food's up!" We got to our feet and made our way down the two levels to the patio.

He'd pulled the two outdoor settings together forming one long table with two long benches astride it. He put a single chair at either end and this was enough to house the fourteen of us left. Michael pulled out a chair and offered it to Irene, who sat down graciously. He then came and sat at the other end of the table with us, scheming in his chivalry. I laughed and grabbed a roll. There was little conversation as everyone ate their fill.

"That was great," said Frankie, leaning back and loosening the Velcro on his board-shorts. "Come on Honey, I need to work some of this off in the pool," he said, grabbing Cyndi. I started to clear the plates. Michael had thought in advance and had bought paper ones, so scraps and all could be dumped straight into one of the bins. A few minutes later, I heard splashing, Cyndi and Frankie were doing laps. *Good luck Frankie,* I thought, Cyndi was an excellent swimmer.

Irene was collecting all the cutlery, plates and platters that held the food. She cleared them off into the green bin and took them inside to stack in the dishwasher. As I was shaking the cans on the table to see which ones I could put in the recycling bin, I noticed how quiet Elijah had been through this process; his was not one of the voices chatting over the table. I turned to find his gaze upon me. I approached him with an armful of cans. "Have you been sitting there watching me work?" I tsked at him. He followed me to the bin and flipped it open.

"No, just sitting there watching *you*." He took my hand and led me around to the side of the house. "I need some of this to myself before I can share you with the others." He pulled me to him, his arms locking around my shoulders as I slid mine around his waist. He was still bare-chested - his back warm and smooth. He played his lips to mine, tasting me. I felt a tingling in my stomach, maybe it *was* love...? Maybe it was hormones. I smiled to myself. "What are you smiling about?" he asked out of the side of his mouth, then drew back from our kiss.

"Nothing, I'm just having a good time is all."

"I don't believe you, there is always more to you than meets the eye," he laughed, and we re-joined the others.

It was getting dark, and Michael flipped on the fairy lights and the outdoor patio light over the barbeque. He had thrown a cloth over the tables and was taking the lid off 80s Trivial Pursuit. "What a surprise!" I said in mock astonishment.

"Are you playing?" he asked, smiling.

"I suppose so," I sighed.

"Are you guys playing?" Michael called to Cyndi and Frankie. There was no answer.

"I'll take that as a no," said Michael. "OK, that's twelve of us so six teams of two or two teams of six?"

"What about three teams of four or four teams of three?" joked Alex. Billy, Alex, Joel, Cherilyn and Irene were the only five still here other than our group of nine. There must have been over thirty people here at one stage or another over the course of the day.

"Six teams of two, I'll partner with you Michael," Irene decided for us. We paired up: Elijah and me, Lorien and Keren, Joel and Billy, Alex and Cherilyn, Bree and Simon; and Michael and Irene. Michael leant over to flick the music system onto the radio. The top one hundred was just starting, that would take care of the music for most of the night.

"Who's not staying?" I asked. Keren and Irene raised their hands. It looked laughable, like we were in school.

"My grandparents are visiting, and I've been instructed to be chipper and social at home tomorrow." Keren made a face. Lorien tightened his arm around her, drawing her nearer. He whispered something in her ear then planted a kiss on top of her head. It was sweet, they looked very happy.

Whilst Michael and Irene were doling the pieces around, a few of the guys went in to get changed out of their swimmers and into something more comfortable and dry. "I'm going to change too," Elijah said, dropping a kiss onto my head.

"I'm staying," Cherilyn told me. "I think Alex is too, but Joel and Billy are being picked up around 11.00 pm." There was going to be plenty of room downstairs in the sleeping quarters.

"Let the games begin!" called Michael. There was no quiz master introduction this time, perhaps as there were other people included, maybe because of Irene.

The game was going to be a battle to the finish. Most teams had three or four wedges, but both Lorien and Keren, and Elijah and I had only one piece to go. Theirs was Sport, ours Music. The twins played carefully, both utilising the green music spaces to get around the board from one wedge to another. Neither of them ever got one of those questions wrong. This is why Elijah had suggested we leave our green wedge for last. They were also good on the movie questions, as was I. Keren rolled and they landed on the orange wedge. Everyone drew in; it was getting exciting. "Who did Bjorn Borg beat in 1980 to win his fifth consecutive Wimbledon singles title?" Michael asked.

"John McEnroe," answered Lorien. He was right. He rolled the dice, moving their piece three spaces toward the middle, heading for their final question. They landed on pink.

"What was 'A Nightmare on Elm Street 2's' full title?" Everyone groaned.

"Freddy's Revenge," answered Lorien.

"Is that your *final* answer?" ensured Michael. Lorien shrugged and looked at Keren, they both nodded. We all knew by now that Michael would sometimes throw a confirmation in as a red herring, trying to baffle you from your correctly stated answer. "I *am* sorry but that is incorrect. The full title is 'A Nightmare on Elm Street 2: Freddy's Revenge." Michael was being ruthless tonight.

I rolled the dice and moved the marker to our last wedge piece required – green. Lorien groaned. A car horn tooted, and Keren got up to see who they were after. It took her by surprise, and I didn't think she was aware of what time it was. I looked at my watch - it was 10.45 pm. "It's your Mum Joel." The boys grabbed their gear and thanked Michael for a great day; they would be back tomorrow.

"OK, what is the complete title of the Eurythmics song 'Sweet Dreams'?"

"'Sweet dreams are made of this'," Elijah sang. We laughed; he was right though. "Go on Ash, roll it again, you seem to be lady luck with the dice tonight." He was right, I rolled a six, and we went straight to the centre…last question.

"What area are we going to ask them?" Michael conspired.

"Not sport, movies or music!" Lorien piped up.

"Hmmm," thought Michael. "The problem is we have our top students for the year all here, and up until Joel left, we had the complete set of five." He was right - Lorien, Joel, Elijah, Irene and I had all been sitting here. "Two of them are in this very team... they have the smarts required between them. Let's remove 'News and Views' and '80s General'. That leaves 'People and Places', what do you think gang?" They all agreed. "OK, for the game, what was the name of the teen movie idol born in Virginia USA in 1964,and co-starred with Demi Moore in movies such as 'About Last Night' and 'St Elmo's Fire'?" I knew this! 'St Elmo's Fire' was one of my few favourite retro movies, not to mention 'About Last Night' and 'The Outsiders'. When Michael flipped the card over and groaned, I knew I was right.

"Rob Lowe." I said. Elijah looked at me and shrugged.

"She's right," complained Michael. We had won and it *had* been fun.

"That's thirty-four to thirty-six," Lorien told Elijah and they both laughed.

"Don't tell me you keep *score*?" I asked incredulously. Elijah smiled back at me.

Keren got up and said goodnight to everyone, Lorien walked her around to the front verandah to wait with her for her ride. We packed up the game and decided to move inside. Michael pointed out the switches to turn off the lights and stereo for whomever was the last one up. We moved the centre mattresses together; no one needed them anyway, and sat in a circle. We'd given up on Cyndi and Frankie, unsure they were still even here. "What are we going to play now?" asked Cherilyn.

"Truth or dare?" Irene suggested. I could just imagine where she was going with this. I groaned aloud. I *hated* these kinds of inane games. All I ever got from them was embarrassed, but no one else seemed to mind.

"OK, I'll go first," chirped Michael. "Irene, truth or dare?" She wasn't expecting her turn so fast.

"Ah, truth," she stammered out automatically. No one ever took the dare unless they didn't want to answer the question.

"Is it true you have the hots for me?" Michael asked blatantly. Simon choked on his drink; coughing so hard Bree had to whack him on the back. I could see how Michael thought this outright attack might shake her off a little. It worked.

"I'll take the dare."

"You have to go and unstack the dishwasher, making sure the kitchen is clean."

"An easy one," she said, getting up and leaving the room. Bree was looking at him with a 'what?' look on her face. It had removed her from the room was Michael's point.

Car headlights swept the front of the house and a few seconds later Keren stuck her head in the door. "Irene, we're taking you home too," she called. Irene came through the room to the front door,

"See you tomorrow everyone." The girls left and Lorien came back in and grabbed their bag. Elijah got up and both twins left the room. "My go again!" Michael sang. "Ash," he said fixing his gaze on me.

"Wait until Elijah is back," chuckled Simon. I could have gladly beaten him to death if he were near enough.

"Good idea." So he did.

A few minutes later the twins returned, both dressed in their silk boxers for bed. Elijah came and lay next to where I was sitting, his head resting in his hands, elbows to the mattress. I draped myself across his lower back, leaning on the other side of him. I traced my fingers across his broad shoulders, lightly scratching. I became self-hypnotised, watching his muscles move to my touch; I had forgotten it was about to become my go again. I wasn't allowed to forget for long, however. "I think it was Ash's go. Did you pick truth or dare Honey?" Michael asked with a lilt of sarcasm in his voice. As per Simon, I could have gladly beaten him to death if he were near enough. I really didn't know which was the lesser of two evils from the choices, so opted for the least likely to be the worse.

"Truth." I covered my face with my hand, waiting for it.

"Have you ever been in *love*?" he asked, stressing the last word. I was glad my hand was at my face. I hoped it was concealing the scarlet colour that had bloomed there.

"Dare." I said, peeking through my fingers to see Elijah looking up at me, smiling.

"Hmmm," Michael mused. Simon went to open his mouth and I told him,

"Don't even bother pal!" he chuckled gently so as not to disturb Bree who was nearly asleep, her head on his lap.

"I know," said Michael getting to his feet. He disappeared into the kitchen and returned with a ball of string and some scissors. He cut a fair length and passed it to me. "You have to thread this around your twin from neck to nuts, *against* the skin."

"Do you have to be so crude?" I asked him, doing my best to avert this into something else.

"Yes Ma'am." He grinned at me. Elijah flipped himself over onto his back, spread-eagled.

"Do it Babe!" he called. They all laughed.

"Excuse me for just a moment," and I too slipped into the kitchen.

Michael didn't say anything about having to use my hands only, so I grabbed a fork, tucking it into my pants at the back under my shirt. I made a face at Michael as I re-entered the room. Elijah was lying there with his eyes closed and his hands behind his head, smiling, waiting. I draped the string vertically up his chest, leaving the majority in my hands. He sat up a little so I could run it past his neck and down over his shoulder. "Lift up your bum." He did, and I tucked as much string as I could down the back of his pants, pushing it as far as I could with the tips of my fingers. "OK, bum back down." This was going to be the awkward part. I moved to the side of him and reached up the back of his boxers to grab the string. I had done a thorough job; I didn't have to reach far at all.

"Well done so far Ash," Michael commented. "You've managed to hardly touch him, what an *exciting* girlfriend you must be." I pulled another face at him. Bree stirred and Simon manoeuvred her to the set of mattresses in the far corner by the patio.

"Good night guys," he said as they trundled off to bed.

I looked back to Elijah laying there. He appeared to have his eyes still closed but I was sure he was watching me through his lashes. Not taking my eyes from his, I reached behind and removed the fork from the back of my pants. His eyes opened widely when he saw what I had in my hand. "You can just use your hand you know. You don't have to shish-kebab it out of the way!" Everyone laughed. Lorien especially seemed to be most amused.

"Just be quiet you," I ordered him. I started to weave the string through the fork tongs, securing it firmly. I then slid the fork up the front of his boxers, tongs pointing upward.

"That's cold!" he laughed, but he could see my plan. I nudged the fork to its very end, and then tucked my other hand slightly into the elastic waist, drawing the fork and the string through to the top.

"Ta da!" I called, and with a few quick finishing movements, I had the fork free, tying the two ends of the string together. Michael clapped, yawning.

"I'm going to bed," he said.

"You always manage to get me a good one and then take off. Typical!" I cajoled him. He just smiled and stood.

"There is bacon and eggs or toast and cereal for those of you early risers; use the barbeque if you like. I'll see you in the morning." That seemed to signal the end of the evening.

"I'll let you get the lights," Lorien said to Elijah, moving to his mattress in the corner. Alex and Cherilyn were also settling in next to each other. I looked at Elijah a little bashfully and he took me into his arms.

"Want to go for a moonlight swim?" he suggested softly.

We turned off all the inside lights, leaving just the range-hood on in the kitchen. This was near where we were sleeping so it would give us enough illumination to guide us when we came back through. I grabbed my pyjamas out of my bag, leaving them in the laundry to change into when we were done. I put them on top of the washing machine and turned to Elijah saying, "I'll just get changed," going to enter the toilet.

"I'll help you," he said, following me. He didn't realise my swimmers were still on underneath my clothes, I didn't really need to leave the room at all.

"We won't both fit in there," I smiled, "I'll just change here."

"I'll help you," he repeated, moving closer to me.

He kissed me, running his hands down my arms, dipping under my shirt. "Bummer." He pulled back smiling, realising, and I stripped off my shirt and shorts, revealing my swimmers. Elijah's boardies were draped over the washing tub. He smiled at me and I watched the smile turn into a grin. He whipped his boxers off and threw them onto the washing machine with my pyjamas. He reached for his boardies, standing there in all of his naked glory. I couldn't help but look.

The moonlight streaming in through the open door painted his silhouette, highlighting and accentuating all the right places of his body; here was the Adonis again, making my head swim. I wanted to go to him and kiss him, but thought I should wait until he'd put some clothes on, imagining us on the cold tiles of the laundry floor, thrashing around naked. He dragged his board-shorts on; it was a slow process as they were still a little damp. When he was done, I went to him.

He wrapped his arms around me as I traced my hands over his firm pectorals, trickling my fingers through the hairs. I looked up at him and he brushed his lips over my forehead, "Let's take this into the pool," he murmured. We turned off the outside lights as we left the laundry.

The stereo was still playing softly as we moved toward the pool. I was surprised at how warm it was as I dipped my foot into the water. I knew it would be cold when we got out, making sure there were two dry towels for us nearby. I waded in to waist-deep, dove under the water, swimming to the shallow end of the pool then tumble-turned and swam back to the deep end. "Burning off some energy?" Elijah asked, sitting on the spa step with his head just above the water.

"Just loosening up the muscles; shaking it off." I joined him at his end of the pool.

"What do you need to shake off?" he asked, running my wet hair behind my ears. I leant into him, still standing on the bottom of the pool,

"You," I answered.

His slow hands ran down my back, curving their way until they met the back of my knees, pulling my weightless body toward him, straddling me over his lap as he had done earlier in the day. We savoured and moved with each other through the deep kisses. Those slow hands were now graduating their way from under my hips, along my thighs and up the sides of my body, tentatively brushing them across my breasts, testing my reaction. It energized me and I didn't stop him, instead kissing him more passionately. I eased away from him and raised my arms so he could draw my tank up. After the tormenting slow peel up my body, its black skin was in his hand, poised to be thrown aside. "Don't you dare," I smiled down at him, my finger gently tracing the side of his face. He put it on the edge of the pool then cupped me, teasing me with light touches of his fingers. The moulding of his hands and my eyes were his only alternating gazes. His pleasure was apparent, a few moments later there was more of him than I had ever imagined. He was hard against me, naturally positioned at the cavity between my straddled legs.

Feeling daring, I leisurely started to flex my hips back and forth in a slight motion. My pressure and movement against him was enough to invoke a groan; he pulled my upper body to him. Elijah's breath started to spiral against my throat as I held his head to my shoulder, running my fingers through his wet hair. My breathing also rose in intensity, not realising at the onset of this luscious grind I would also receive the pressure back from him. As he leant his neck against the edge of the step his extended arms reached for and found my breasts, playing them rougher than before. The new angles of his body created added force against me; his breathing hitched. He captured my gaze, holding my eyes with his until they snapped shut, his face distorting into a grimace. He pulled me to him tightly as he exhaled against my chest, his breath still sprinting although the pressure had been subsided.

He held me like that for a few moments, his hands sliding gently over my back. "Oh my God Ash," he murmured, my head firmly between his hands as he leant in to kiss me. Drawing back several minutes later he looked into my eyes, smiling gently. "That was wonderful," he said, running his hands along the thighs still straddling him. My breath drew in quickly and a jolt shuddered through my body. One of his hands had crept between my legs to play against the fabric. "Can I ask you a personal question?" he whispered, bringing his arms up to hold me tightly once again. I nodded. "Have you ever, ahhh, masturbated?" he asked a little timidly. I wasn't embarrassed to answer a question about such personal self-ventures, especially since I'd never been a participant. I shook my head. "So you've never had an orgasm?" he asked, his lips at my ear, teasing with his tongue.

"No, but nearly," I answered breathily.

"Nearly?" His mouth lazed sensuously down my neck, his hands seeking the contours of my breasts again.

"A few minutes ago," I admitted a little shakily. He grazed his fingers between my legs again before he lowered one of his knees, centring me, tightening my straddle. He drew my face down, kissing me deeply. With his hands on my hips, he started to grind me slowly back and forth.

"Want to try?" he sighed into my mouth. I did.

We stripped off under the moonlight and proceeded to towel each other down, leading to another heated embrace. Pressed against each other we were equally wanting but eventually Elijah eased away. "I think this is far enough for tonight, don't you?" I agreed. I didn't think I was ready for sex although after tonight I was not so quick to judge. I *wasn't* ready to have sex for the first time on a mattress surrounded by five other people, nor in a pool where our friends would be swimming tomorrow. I thought back to Michael's comment about the gene pool and laughed, mentioning it to Elijah as we started gathering our clothes. "Lori won't be happy either," he held up the boardies he'd been wearing - he had put on Lorien's by mistake. "Oh well, what he doesn't know won't hurt him." We switched off the stereo and as I went to turn off the waterfall, I realised it hadn't been running all day, briefly wondering why. I looked back toward the pool, now a motionless piece of glass, as we crept back inside.

Elijah's arms circled around me from behind as I climbed under the covers; he kissed me softly, his mouth at my nape. He drew me to him tightly, leisurely wending his hand under my PJ top, cupping me lightly. I felt his mouth curve upward against my back and I knew he was smiling. The feathered kisses started to trail across my shoulder blades; sleep stole in upon us at some stage.

Day Two

Music Selection: Billy Joel, 'Uptown Girl'
Diary Entry: In waking realisations, it prompts you to have to make a choice and stand by it.

I WAS DREAMING. This wonderful experience couldn't be happening to me for real if I hadn't been dreaming… I was laying on my bed, dressed only in my bra and briefs. Elijah was lying with me. I was certain it was Elijah - it felt like him, I wanted it to be him… Why *wouldn't* it be him? Stretched out on my back with my arms draped above my head, he caressed his fingers down the underside of my arms, playfully, knowingly charging my body. His body weight shifted to reach my face better. Placing both hands on either side of my jaw, he drew my lips to his. My body reacted immediately, and my breathing raced, my heart cantered, my lips sought his - stronger, open, flicking my tongue over his teeth and into his mouth. A low groan escaped his lips, sending his sweet breath into mine. I didn't know I could hunger for anyone in the way I hungered now, for him. As he rolled on top of me, my hands braced his lower back before sliding them further down to trace the rounded curves of his body, forcing him to me. *What the hell was I doing*?

He shifted slightly to my side, not breaking the kiss. His fingers were at my jaw, throat, shoulders… moving down… always moving down. He had the catch of my front-hooking bra open in one quick snap, slowly peeling the fabric away to expose a readied breast. *Find some control woman*, I berated myself, yet found none. As his fingertips brushed over me, they sent the most delicious shivers through my entire body. I was happy for him to keep leading this dance. The source of the energy was his fingertips, the finale was begging from my centre; he was the electricity and I, his conductor. "We don't want this one getting jealous, do we?" Without expecting an answer he slid the veil away from my barely secreted other breast. Only for my erect nipple had this cup stayed in place. His greedy mouth took over when his sensitive fingers had their fill.

My breathing took on a whole new rhythm and I knew I couldn't stand this much longer. I was ready to flip him over and take him right then and there. Sensing my intensity he slowed the pace, kissing his way back up to my chin, out to my jaw, to my ear. His breath stayed there, in line with my own, bringing the panting to a less hectic speed. "Shhhhhh," he soothed, "we have all the time in the world Ash." The fire was too far ablaze, and I couldn't relax.

The heat became a deeper, burning torment as he kissed me again... softly, slowly; I had never felt this way before in my life and wanted him so totally. *What am I thinking!* I was his puppet, I wasn't thinking, and as far as I was concerned, he could pluck the strings in any way he chose. I was his for the taking, for the making; yearning for him to make the marionette dance...

He avoided my areas of tumult as he dragged his lips oh so slowly down my frame. He lowered himself to kiss between my breasts, grazing his hands down to form themselves to the sides of my body, teasing them from my waist to thighs and back. Kneeling over me, his tongue lapped sensuously at my navel.

His fingers gripped onto the top of my briefs, starting to slide them down as his mouth continued to circle lazily around my stomach, back to my navel, alternating between kisses and tongue. He stopped, chuckling deeply and chose a different move. What his teasing hands had been doing he replaced with his tongue, working his mouth past my hips and to the inside of my thighs, down to my knees and back; frustratingly overlooking the area of impact where I most wanted him to be - his hands, his mouth, himself. I felt my grip on life starting to slip as he tortured me toward insanity.

He stripped off his shirt and came back to lie with me, on me, writhing our naked upper bodies together. He was so majestic, so muscular, and so *desirable*. Our mouths worked together, crushed together, breathed together. The crescendo of groans continued to grow, not coming from him alone as he started to trek back down my body with his fingers, his lips, his tongue.

He lightly caressed a finger across my stomach before tucking it into the waistband of my briefs, another finger joined it, and in one fluid movement, they were reefed down to my knees. I gasped as he looked up at me, smiling a coquettish grin.

It was for different reasons I now gasped. I was sitting bolt upright on the floor, the covers pooled around my waist – I yanked down my pyjama top covering my half-exposed body. It *had* been a dream, but *what* a dream. I laughed self-consciously realising I had eased up my own pyjama top during the course of this dream - there never was a bra. *Ashlyn*, *meaning 'to dream'*, I though wryly. And, in this dream, it was *I* who was about to hand over my very being for the first time. Also, I had fallen for the wrong brother! It had been Lorien in my dream and I noted the irony, the 'God of dreams'…

Elijah's eyes were wide as he looked at me, a smile playing at his lips. "Good morning," he growled, burying his face into my neck. I bit my lips between my teeth feeling wretched, feeling guilty. I looked around and no one else was stirring yet, *thank God*! Elijah moved in to kiss me, winding his arms around me, dragging me back to a laying position. This was all wrong and I struggled to sit back up. I fought with the unease and panic trying to take my control. I had to shove them deep down, knowing I had to regain my composure. "What's wrong?" Elijah whispered as he rubbed his hand over my back, looking at me with concern yet allowing me to sit up. We had shared such an amazing night together, *could it have only been last night*? I was the most horrible person in the world; already knowing and accepting it was over. I'd not only turned him on and off like a tap, but I had disconnected the water main and hacked at it with an axe. I leant down and kissed him gently, lying with my ease and actions.

"I just need to use the bathroom." He relaxed a little and I grabbed my bag, heading for the staircase to lock myself in the bathroom upstairs. I ran into Michael at the top of the stairs, and he grabbed me, centring us before I could topple us over.

"Whoa, what's wrong?" he asked laughing, and then held me at arm's length, peering into my face. "Ash?" I threw him a grin, not allowing him the chance to become too aware of my raw feelings.

"I need to use the bathroom." Although not looking overly confident at my answer, he let me go.

Locking the door behind me I knew my lame excuse, now used twice to a somewhat level of believability, was not going to wash for long. I sat on the edge of the tub *oh no, oh no, oh no, OH NO!* What was I going to do? I couldn't go down to Elijah as if nothing had happened. I was in a whirl of confusion and eddying emotions, all ending with the same simple realisation - I was in love with Lorien - hopelessly, emphatically, categorically. I had wondered whether it *was* love I felt for Elijah and couldn't answer the question as yes. I now realised why.

I accepted I didn't need to take anything away from those sweet and passionate moments I'd shared with Elijah, and were correctly shared with him; I hadn't been thinking or wishing I had been with Lorien. I had wanted Elijah. What I didn't want was my interfering subconscious that had dragged me down this path, kicking and screaming, clawing for its blood. It was hopeless though; none of this changed the fact it was Lorien who was my jigsaw puzzle piece. Elijah and I may have formed a tight corner section, long lines with one connecting portion, but it was Lorien who was meant to be intricately interlaced over and over against my crazily shaped edges. Of this, I was sure, even as I tried to push it away and shove the thoughts angrily out of the room, slamming the door.

Maybe it was *only a dream*, I hoped, very quietly to myself. I allowed this to develop a little more… Maybe the shock of waking up with the vision dancing so close to my first conscious thoughts of the day *had* set this panic in motion. Could this be possible? Of course it could, I reasoned with myself, feeling a little better. I started to dress, as I would have to leave my fortress of solitude eventually. I'd think no more of it. I would under no circumstances base the rest of my day, *or life*, I reminded myself, on this initial reaction. Nothing could be that set in stone.

I brushed my teeth and hair, looking at myself in the mirror. I gathered up all of my things and threw them back into my bag. I took it into Michael's room and left it on the floor, knowing I would need nothing else from it today. I caught a glimpse of myself in his mirror as I went to leave; *you love Lorien*, I reminded myself, almost in a children's chant. Great!

Elijah was waiting at the base of the stairs when I came back down. I was convinced by now I'd just been silly - here was the man I wanted. I looked around the room to see where Lorien was and caught myself doing so. Elijah was looking at me, worried. It didn't matter what I thought, I was *not* going to hurt this man; a man I cared very much for. I knew that *was* the simple truth. An old song fragment jumped into my head about loving the one you're with. I would make this my mantra, and accepting this I smiled genuinely at Elijah. Everything was going to be OK. He took one of my hands in his and sat on the stair, bringing me with him. I could see Michael watching me from the kitchen as he pretended to busy himself grabbing bacon and eggs from the fridge. "Everything OK?" Elijah asked.

"Everything OK," I smiled at him, possibly a little more dazzlingly than was necessary. I stood, bringing him to me this time; pressing him against me, *trying to erase the doubt from both of our minds*. But, it worked, and Michael also visibly relaxed. Crisis narrowly averted.

"If you two are finished welcoming the new day, we need some more ice Ash. Can you run down to the service station and grab another six or so bags?" Michael called. I led Elijah into the kitchen so I could grab my car keys and wallet.

"Coming?" I asked.

"Just give me a second," his face broke into a grin. "I think I should change first," motioning to the silk boxers he still wore.

When we were in the car and driving, he took my hand again. "I'm sorry Ash," he said quietly.

"Whatever for?" I asked in all curiosity.

"Last night, it was too much wasn't it?" It was all I could do to restrain myself from throwing my head back and laughing loudly. He had no idea of how far from the ballpark he was.

"Oh Honey, no! Last night was incredible, don't ever think that."

"I just thought when you seemed a little... *awkward* this morning," he chose his word carefully, "that it may have had something to do with it."

"No, that's just me," I assured him. "I woke up not knowing where I was at first, a little disorientated, and *desperately* needing to use the bathroom." He curled both of his hands through my free one, accepting this, a smile back on his handsome face. But, still the wrong face. I was glad he didn't make the connection this had *not* been my same reaction when I woke up against him in his bed yesterday morning.

When we got back to Michael's, the delectable scent of frying bacon assaulted me. "I'm starving!" I told him.

"Me too," he purred, coming to me for our second kiss of the day. We staved our hunger by feasting on each other for a few moments - I knew it was going to be OK. I also knew if I kept telling myself this it may actually become a fact.

"Stop melting that ice!" Michael called from the kitchen window. Elijah leant back from me, smiling. I followed him to the back door of the car to help him get the ice from the seat.

"It's OK, I'll make two trips." He hauled three of the bags onto his shoulder, heading for the back yard. I went in to help Michael in the kitchen, who was already starting on the platters for the day.

"Who's on the barbeque?" I asked, reaching for the fruit.

"Keren's twin. He's under strict instructions to cook the bacon only and to press the flesh of any wandering fingers that come his way. When we're all ready, he can throw the eggs on at the last minute. There is nothing worse than intermittent eating!" he concluded. I smiled, Michael had his ways about him, and once again, this was one of the small nuances that made him an excellent host. It would be a group breakfast.

Bree wandered in with the covers still wrapped around her. "'...time izit?" she asked, rubbing her eyes.

"Nearly 9.00 am," Michael told her. "Wow that's like dawn for you isn't it Bree?" We laughed; she did not.

"...shower," she mumbled and made her way to the staircase.

"Morning!" Simon rounded the corner. They were the last ones up, so he grabbed all the bedding and stacked it in a corner to put away later. They were complete opposites at times. He was a bright waker whereas Bree was not. "Want some help?" he asked Michael.

"You can take the soft drinks out and repack the eskies if you like." Simon reached up and grabbed three cartons off the fridge, disappearing from the kitchen.

"OK," Michael gushed, "drinks, check; food, all-but check; breakfast, check. That's check-mate!" I laughed with him. Most of the guests who were not already here would be arriving late morning or early afternoon. There was no need for a big meal again today. We were all-but 'checked'.

"I might start putting some of this away," I pointed to the stack of mattresses, pillows and bedclothes. "Do you want any of the bedding washed?"

"Does any of it need it?" he asked pointedly.

"No!" I said.

"Everything goes back into the two spare bedroom cupboards except the mattresses, they came from the garage." I shoved all the pillows into a pile and took my first armful up the stairs.

As I started to fold the covers, Simon and Elijah came back into the kitchen. "Anything else you want us to do before we have a swim?" Simon asked. Elijah looked over to where I was standing. He winked and smiled.

"The mattresses can be stacked back in the garage if you don't mind."

"Not a problem," Simon said, and they came over to where I was standing near them. "Only three trips you reckon?" he asked Elijah.

"Definitely!" They then proceeded to stack five of the fifteen mattresses together and swung the pile up and between their shoulders, carting them out the front door, which I ran to open for them.

"Why does he have so many?" Elijah asked as they exited the door.

"He was a bed wetter," laughed Simon. "A new mattress every year!"

"Shut up Simon!" Michael called from the kitchen. We all knew Mr Lennox was a scout leader, but Elijah didn't. Any time a camping trip was called off due to the weather, the camp took place on the Lennox's lounge room floor. Michael being the campest thing there.

I was still sorting and folding the last of the bedclothes when they came back for their third and final load. Simon was obviously part way through a joke of some sort; he interrupted himself as they loaded up the final five. As they headed out the door, I heard him say "And the duck said, 'what would the circus want with a brick laying duck'?" They both laughed hilariously. I smiled and shook my head.

"The bacon is all done - it's in the server under foil. Anything else need doing?" Lorien had come into the kitchen.

"You can stick those in the fridge," Michael motioned to the four completed platters with his chin, "and then it's dismissed, thanks twin." I kept quietly stacking the covers, ready to take them upstairs, hoping to go unnoticed.

"Morning Ash," Lorien called and then ran up to me, seeing my pile about to slip. "Whoa, need a hand?" he asked smiling.

"Ah, OK." He took half and followed me up the stairs.

When we reached the top, I led him into the room off the deck. We heard a massive splash; Simon and Elijah had obviously finished their cartage. With everything away, we walked out onto the deck. "Coming in?" Lorien asked, stripping off his shirt. He already had his board-shorts on, and my stomach curled when he patted them saying, "Thought these would be dry by now." He ran down the stairs and dove into the pool. I heard the bathroom door open, and Bree was at my side.

"Looks like Cyndi and Frankie made their escape at some stage over the evening." She pointed to where their bags had been yesterday; they were gone. "Simon in there?" she asked, smiling.

"Yes, with Lorien and Elijah. I think they're waiting for us." Bree sighed and said,

"I don't know why I bothered to wash my hair, hang on, I'll get changed." I trotted back downstairs and into the laundry, my tankini and overshirt were still where I'd left them last night, draped over the wash tub and on top of the washing machine respectively. I changed in the toilet and entered the kitchen as Bree came down the stairs.

"Can you do me?" I asked her, handing her the sunblock from off the fridge. Michael looked at us lewdly and went back to stacking the dishwasher with the latest grimy residents. We coated each other in sunscreen and went out to face the boys. We knew they were waiting on a challenging game of 'double-storey', with Bree and me as the duelling pawns.

"Babe, Babe!" they called in unison as they saw us near. "Babe!" They were motioning to their shoulders, jumping around like kids. "C'mon Babe!"

We dropped our towels and clothes far enough away so they wouldn't get wet and went to the side of the pool. Lorien dragged himself up over the edge and sat, waiting to referee the game. He glistened, his wet hair in his eyes. As if in response to my thought, he reached up and dragged it back over his head. "Umm how do we do this?" I asked nervously, not sure how I was going to climb on from this height. Simon solved that problem with Bree. He launched himself out of the pool at her, grabbing her around the waist and throwing himself backward, ensuring she would land on top of him. When they resurfaced, Bree was already balancing herself on Simon's shoulders.

"Bring it Ash!" she goaded, enticing me with a flick of her hands; beckoning.

"Yo! Bring iiiiiii-T!" agreed Simon. I couldn't help but laugh.

"Just jump in Ash, I'll take it from there," Elijah said. I slipped into the water. He bobbed under and was suddenly between my legs, placing one on either side of his neck but not before quickly teasing the same area of fabric as he had done so masterfully the night before. He broke back above the water. Could anyone tell I was blushing?

Alex and Cherilyn came jogging up the driveway as we were about to start. I'd forgotten they were even here. "We'll take on the winner!" called Alex, as both of them stripped down to their suits. Cherilyn beamed at him; they were obviously getting on well. Lorien whistled between his teeth and the battle was on.

Bree and I grappled for several minutes with the boys trying to jockey us into better positions for attack. We knew it wasn't going to work - we were too slippery to get a good grip on each other. "Game off!" Bree finally called, dropping off the back of Simon's shoulders into the water. I did the same. Elijah scooped me up and plonked me back onto his hip. He smiled at me and kissed me. I kissed him right back.

"Why?" asked Simon, clearly confused as to why the fun was over already. "You can't call a draw in 'double-storey'!"

"I didn't call a draw," Bree explained, "I called game off. We need to de-sunscreen a little before we can try again." Michael joined us with a tray of coffees.

"You missed it Simon," Michael regaled. "Some girl-on-girl lathering action was happening in the kitchen, and *you* missed it!" He laughed at his own comment, as did we all.

Michael passed my coffee to me in the pool. Everyone else got out, dried off and moved up to the decked area to drink theirs. Lorien was suddenly beside me. He'd slipped back into the pool, joining me against the edge in the deep end. Michael passed him a mug too. He hooked his arms over the edge to hold him in place whilst he drank, although he could have easily touched the ground. I wish he'd swum to the other side of me, so I didn't have to look past him to see the others. The edge of the pool forced his bi and triceps out into a most appetising feast of eye-candy; they were all I could see in front of me. I was thinking of how they would feel wrapped around me when I accidentally flicked him with my waving feet. "Oops, sorry!" I said, "I should get out to drink this."

"Here," he said taking my mug from me. "Get on." He offered me his back to climb on, smiling. I thought quickly, *would I have done this yesterday*? I couldn't stand there thinking about it all day so resigned myself and got on. He waded to the shallower end of the pool and turned so I could drop off onto the dormant spa seat.

He pressed both mugs into my hands and turned to dive back into the pool. I moved into the corner, crossing my legs, and turned my body to face the rest of the group. Elijah winked at me from the deck. *Whew, good!* Lorien birthed himself through the water, coming to sit next to me. His hair dead straight again and hanging down his back... I wanted to touch it. *You love Lorien!* my self-conscious sing-songed at me. I dragged my eyes from him, picking up the thread of conversation happening above. "But why?" Bree was asking Michael for an explanation on something.

"Because one of the awards is for her and it's titled the 'best "Frencher," and we are not talking the language' award, you know, a play on her giving me my award at the dance," he concluded.

"Just kiss her again mate," Simon chuckled.

"*You* kiss her if you think she's so kiss-worthy." Michael huffed.

"So there are no awards then?" I asked, getting the gist of their conversation.

"Not if she turns up again today!" Michael called down to me.

At about 10.00 am we sat down to breakfast. Michael had ended up taking over the cooking of the eggs; Lorien wasn't 'doing it right' apparently. He didn't seem too worried about losing his job as head chef. Everything was delicious and we ate every single bit.

Lorien got up and started to clear the plates. He and Michael were the only ones currently 'stag', so left the duos, to do. "I bet you're glad the awards have been cancelled," Elijah said, leading me to the upper deck so we could be alone.

"Why do you say that?" I asked as he pulled me onto his lap. I tucked my legs up and circled his shoulders with my arms.

"You're his favourite target, I'm sure you would have been the receiver of more than just one." I laughed; he was right!

We sat silently for a while, my jaw nestling against his forehead, thinking our own thoughts. *You love...* I shut it up immediately. I looked down at him; he was watching me, smiling. He slowly traced the heart outline of my facial shape with a finger, lightly kissing me when he was done. He exhaled, pulling me closer. I tightened my arms around him also. "What I wouldn't give for it to be yesterday," he mumbled against me. "I'm going to miss you when I leave this afternoon."

"You will just have to dream about me tonight," I offered, immediately wanting to swallow my words.

"Oh I will!"

Several minutes later he asked, "Are you going to school this week?" It felt like we were already finished for the year; I kept forgetting we still officially had another week to go.

"Maybe, I haven't really thought about it. I won't be going tomorrow though."

"Let's make some plans for later in the week… I know!" he sat upright, nearly knocking me from his lap. "Sorry Ash," he said laughing, righting me again. I swung my feet back to the ground, smiling at him.

"You were about to say?" I asked.

"How about we go to the beach on Wednesday? You can get in that surfing lesson I promised you." I pulled a face, but he continued, "Oh come on, you have to try it."

"OK," I agreed. He smiled, content.

People started to arrive. "I suppose we should go down and be sociable," I offered with a dramatic sigh, climbing from his lap.

"I suppose so." As we reached the pool level, a game of Marco Polo was starting,

"Marco," called out Cherilyn, a bass reply of five male voices answered her,

"Polo!" Joel and Billy were back and had joined Alex, Lorien and Simon in the pool. Elijah kissed me and jumped into a vacant spot.

I sat with Michael and Bree near the shallow end, watching the action, laughing now and then. I realised it was *very* quiet, neither Bree nor Michael was talking. I turned to them and they were both looking at me. "What?" I asked.

"That's what *we* want to know," answered Bree. She knocked on my forehead lightly with her fist. "There's something going on in here that has our senses overloading." They knew me so well; there was no point in putting up a fight over this.

"Can we talk about it tonight, when everyone has gone?" I pleaded. They were fine with that.

The clouds that had slowly formed over the course of the afternoon were now dark and menacing with their threats. It was going to storm and big time. As the twins, Simon and Michael started to check all the loose furniture was stowed in an acceptable manner for the coming onslaught, Mrs Standish pulled into the driveway. Lorien grabbed their bag, calling, "Thanks for the great weekend Michael!"

"Anytime twin," he said and followed him to the car to say hello to Mrs Standish. Elijah came up to me, pulling me into his arms.

"I've had a great weekend too," he growled as he leant in to kiss me goodbye. He nuzzled his lips to my neck, sighing, "I wish it was Friday all over again and we had the next three days still spread out in front of us." I did too and this disclosure from him would have thrilled me on Friday. Now, however, the wonderment of him still existed but the ecstasy was gone; it packed its bags and crept out in the wee hours of Sunday morning.

He took my hand and I walked him to the car. "Hi Mrs Standish," I said.

"Hello Ashlyn, did you have a good time?" she asked, smiling. Elijah gave me a lecherous grin and kissed me again before climbing into the back seat.

"Everyone had a ball; Michael is an excellent host." I was blushing slightly as she had obviously seen the final kiss goodbye, albeit a *lot* calmer than previously shared ones. It didn't seem to faze her at all; I guess that came from having two such handsome sons; there was always some girl or other kissing one of them, or wanting to.

"Michael was just giving me some of the highlights. I understand you and Eli put Lori in his place?" I must have looked at her like a moron as she added, "Winning the trivia?"

"Oh yes, a masterful and well-deserved win," I agreed.

"See you in school," she waved and backed down the drive. As she left, she tooted the horn. Elijah was hanging out of his window blowing kisses to me with the full extent of his arm, great big 'Mwuahs'. We stood there and waved until they were out of sight.

CHRISTMAS HOLIDAYS

Awakenings

Music Selection: Culture Club, 'Time (Clock of the Heart)'
Diary Entry: We could have made this something special, if we had enough blocks to build with. Alternatively, we may have still had nothing to show for it in the end - seasons will always be subject to change.

"OK, SPILL IT." Bree let me have it before we'd even turned to walk back up the driveway.

"Let's get the yard secured first," Michael suggested, looking up at the inky sky. This thankfully kept us busy for fifteen minutes, giving me time to think about what I was going to say to them. What not to say to them.

As we walked into the kitchen, Michael flicked on the kettle. "Sit," he ordered, pointing at a stool. Bree came and sat next to me. They both looked at me expectantly, knowing I would talk sooner or later. I relented after several minutes and simply said,

"I had a dream last night." They looked at each other and then back to me.

"This is all about a *dream*?" Bree asked. "It must have been some dream." I went on to explain how Elijah and I had taken a midnight swim, carefully editing where necessary, and then described in fairly accurate detail the essence of the dream.

"So what's the problem Ash," said Michael, handing me a mug. "I must be missing something. You two have been getting on so well I thought you'd actually fallen for this guy. Then you tell me about your dream and you're having the opposite reaction to what I would expect." I didn't let him continue.

"It wasn't Elijah." They looked at each other again. "It was Lorien."

"I think you're making more out of this than necessary," Michael waved it off. "You love him, don't you?" I shook my head, no. "Since the dream or before it?"

"That's irrelevant; I won't ever love Elijah now. I still care for him a lot, he's a wonderful guy, but I know it will never be love."

"You're in love with Lorien?" Bree asked. I nodded my head, yes. My body and mind felt battle-worn; I was void of energy and emotion at this stage. "What are you going to do Ash?"

"I don't know. What can I do?"

"What are you going to *do* Ash?" Michael repeated. "I mean you've obviously had all day to consider this. Have you made any decisions?"

"I'm going to get on with it and try to put it behind me."

"Get on with it as in keep seeing him and try to ignore this whole thing?" Michael confirmed. I nodded. "Do you think that's wise *or* fair?"

"What he doesn't know won't hurt him."

"And do you think you're being fair to yourself?" Michael suggested.

"No, not really, but what other choice do I have Michael?" I turned to Bree and said, "What do you think?"

"I'm not sure which one of them you want us to cheer for? Do you actually want Elijah or Lorien?" Before I had a chance to answer, the heavens opened up with a brilliant strike of lightning followed instantly by an almighty crash of thunder. The rain bucketed down.

"I'm going to love the one I'm with."

"Do you think you're mature enough to make that work?" Michael asked speculatively.

"I don't know, but can it hurt to try?" Neither of them answered me. I asked again, inflicting my point moreso, "*Can* it hurt to try?"

"I suppose whatever you decide to do will hurt him, whether now or at some stage in the future…" Michael mused.

"But if it's in the future, don't you think that's unfair on him, not knowing now that there's no hope for this to ever become anything more? Don't you think he'll be falling more and more in love over this time?" Bree asked.

"So you don't think it's possible for me to get over this and love Elijah enough, maybe in time fall back into pace with him?" I asked hopefully.

"Only you can answer that Ash," Michael reasoned, "but Bree is right. He needs to be considered in this too. Can you see yourself realigned with him?"

"Maybe…" I started, and then shook my head, "No."

"You'll do what you think is right Ash." Bree put her arm around me and squeezed reassuringly.

"You always have," Michael smiled at me. "We'll always be here for you when you need us." He came over and wrapped his arms around both of us. They allowed me to cry against them until I was done.

I played 'possum' for the next three days, feigning a sickness that was only in my heart. Mum tended to me as only a Mum can. Her nursing made me feel safe and secure, that nothing outside these walls could ever cause me or anyone else pain. My conscience begged to differ.

There was a knock at my door late Wednesday afternoon. When Mum opened the door, I could see Elijah standing behind her. "Thanks Mrs Mercy," he said as she smiled at him and left. Elijah closed the door behind him. "How are you feeling?" he asked, coming to sit next to me on the bed. He leant down to kiss me and stopped. "Are you infectious?" He grinned and kissed me anyway, he obviously didn't care. He moved in behind me, cradling me in his arms from behind. "Do you think you'll be feeling better by Saturday?" he asked quietly, his lips playing across my hair.

"I think so, I feel a lot better today. What did you have in mind?"

"I hoped for it to be just us two, but not knowing if you were going to be up for it, suggested a day at the beach to the rest of the group. Give you a chance to get on my board." He chuckled at his innuendo.

"In front of the rest of them?" I teased. He hugged me tightly, laughing softly. "What time and where?"

"Now that you're coming, do you mind driving? It'll make transporting my board easier." I shook my head; that was fine. "We were all going to catch the train at 10.30 am on Saturday morning, the same train we took…" He looked down at me. "Remember that train ride Babe?" I smiled up at him, I did. "We can load everything from my place and meet them there. How does that sound?"

"Perfect," I sighed, and it did. It would be a wonderful day, could be. I shook that thought off, reinforcing *would be* to myself.

I arrived at the Standish's at 10.00 am on Saturday morning. Dad had put the roof racks on to store Elijah's board and I'd emptied everything out of the car and boot except for the blanket I always kept in there. It would probably come in handy today. It was just as well too, as Mrs Standish had packed two eskies full of food and drinks. I laughed as Elijah swung me into his arms, noticing the pile of things to go into the boot. There was also an umbrella, several rugs, a ball, volleyball net and two sets of goggles, snorkels and flippers. "You have a big day planned for me?"

"Huge!" He put me down and gently kissed me. After several minutes, Mr Standish was at the door.

"Need any help packing the car there, son?" he asked Elijah with a smirk.

"I've got it under control, Dad," he grinned back at him.

We were the first to get to the beach. I checked the clock on the dashboard; their train wouldn't arrive at Castlebrook for another twenty minutes, and then it was a good ten-minute light-rail ride. We grabbed as much as we could on the first trip, which was most of the loose stuff. Elijah erected the net several metres away from where I was spreading out the rugs. We went back to the car and got a second load - all the bags, the umbrella and his board. He slung a few of the bags over his shoulder and hooked the umbrella and his board under one arm comfortably. This left me with only a few bags to carry. I watched him as he readjusted the board to a better position under his arm before starting the walk back to our spot. His muscles moved captivatingly, capturing my gaze as they had done what seemed like a lifetime ago in his kitchen. He was still so hot and very sexy. I knew with that thought I *could* make this work if I tried hard enough. On such a glorious day as this, nothing was impossible.

Elijah decided to leave the eskies in the boot until Michael, Simon and Lorien arrived to help carry them. I had offered, but he told me I'd done more than my share and the other three lazy lads could put in their effort. He was such a gentleman and as if in direct contradiction to him I took his hand and pulled him to the rug. "Get your board out!" I ordered. "Quick, before they all get here." He laughed, rolling me on top of him and kissing me lightly. I *could* do this... His concern from Sunday was absent from his thoughts. We were back to how it had been prior to the dream, not that he was aware of this division in time. *Pre-dream: post dream*, which is how I now thought of my life with Elijah. He stood up and angled the umbrella to best cover the rugged area in shade.

"I think I'd better lather you up," he suggested provocatively, grabbing the sunblock from his bag. This time I allowed him to apply it to my entire body, not just my back. After a few minutes of him teasing his fingers in and out of my tankini top I told him,

"I don't think they'll burn too badly do you?" He laughed and said, "Just making sure!"

"I'm going to have to blame this on the cold water," I told him, pointing out my pointer-outers. He passed me the sunblock and leant his back against my chest, wriggling his shoulders.

"Great massage therapy," he said, laughing.

"Thanks, that's *not* helping them subside any is it?" I asked as I pushed him forward so I could sunscreen his broad back. After a few minutes he said,

"That'll do," and scooped me up, running towards the water with me in his arms.

"No!" I called, laughing, knowing my pleas would go unheeded. He ran until he was thigh-deep and then threw me out in front of him, diving under the water behind me. He surfaced next to me, pulling me around his hips.

"This brings back pleasant memories," he growled as he drew in to kiss me. The waist-deep waves rocked us gently, mesmerising us into their trance.

We chose South Castlebrook Beach for this very reason. It was secluded, and due to the rocks, very few swimmers or surfers came here. I felt bad initially as I thought this location would hinder his surfing, but he assured me he could still 'catch a set' out past the rock formations, and, it would be a better environment for my first lesson. I looked at him dubiously when he added that, unsure whether I wanted to go through with it after all. "You'll see," he promised, drawing me to him again.

A whistle cracked through the smooth sounds of the ocean and we looked up to see the five of them standing next to the car. Elijah motioned to the boot that we had left ajar, and they got his message. Michael and Lorien grabbed the eskies and Simon shut the boot securely. We made our way back to the rugs to greet them. I deliberately averted my eyes from Lorien carrying the esky, his brown muscles flexed way too enticingly. I turned my focus to Michael; his body even more bronzed than when I last saw him.

"Sunbaking much?" I asked sarcastically as he put the esky down. He knew how averse I was to him lying out under the hot sun, especially during the worst of the summer months.

"I use protection," he quipped, turning a simple statement into an innuendo. He flopped onto the rug, dramatically.

"What's wrong with you?" I asked, settling in next to him. I looked at Bree and she smiled before grabbing Simon's hand and running into the water. Elijah had gone to sit with his brother for the moment, his brother who had wrapped his form around Keren from behind. She lifted her hair out of the way as he started to apply sunscreen to her shoulders.

"Back to me please!" Michael said. I smiled apologetically and lay on my stomach facing him.

"Sorry Honey, come on, tell Aunty Ash all about it." He rolled onto his back, throwing an arm over his face.

"Mum has a new boyfriend," he sighed significantly. I knew what he meant by this. Since the Lennox's divorce, Michael had been very protective of his mother and the 'new' boyfriends did not last all that long.

"What's so different about this one?" I asked, tousling his hair. He sat up,

"I think I actually *like* him." He sighed again. "He treats Mum really well, is considerate and thoughtful, he even tries to get along with me too. He may be a keeper..." More sighs resounded.

"What's his name?'

"Walter Mellons if you can believe it." I had to say it over a few times to get his meaning and then laughed. "Fortunately everyone calls him Wally. I'm not sure if that's better," he confided, also laughing.

"If you get on with this guy, what's the problem?"

"None really, but what's a Saturday at the beach without a little drama?" he asked playfully. "Speaking of which," he looked up at Elijah and said, "how's it going Ash?" I'm not sure if anyone else noticed the undertones of his open-ended question, but I understood.

"Great, unbelievably great. I think this can work."

"If you say so, you would know. I'm just glad that you're back on the ground again." He pulled me over to him and quickly hugged me.

"It would've been so much easier if we had fallen in love Michael, don't you think?" I offered insincerely. He rolled his eyes at me,

"Yes, *much* easier." He stood, poised to run at the water's edge. "But I wouldn't have ya!" he baited before running to the ocean. I was on my feet chasing him.

After we had all stopped to eat, Elijah brushed his hands across his boardies and took my hand. "Where are we going?" I asked him.

"Lesson one," he replied with a wide grin. I rolled my eyes at him but stood, ready for the inevitable. He went through the motions with me on the sand first, showing me how to paddle and flick my feet through to stand on the invisible board. After several attempts on dry land, I was ready to try it in the water, apparently.

I lay across his board and he held it for me whilst I went through the motions again, unable to get to my feet. "Don't worry about that Ash - no one can do it without a wave. Try catching a few in just lying on it," he advised.

The swell was not great as there was only about a two-metre gap in the rocks so most of the breakers were happening further out than my sheltered area. I rode the board in lying on my stomach for a few goes and Elijah coaxed me into trying to jump to my feet. After half a dozen disastrous attempts, I gave up. "You did fine Babe," Elijah told me, grabbing the board in one arm and me in the other.

"You can all just shut up too!" I called to our friends who had enjoyed the lesson a lot more than I did. They were laughing hysterically.

"Ash, you were just *too* funny!" Michael crowed. I knew better than to order him to try. He would no doubt take to it like a duck to water.

"You go out and have a surf, show me how it's done." I told Elijah. He planted a kiss on my forehead and started to paddle out through the break in the rocks. I sat down on the rug and towelled myself off, watching him.

He was good; caught many waves and rode them smoothly. I turned to Lorien to ask whether he surfed too. The thought had not entered my mind until now. I noticed Keren was watching Elijah with great interest, remembering who had been her first choice. I wished we could just swap.

Lorien was lying beside Keren with his eyes closed, his finger lightly running the length of her outer thigh. I took this opportunity to study him further. A small patch of sand was stuck to the stubble on his chin, I wanted to reach over and brush it off. I ran my eyes down his body, taking in his hairless firm chest, his flat stomach. His abs were so well defined I could follow the contour line on either side of them to where they disappeared beneath his board-shorts; knowing where this definition ended up.

I hadn't noticed throughout my examination of him that he'd opened his eyes; my gaze had not been directed to his northern region for some time. When my analysis of him finally did return to his face, I realised he was looking at me and I quickly turned away, *so* busted. He had no reason to believe I was perving on him, but would he make the connection? I kept my focus on Elijah from that moment on, even though in my mind I was writhing on the sand with Lorien. *It isn't going to work*, I confirmed to myself, knowing there was nothing else I could do. At least I had come to a conclusion, pleasant or not.

I distanced myself a little from Elijah for the rest of the afternoon by busying myself with volleyball, building a sandcastle with Bree, pretending to sleep. I felt him sit beside me at one stage, "Everything OK Babe?" he asked, rubbing his hand over my back. I mumbled sleepily and turned my face the other way. I knew if I broke up with him, I would need an explanation. I wanted him to make the final call. I hated myself.

It was a quiet ride home in the car. He didn't take my hand once, instead staring straight ahead at the road. I wondered what he was thinking as he'd obviously realised something was wrong.

When we got back to his place, we unpacked the car and he led me out onto the verandah. He sat down; his arms firmly crossed over his chest. "What's going on Ash?" he asked, surveying my face for any hint of underlying trouble, any trace of secrecy.

"I don't know," I answered truthfully, and I didn't; didn't know how to answer his question without hurting him so terribly.

"Well you have to know. There's been something going on for nearly a week and I don't understand. You seem to be so far away at times, and I know you've been making excuses to me. It feels like you're avoiding me and that's something I can't comprehend. Is something wrong? Can I help you with it? Ash you have to talk to me, this is tearing me up!" He stood and started to pace back and forth across the verandah, finally leaning his hands against the railing; his head lowered, frustrated. "Is there someone else?" he asked so softly I could only just hear him.

"No Elijah." I went to him and tried to soothe as best as I could.

"Then *what*? Have you simply stopped caring about me? What did I do? What *can* I do to reverse this? We both know things have changed and I don't want them to." He turned to face me and embraced me tightly. "I don't want this to be the end Ash," he whispered.

"It doesn't have to be Elijah," I told him. "I just need some time to get my head around things."

"What *things* Ash? Why can't you talk to me about it? Why have you got me at arm's length?" Too many questions, no answers I could give, none that mattered anyway.

"I wish I knew," I told him. "I don't know if I can find the words to explain it to you Elijah."

"Can you please try? This running hot and cold is making me crazy!" I sighed deeply, and said,

"I just don't feel like I'm a whole person at the moment, which makes it impossible to be able to share anything with you, feeling this way. I seem to be fading away; that I don't belong anywhere, and it has all happened so fast. It's not that I don't care for you anymore, I do. I just feel... vacant." I looked at him to see if he'd made any sense of what I had just described. I was not proud of the way I had artfully danced around mentioning any form of catalyst. His brow was furrowed, mulling it over.

"So you're not seeing anyone else?"

"No."

"And there is nothing I can do to help you through this?"

"No."

"Then I guess I'll just have to be here supporting you until you're through the other side." He hugged me again, his face against mine. He drew back and asked softly, "Can I kiss you Ash?" This made me smile, thinking back to our first date on the train. I didn't answer him, but pressed my lips to his, silencing him. Tears started to run down my cheeks and when he felt them, he drew back, scanning my face.

"Shh," he whispered, brushing the tears away before pulling me to him. He let me cry on his shoulder, having no idea as to their source.

The Fat Lady Sings

Music Selection: Cyndi Lauper, 'True Colours'
Diary Entry: Hey, don't give up even though it's difficult to be strong in an assembly of whimsical entities. It's hard to retain your vision and in the internal blind harsh light, it can create a feeling of nearly non-existence.

WE DANCED AROUND LIKE THAT for another week and finally I got a call on Monday from Elijah asking me to come over and see him. When I saw his face, I knew this was the end. He sat next to me on the sofa, taking my hands. "I think we need to take a break for a while, don't you?" he asked. I nodded, my eyes already starting to glisten with moisture. I didn't think I'd actually take it as hard as I was, thought it would be easy in fact. I'd forgotten though that we'd spent many wonderful times together and I was about to lose one of my best friends. I hadn't thought of that.

"I'm so sorry Elijah, I just don't know what's wrong with me," I lied. "The thought of not having you in my life, even as a friend is impossible to imagine," I said truthfully. He hugged me to him, allowing me to cry once again on his shoulder.

"I'll always be your friend Ash," he said quietly, rubbing my back. He was such an amazing guy. He held me like that for several minutes, then I felt him flex, motioning with his arm. I looked up to see Lorien halfway down the stairs. The look on his face made me cry even harder.

When I had calmed down, Elijah walked me to the car. "We'll see each other over the holidays," he promised. "Still going to the movies on Wednesday?" I nodded. "I'll see you there then," he smiled. I went to kiss him, one final sweet kiss but he put his hands on my shoulders, stopping me. "Not the best idea hey?" He held me to him one last time, hugging me fiercely. "I'm so sorry Ash," he whispered. These were not the words of someone taking a break. These words meant it was over, completely and irrevocably over. I pulled away from him and got into the car. I drove off and didn't look back, fresh tears already starting to form.

I wasn't sure where I was going until I took the Gracey turnoff. When Michael opened the door, one look at my face explained the situation. He took me in his arms and held me until I had calmed down enough to speak. "You broke up with him?" he asked gently.

"He broke up with me. I don't know why I'm so upset, this is what I wanted."

"I don't think seeing anything end ever comes without some form of pain," Michael said with the wisdom of a sage. "Want me to get Bree over?" he asked. I shrugged my shoulders,

"If you want." I left it up to him. He reached for the phone and I excused myself to use the bathroom. I could hear him mumbling into the handpiece to whom I assumed was Bree.

When I returned, he'd made coffee and was texting on his mobile. "I rang your mother and told her what happened," Michael said, "and that you'd be staying here tonight. She said to tell you that she loves you and asked me to take care of you." He smiled at me.

"Who are you texting?" I asked, feeling a little better after washing my face.

"Bree. There was no answer at her house." A few minutes later, he got a message. "She'll be here in an hour or so, she's out Christmas shopping with her Mum." As he put his mobile back on the coffee table, it rang. I couldn't see who it was before he picked it up. He answered, his eyebrows raised at me.

"Hi… yes, she's here…" *Who is it?* I mouthed. He just shook his head at me. "Do you want to talk to her?" This was so frustrating only getting Michael's end of the conversation. "No, she's OK now, the floodgates have closed for the time being," he looked at me and smiled. "OK, I will. Bye." He hung up. "That was bachelor number two," he said before I had a chance to ask him.

"Who?"

"Lorien."

"What did he want?" This was *not* a phone call I'd expected.

"Elijah filled him in on what happened when you left, not that he didn't already have an idea. He tried your place and then rang me when your mother said you were here."

"What did he *want* Michael?"

"To see how you were, to let you know he's thinking of you."

"Is that normal?" I asked.

"Anything is possible with those two, but I must admit, it does seem slightly out of the ordinary," he said. It was the first time I could remember hearing Michael use the twin's actual names.

Bree arrived within the hour and my tears started all over again. What was wrong with me? "Fate is a funny thing Ash; you got what you wished for. Maybe there's a greater knowing we aren't aware of and it's working for you unseen," Bree suggested. I hoped she was right. Michael told her about the phone call he'd received from Lorien earlier; Bree also agreed it was a strange response.

"I don't know though," I sighed, "like Michael said, anything is possible when you're talking about a Standish. They don't do things like everyone else."

"The important thing is that you deal with the here and now, get one twin out of your system before you go launching yourself at the other," he grinned. Bree and Michael could always make me feel better; give me hope or shake me down when I was being stupid...

"Something you're both forgetting is Lorien has a girlfriend. What kind of friend would I be to Keren, sidling in and stealing her man?" I posed to them. Even though I knew Elijah had been her first choice, I couldn't see her dumping Lorien on the off-chance Elijah was interested in her. Keren was many things but being a selfish and irrational person was not part of her make-up.

I knew there was no happy ending necessarily waiting for me either. Just because I was no longer with Elijah didn't mean Lorien was champing at the bit waiting on his turn. He'd asked me out once, a long time ago. There was no guarantee he even had any feelings for me anymore. They were never given the chance to develop all those months ago. He was probably used to thinking of me as his brother's girlfriend and nothing more. I sighed again. This roundabout conversation in my head was not going to resolve itself, nor find a conclusion. "Cheer up Ash," said Bree. "I'll show you what I bought you for Christmas if you like." I laughed and then felt a small wave of panic. Christmas was Friday and I had bought nothing for anyone. I always shopped for Mum and Dad, Michael, Bree and her sister Sara. Michael understood from my expression that I'd obviously let it slide so far this year.

"Want to go gift-buying tomorrow?" he asked. "I need to get something for Wally..." he pulled a face.

"Now you're shopping for him?" I asked impressed. "Looks like he *is* a keeper." I smiled at Michael. I was very happy for him and especially his mother. It was time for their family to move on, as hard as that had been for Michael in the past. It looked like he'd resolved some of his issues with the new beaus. Well at least with Wally.

"Oh, I nearly forgot," Michael said as he got up, heading for the TV cabinet. He slid a handful of paper sheets out from between the TV and the edge of the cabinet. "I bet you're glad I never got the chance to hand these out," he said, passing them to me. They were the mock awards that went un-presented, and I *was* glad they hadn't been, as I was the receiver of three of them. Elijah was right; I was Michael's favourite target. They were titled: 'Double your pleasure, double your fun award – for: keeping a spare on hand', 'What a girl wants award – for: being asked out by both twins on the same day', and finally the 'Has she or hasn't she award – for: the question that everyone wants answered - has she slept with him yet?'

"Jesus Michael, I would have killed you for these, even if it was still business as usual."

"There's one more," he said dejectedly, "you're just going to *love* this one." It was an award to be given to both Lorien and Elijah, 'It takes two award – for: if you'd learnt to share twins, you could have shared her, twins'.

"Keren would have skinned you alive if you'd actually gone through with this you know." Michael just grinned at me, obviously prepared to have taken that chance at the time. I thanked my lucky stars

Irene had put the moves on Michael that night, preventing this from ever occurring. "Can you burn these or something please?" He took them from me and tore them into pieces, throwing them at me like confetti.

We headed to Castlebrook the next morning, bright and early. Bree ended up staying the night at Michael's too, so we swung by Simon's place on the way out, to pick him up. I made sure I took note of all the things Michael and Bree had expressed any desire to own, making my selection a lot easier to choose for them.

I got a pair of earrings for Bree, a music gift card for Michael and a game for Sara. Mum and Dad were easy, they both loved to read so I got them each a gift voucher from Amazon Books online. I felt a lot better having this out of the way. I knew I would have put this off until Christmas Eve smacked me on the forehead, forcing me out in a frenzied shopping spree, grabbing at anything in desperation.

We were done by lunchtime, so went to a café to get something to eat. "Don't look now..." Michael started, "but there are twins at 11 o'clock," he pointed. Sure enough, there sat Elijah, Lorien and Keren, waiting to order. Keren waved us over; it was the natural thing to do. "Are you OK with this?" Michael whispered before we moved towards them.

"Now is as good a time as any to get this over and done with. I was going to go through it tomorrow at the movies anyway. Let's go." I followed them through the crowd. Michael was particular in selecting his seat, ensuring I was not crowded in with Elijah and no one else.

"Hi," I said, with bravado I didn't feel as I took a seat opposite Elijah.

"Hi Ash," he smiled gently at me. "How have you been?"

"Well, since yesterday - great, horrible, OK, messy. You?" I only just managed to keep the sarcasm out of my voice - this was *not* his fault. It was all well and good that I wanted to play the victim in this scenario, but Michael and Bree knew better, as did I. He smiled at me sadly and I noticed his hand steal across the table toward mine. He caught himself doing it and snatched it back quickly. Sometimes it was hard to restrict natural instincts and I knew he was not elated about my being upset over our break-up.

Michael went into damage control and soon had the table laughing. I could have kissed him; so grateful was I. He took all the pressure and sent it flying with a casual flick of his finger. Lorien caught my eye, smiling at me. *You OK?* he mouthed. I nodded and smiled back at him. He was just so considerate and thoughtful. What I wouldn't give to be able to reach across the table and trace my finger over his mouth. His lips looked so soft and vulnerable. I wondered how they would feel pressed against my own. I sighed again. Michael took this as a sign to move on so stood and went to organise the bill. "Sorry I can't offer you a lift but there isn't enough room in the car," I explained to Keren, primarily for Elijah's benefit, however.

"Not a problem Ash, we all live so close to Sommersett station it would be a pointless trip for you to make anyway." She smiled at me and took my hand, patting it gently. Her sympathy was enough for the waterworks to start again, so I drew away from her and stood as Michael came back to the table. We said our goodbyes and walked to the car.

"How was that?" Michael asked when we were out of earshot.

"Bearable," I told him. He put his arm around me.

"You'll be fine," he reassured. At least this time there had been no raging tears and, considering it was only yesterday we split up, I was feeling OK... for now anyway.

All By Myself

Music Selection: Bonnie Tyler, 'Total Eclipse of the Heart'
Diary Entry: I had it all; it's all gone. There is little I can do to change the situation and I feel so empty and miserable.

I PICKED UP BREE, MICHAEL AND SIMON on Wednesday morning and we headed into Castlebrook to meet the twins and Keren who were taking the train. On the way in, we discussed the best formation for our seating, as I didn't want to be too near Elijah. When we got to the cinema, they were waiting for us in the foyer. We bought tickets and took our seats. Elijah went in first, then Simon and Bree, followed by Lorien, Keren, myself and then Michael. I realised this still wasn't a great arrangement. If Lorien and Keren started to get all kissy-face I didn't know what my reaction would be. When had I become such high maintenance?

Fortunately, the movie we had chosen was non-stop action from the onset and I was quickly absorbed in the storyline. At some stage through the movie though, I felt a nudge from Keren. When I looked over, I noticed this had happened out of abstract movement and not because she was after my attention. She was pressed against Lorien, body and face, and I didn't know where to look. Michael noticed too and put his arm around me, drawing me under his arm. He took my left hand and asked me if I wanted to swap seats. It would have been way too obvious, so I shook my head.

He kept me wrapped up for the rest of the movie, doing his best to avert my attention when he could, allowing me to sit quietly crying at other times. All I wanted to do was leave, but once again, the obviousness of it all prevented me from doing so. "Are you OK Ash?" Keren whispered to me some time later. I looked over to see her smiling at me. "You're the only person who can cry through a 007 movie," she laughed quietly, not having a clue what had brought on my silent tears. I noticed Lorien was also looking at me, checking out the embrace Michael had me in. He seemed perplexed. This was never going to get any easier I realised, yet I had suspected that it may have been the case - Lorien was *not* single. Would it matter if he were?

We didn't hang around after the movie, although the twins and Keren wanted to goof off around Castlebrook before going home. Thankfully, Bree feigned a headache, giving us an excuse to get out of there. She'd been sitting on the other side of Lorien so would've been privy to what was going on too. Before we climbed into my car, Bree gave me a quick hug. My friends were so special to me; I didn't know what I would do without them.

Simon, not usually one to get involved in this kind of soap opera, surprised me when he told me Elijah's reaction to the scene. "So no one watched the movie, instead I was the main attraction? How on earth could he see Michael's arm around me from where he was sitting?"

"I think he was jealous *and* was certainly confused about what was going on."

"And what did you tell him?"

"That you and Lennox had been going at it hard since the break-up," he laughed.

"Simon *don't* tease her, can't you see she's upset enough," Bree chastised.

"What can I say," said Michael. "Chicks dig me." He reached over and took my hand, holding it over his heart.

"Sorry Ash," Simon said, "I didn't mean to upset anyone, but I couldn't help myself." That was Simon to a tee – no tact or thought processes, he just ran on primal instinct, saying whatever popped into his mind.

"I was already upset Simon, you had nothing to do with it. You didn't really tell him that though did you?"

"He did," Bree said, pulling a face at Simon. I had to admit, it was pretty funny. I started to laugh, unable to stop myself.

"I'm sorry Michael," I apologised, not wanting to hurt his feelings, sure that I had not.

"Well *other* chicks dig me." He laughed with me; we all knew this was a fact. "*I* noticed something else too…," he drawled. "But I don't think I should tell you…" he teased. I gave him a stern look and he relented. "Elijah wasn't the only one keeping tabs on us during the movie. Lorien was taking a keen interest too. *And*, Keren was taking a pretty keen interest in Lorien taking a keen interest," he chuckled. "At one stage I caught his eye and winked at him."

"What did he do? Why did *you* do that?" I asked, unsure how it would make a difference.

"I just wanted to let him know all bets were off, that you were free to do what you wanted, with whom you wanted. He sort of just snorted and went back to watching the movie. Would you rather him think you were sitting there crying over him?"

"No, I guess not, but what on earth did you hope to achieve from that interaction?"

"Jealousy Babe!" Michael answered positively.

"Michael, Honey, I don't think you're much of a threat to the Standish twins, they know you too well."

"All I can say is that Elijah wasn't all that happy either," Simon piped up from the back seat.

"What our senses tell us, what we *see* or possibly smell can affect all the things we profess to know."

"For example?" I prompted.

"OK, let's say there's a delicious looking piece of cheesecake in the fridge and you want to eat it *so* badly. However, you can tell by the smell it's gone off. Looks can be deceptive…"

"That explanation sort of takes on the opposite side of your intention though, doesn't it?"

"It may not be the best comparison, but do you get my meaning? When you know you can't have that slice of cheesecake anymore, you'll find yourself out buying another as you will *have* to have the cheesecake." I supposed so.

"I don't like being thought of as a dessert though," I laughed.

"Why not?" Simon scoffed. He had a point there.

"However," I continued the debate with Michael, "what if the cheesecake had someone else's name marked on it and you were unable to eat it in the first place, regardless of it having gone bad?"

"I still say that makes you want it even more, especially if the person who it belongs to doesn't want it anymore."

"So now I am unwanted, rotten cheesecake." We all laughed.

Michael rang on Boxing Day, brimming with excitement. "You will *never* guess what's happened!"

"Do I get a clue?" I teased, knowing he would burst if I taunted him too long.

"How's this for a clue? Keren and Lorien broke up!" I didn't know how to feel about this.

"What happened?"

"Personally, I think she always preferred Elijah..." I knew this to be true.

"What *happened* Michael?" I asked again.

"Well, so the story goes, Keren had been sulking all afternoon after the movie and when Lorien asked her on the train ride home what was wrong she got stuck right up him... Said he didn't care about her and was more interested in you now that you were no longer going out with Elijah..."

"Wow!"

"You bet, and she broke it off with him, right then and there."

"Who told you?"

"Elijah told Simon, Si..."

"Simon told Bree and Bree told you right?" I interrupted him, laughing.

I felt elated and was not sure why. This news was certainly no guaranteed escalation for my situation. Lorien still had no idea how I felt about him. Well I didn't think so... I debated whether to ring Lorien or send him a text message. I wanted him to know I was there for him and to show him the support he gave to me when Elijah and I broke up. I decided on a text message. This way I could say what I wanted without the need to make strained conversation. *Hi lorien, hope u r ok let me know if u need anything, ash xxx.* Straightforward, to the point and obvious as to the issue. A few seconds later, I got a reply,

Meh, u know how it is. I may take u up on that offer. L ☺ A few simple words from him and my day was suddenly sunny. I didn't delete the message. I knew I would want to read it again; torment myself as to all the various undertones I could imagine.

The Brick-Laying Duck

Music Selection: Irene Cara, 'Flashdance…What a Feeling'
Diary Entry: On my own I let my tears fall, tears full of silent regret. They go unheeded however in our society made of concrete.

I RAN SMACK BANG INTO LORIEN as I hurried out of the Post Office the following Tuesday morning. I managed to drop my bag during the kafuffle, knocking its contents all over the ground. He stooped and helped me collect everything and as he handed it back over asked, "Where are you going in such a rush?"

"Nowhere in particular. Where are you going?"

"Nowhere in particular."

"Want to get a coffee?" I suggested.

"Sure."

We walked a few blocks down the street to the coffee shop, which was virtually empty. Just because we were on school holidays didn't mean the rest of the world was on a break. It was also well before the lunch crowd would start to assemble. "How have you been Lorien?" I asked, knowing what a sensitive person he was.

"Fine I suppose. It wasn't like we were as close as you and Eli; it came as a shock more than anything."

"It's very easy to love a Standish. I'm not sure what Keren's problem is."

"The possibility she was going out with the *wrong* Standish I presume," he smiled. He didn't seem to be overly concerned about their break-up at all.

"Are they going out now, Elijah and Keren I mean?"

"Do you care if they are?" he asked, although I was not sure why.

"It's none of my business what Elijah does or with whom," I answered honestly. I knew it was not an issue for me either way; it was the Standish sitting across from me right now I had issues with; issues of which he was not even remotely aware.

"I thought you may have had a jealous streak coming out in you, and no, they aren't. I think Eli would give me a little more breathing space before he allowed himself to seduce or be seduced by her, assuming that happens," he finished, laughing.

"I still can't believe how well you're taking this," I reiterated. "I know what it's like being the dumpee, even though I *wanted* to be the dumper. It still isn't a pleasant feeling when it happens." When he didn't answer, I looked up at him; he was eyeing me strangely.

"Want to run that by me again?" I quickly thought back over what I'd said, scanning for the confusion. I realised that my wanting to break up with Elijah was not a published fact and he'd picked up on that; now looking for the underlying explanation. "Ash?" he prompted when I didn't answer. The waiter bringing our order to the table, which gave me an extra few seconds to get myself a story together, interrupted him. Fortunately, she took her time, taking the opportunity to flirt with Lorien. Typical Standish though, he shut her down quickly and refocussed his attention to me. "Ash?" he asked again more firmly.

"What?" I answered in what I hoped sounded like honest confusion.

"Were you using my brother?"

"No Lorien, I'd never do anything like that. I was pretty much a full-time single girl until you moved here. I can't believe you'd think that about me."

"What else can I think after the bombshell you just dropped? Can you explain to me what you were referring to if it wasn't about taking Elijah for an emotional hayride?"

"Not really," I mumbled.

"Not *really*?" he said. "What does that even mean?" He was starting to get angry, and I needed to quell that immediately. I couldn't stand the thought of having Lorien upset with me or thinking of me in that way.

"I cared very much for Elijah," I told him truthfully.

"Then why did *you* want to break up with him? I thought he'd truly broken your heart when you split up. I can see now that my concern was completely unjustified!"

"Lorien," I started, trying to find something to say to appease him, without having to spill the beans entirely.

"I'm listening." I sighed, and tried...

"The beginning of the end started on the Sunday of Michael's party." I could see him working back through the days, trying to find the trigger that had started me on a self-destruct course with his brother. He obviously came up with a blank as he prompted me to continue. "On Saturday night when everyone else had gone to bed, we had such a special moment, a moment that would have taken us in new directions if it'd been given enough time to develop."

"You had sex?" he asked, a little surprised.

"No, nothing that extreme," I laughed. He was looking at me impatiently. "Anyway... I had a dream that night, a wonderful dream, and without going into too much detail, Elijah was doing amazing things..."

"Ash, I still can't see the problem. Did it scare you? Was he cruel?"

"*Amazing* things I said, I don't think that word conjures up fear or cruelty, do you?"

"Will you stop beating around the bush and tell me what the problem was."

"Just as it was getting to a more intimate part... I can't believe I'm telling you this." He waited. "Elijah looked up at me..."

"What's so scary about Eli's face," he laughed.

"It wasn't Elijah, I had thought it was, but it wasn't," I ended lamely.

"So who..." he didn't finish the question. I couldn't look at him, I was completely vulnerable now, and all the cards were on the table. "You don't mean..." he seemed to be having difficulty finishing his sentences. "Me...?" he asked, a hint of disbelief in his voice. He moved to the seat beside me, making the conversation more confidential. "Ash, I don't know what to say."

"You don't have to say anything Lorien; it's just the way it is. I don't expect anything from you and in fact had no intention of *ever* allowing you to know anything about this."

"It just slipped out."

"Yes, it did. I'm not Freud you know." Now I was starting to get angry, possibly because he hadn't swept me into his arms proclaiming his eternal love for me.

"What was the situation with you and Michael at the movies about then?"

"You listened to Simon…" I sighed. "I'd been witness to you and Keren swapping saliva and I got upset. Michael was being my friend. I don't know what I would have done without him and Bree over the past week or so." He smiled a little and said,

"You *were* perving at me that day at the beach." He realised that this was neither the time nor place to be swapping such pleasantries and the smile faded. "So is it still the case?" he asked softly.

"Lorien, do you think I would have stumbled around blindly in confusion after the dream not knowing what to do about Elijah if it wasn't *always* going to be the case?"

"I guess not. Does Eli know?"

"No, I wouldn't do that to him. He was aware I'd pulled away, but he couldn't understand why. There was no way I could tell him I'd fallen instantly in love with his brother," I laughed, a little hysterically. "It's been a very difficult few weeks for me…" I sighed. I pulled a five-dollar note from my bag and put it on the table, standing to leave.

"Where are you going Ash?" he said grabbing my arm. "Can't we talk about this a bit more?"

"What for Lorien? I love you and you don't feel the same way about me. All we would achieve is to draw out a conversation I already consider awkward and embarrassing. You may have only had five minutes to deal with this, but I've done nothing but deal with it for weeks.

To tell you the truth I'm *over* thinking about it. I've never been more miserable in my life and there is nothing I can do to change that." I pulled my bag over my shoulder and leant down to place a soft kiss on his forehead. He let me.

My mobile phone chirped an hour later; it was a message from Lorien. *Can't we talk about this ash? I don't want u hurting, L* ☹ No, we could not talk about this, I would end up simply hurting more. I turned off my phone.

BACK TO SCHOOL

Making it Through the Week

Music Selection: The Eurythmics, 'There Must Be An Angel (Playing with my heart)'
Diary Entry: Am I dreaming? An angel has shone its light upon me, making me think back to our beatific juncture.

IT WAS FINALLY FRIDAY, the last day of the first week back at school. We were now in Year 11 and our lives had changed so dramatically since the return to school after the October holidays last year. Nothing seemed the same. Our two hundred enrolments in Year 10 had shrunk to about one hundred and forty; the only two from our group not to return was Cyndi and Frankie. Cyndi was going to be a kindergarten teacher and had enrolled in TAFE. Frankie had also enrolled in TAFE, doing his builder's trade certificate and working alongside his father as an apprentice. They were planning to move in together in a few weeks, to be nearer the TAFE, they told everyone.

I was sitting in Maths class hot, bored and still full of the anguish I'd tried to hide throughout the week. I didn't know where to look when I first saw Lorien, him being the only person to know how I felt about him with exception to Michael and Bree. I didn't count Simon. They were considerate of me during recess and lunch, keeping me chatting and active, not allowing me to feel uncomfortable. This performance continued throughout the week and I was thankful, it had made a difficult situation easier to endure. Other than that, I managed to prevent myself from looking at Lorien or taking notice of him in any way during classes. This was especially difficult in Music as there were only nine of us. I knew it would smooth out eventually and everything would go back to normal. It was just going to take some time. Fortunately, Keren had dropped Music this year, making it only an uncomfortable duo instead of a trio.

I decided to skip the usual routine with Michael and Bree when the bell rang for lunch. I had Music next period so would spend the break hidden away in the classroom, expressing myself through the strings and bow of my violin. I didn't feel like eating or playing when I got there and sat leaning on the desk with my chin in my hands, wondering again how I'd managed to find myself here, so miserable and alone where once there was rhapsody. I knew it would be rough when I got back to school. In the very smallest and tiny way though, a torturous way, I was glad. I would get to see Lorien again on a daily basis – dually adding to the agony and lessening the pain.

I finally broke down a few weeks ago and filled Mum in on exactly what had happened. 'There was no better cure for an old love, than a new love,' she had advised me. I would have laughed if it hadn't been so ironic. There are some things though you just can't discuss with your mother. The fact that I'd managed to get her advice in reverse order was a primary reason for not doing so. I *had* the new love, throwing it away for no love.

Lorien came into the room whilst I was tormenting myself with these thoughts, heading straight for the piano. He launched into a rather tender sounding piece, something new I presumed, as I hadn't heard it before. He hadn't noticed me. I didn't want it to appear I was racing out of the room because of his arrival so stayed motionless. Eventually, I gave my E string a pluck to announce my presence and he stopped playing immediately. "Ash," he said, "I didn't see you." He rose off the bench and came to lean on the back of the chair in front of me. "You're a hard woman to catch on your own, you know that?" I wasn't sure if he expected an answer, none was offered. I just sat there tightening and relaxing the E string peg; plucking the string and listening to it go sharp then flat. He took the violin from my hands and moved it to another table, out of my reach. This made it very difficult to avert my eyes and be the focus of my attention, not to look at him.

"How have you been?" he asked as an apparent icebreaker.

"Fine I suppose. It's hard to determine though as I have to wade through the layer of embarrassment to get to any other feelings." His eyes were sad as he asked,

"Are you embarrassed because of what happened the last time I saw you alone?"

"Yes that *and* you can add 'right now' to the equation too if you like." I wished he would just ignore me, kick me out of his life and pretend I didn't exist. So close but an eternity away from me. It would have been easier to deal with that rather than him being sweet.

"I don't think you've noticed through the veil of shadow you've cast over me this week, but I've been *trying* to get your attention, without getting everyone else's at the same time."

"Oh?" Was he about to suggest another duet, perhaps accompanying him on the new piece he'd written during the school holidays? I looked up at him, waiting for him to continue. He appeared to be choosing his words carefully, his brow drawn in thought.

"I've had a hard time not thinking about what you said to me at the coffee shop, in fact it's been a constant torment."

"I'm sorry Lorien," and I was. "It was never my intention to make you feel uncomfortable. I'll get over it eventually, it's just hard speaking to you about it, especially now, this first time." I was hopeful something could be saved and said, "I want to put this behind us and still be friends... I miss you."

"You need to let me finish, Ash. You're making assumptions, wrong assumptions, and I need to explain some things to you."

"So we can't be friends," I muttered in rejected acceptance. I seriously needed to stop throwing suggestions around in his vicinity. I only ended up hurt again... and again.

He laughed. I couldn't believe what I was hearing. Lorien was always so sane and considerate, and here he was laughing at me. Didn't he realise how hurt I was, how his reaction was affecting me? As if in sympathy, slow, fat tears started to make their way down my cheeks. I lowered my face to conceal them as he came around the desk and sat facing me. "Ash," Lorien urged, "look at me."

"I can't." I couldn't. The embarrassment of the past several weeks, the torment, the wanting, the knowledge that I would not have my prince... Life was so unfair.

"Ash," he breathed into my ear, his hands moving to my face, trying to force my eyes to his. I kept them lowered; more tears were starting to build there, and I didn't want him to see them. "Please look at me," he tried again. I shook my head. He lowered his cheek to mine, his mouth aside my ear. I thought he kissed there softly, secretly. I had myself so convinced this was impossible, scoffing at the memory of moving my own clothing in a wonderful, if not misleading, dream. "What?" he questioned, moving his face back to read my expression better, his brow furrowed.

"Nothing," I mumbled and stood to leave the room.

"Hey," he reached out to capture my hand, "where are you going?" He drew me back to him, wrapping his arms around me and pulling me close. I couldn't calculate this. What was happening? Why was he doing this, making it even more painful than need be? I still wouldn't meet his eyes, as I didn't want to see the pity brewing in them. "Will you look at me Ash," he said again, more forcefully. I looked.

His hands moved into my hair, his lips centimetres from mine - his eyes scanning my face, drinking it in. He kissed the tears from my left lid and then my right, brushing his now wet lips against my cheek, and then holding me to him again. His breath was a husky whisper in my ear. "It's always been you Ash." I looked at him then alright! I searched his face for the hint of a smile to say this was all a lie, that he was just tending my feelings. But why would he do that? "Did you hear me," he laughed, "I *love* you."

"No," I shook my head. This can't be happening. "*Ow!*" he pinched me lightly but enough to bring my attention to the reality he was creating, trying not to smile at my reaction. "No," I answered again. "It can't be real, but I can't be dreaming either. Lorien what are you doing?" I started to weep, real heart-wrenching sobs. However, I held him closer. I clung to him, desperate for it to be true. He gently brought my hands from behind his back, kissing each of my palms before draping my arms around his neck.

"If there's only one way I can prove this moment to you, then here it is; much to my detriment of course," he chuckled lowly. I raised my eyes to his in confusion, in hope, my arms now locked around his neck. He stared into my eyes as he brought his hands to my face again, softly brushing away the tears from my cheeks with his fingers. I felt like he was inside me, so intense was his gaze. Then he kissed me.

"Wow," he murmured a few minutes later, "you've been holding out on me." He drew back, smiling lazily. I must have still been wearing a mask of shock or disbelief, as he said, "Ash, Ash*lyn*, I love you, do you understand?" he asked, laughing softly. I nodded. Then I felt him tense. "Am I assuming too much, am I being a fool to think this is how you still feel about me?" he asked, looking into my face for the disappointment he was not expecting. Instead, he saw a smile.

"I've loved you since Michael's party, ever since I dreamt about you and even unknowingly before then. I've not been able to dismiss it since - it was having you or going crazy. All the things I told you at the coffee shop are still true, would always have been true..." I smiled, shyly. I still couldn't believe I was in his arms; arms that now belonged to me, which would always hold me and keep me safe.

He lowered his lips to my forehead, pressing them warmly against it, then to each of my cheeks. He grazed his lips over mine, groaning slightly. "Now don't start that again," I murmured out of the side of my otherwise entwined mouth. He pulled back looking at me curiously, a half-smile playing on his lips.

"The dream," he guessed.

"Hmmm," I sighed, seeking his lips once more.

At some stage, I heard bells ringing and thought they sounded so surreal and strong. Then, when I heard the catcalls and wolf-whistles from the doorway I realised the bell was signalling the end of lunch. Music, period seven was about to commence. I pulled away from Lorien embarrassedly. Looking at the ground, I hurried off to take my seat. As always, Joel and Billy had plenty to say but I ignored them. They eventually saw they weren't going to get a rise from me and decided to leave me alone. I was sure *that* was only for the moment, however. They would be back, but who cared, I was so happy. Lorien shifted into the seat beside me. "What are you doing there?" I smiled. He had previously sat in a row behind me earlier in the week. When our kiss was interrupted and he disappeared, he had gone to retrieve his bag from the desk where he put it as he entered the room earlier.

"With only nine of us in the class I don't think Mr O'Dowd will have a problem with it, do you?" Mr O'Dowd was not one of the teachers who liked to have his students move about.

His eyes never left mine throughout the entire Music period. I blushed regularly, and once he caught himself as he went to stroke my cheek. He tucked the offending limb into his armpit, grinning. *Beautiful…* he mouthed, and I knew another blush was heating my face.

As soon as the bell sounded, Lorien was standing at my side, his eyes luminous. "Let's ditch last period." I nodded, taking his hand and dragging him to the door.

"Now don't you two be late for English," drawled Billy with a smirk on his face. We ignored him, losing ourselves among the departing crowd.

"Where are you taking me?" Lorien asked casually as I led him by the hand toward the parking lot.

"I thought we'd drive somewhere, sit... chat..." We both knew what we were doing, regardless of the venue.

"My house is a lot closer and more comfortable than the car, don't you think?" He ran the back of his hand lightly down my cheek, looking intently into my eyes. I was at such a dire level after the slow growing crescendo of looks and nuances during Music class. I'd waited so long to be with Lorien, I wanted more of him immediately. Our first kisses were interrupted, and I needed to have my initial fill. The endless weeks of bleakness had unbelievably ended abruptly. I didn't care where we were, I just needed to be with him; attracted like opposite ends of the poles.

I fought a slight wave of anxiety and I wasn't thinking straight. "What about your mother? Isn't it possible she *could* come home to grab something? Maybe she doesn't have a lesson and chooses the comfort of your living room over the History staffroom." I couldn't believe how rapidly I was speaking, not wanting to waste even a second.

"Not a chance." He was already guiding me to the canteen entrance. Just a quick jump across the road where we could seclude ourselves for half an hour or so and he obviously felt the same way. The thought made my heart skip a beat. How long had I been waiting for this? If the prelude during Music class was anything to judge by, I was uncertain I could ever face the world again. Just Lorien and I, forever locked away in our own personal bubble... "Ash," he said. I turned to face him. "We cross the road here." I was on my way past the school entrance, just walking in a daze. "I can *imagine* where you were and what you were thinking... luckily one of us has the ability to get us safely across the road." With his mouth slightly open, he ran his tongue over his bottom lip, his eyebrows slightly raised, eyes smouldering. *I want to launch myself at you right now* was my immediate new thought. Just a few more metres...

He glanced quickly over his shoulder as we reached the other side of the road, making sure we had gone unnoticed. "Let's go around to the back door, it's a little more secluded to enter by." We darted around to the left-hand side of the house - the garden side. I couldn't believe the difference.

"Oh Lorien!" I cried, "What happened to your mother's beautiful garden?" Most of the flowerbeds were wilting and starting to brown, the end-of-summer heat had taken its toll.

"She hasn't had the time and Dad has hardly been home over the last few days. It doesn't take long to lose its shine," he reasoned. "Look," he said pointing; clusters of marigolds were still in full bloom with many buds just about to open.

"Promise me you'll water the garden this afternoon? Please?"

"Of course Ash, if that makes you happy." He put his hand to my chin smiling slightly, moving in to kiss me. He paused with only a fraction of space between us, looking thoughtful, "I can do it now if you like."

"I think we should get out of sight," I said, pulling him onto the verandah. He chuckled, exhaling the laugh into my mouth, already initiating the next kiss. Heaven had found a place on earth. We moved as one person, re-shifting weight, alternating face angles; our hands slowly sampling each other's hair, faces, waists and hips. It was a slow, intoxicating waltz and I danced...

The sound of a passing motorbike finally cast us from our spell; we'd been standing there for nearly fifteen minutes. He looked into me as his dark eyes surveyed my features, moving a strand of hair from my forehead, tracing a finger over my cheek, taking in my mouth. That made me blush and I couldn't help but lick my lips, knowing they were being analysed.

"Are you thirsty?" He breathed the question into my ear, kissing the side of my neck. It was doing fantastic things to me. I nodded, eyes closed, head moving to angle my neck toward him as he kissed a slow trail around my throat. "Me too," he sighed deeply against me, and finally drew his face away from mine. "A little revitalisation of the body and then we can return to the rapture." He opened the back door for me to enter the small hallway at the rear of the house and I took this advantage to use the bathroom as I passed by.

When I went into the kitchen, he wasn't there. "Lorien?" I called quietly.

"Over here." He was sitting on the arm of the sofa, two glasses sat on the coffee table. It felt a little weird being here, as I never thought I'd see the inside again. It also looked so out of place without the vases of colourful flowers everywhere. I suppose winter came eventually, even to Paradise. "You OK Ash?" he asked with concern.

"Perfect," I told him, smiling brilliantly. I didn't want to spoil our afternoon. I also realised how many times I had been asked that very question over the past few weeks. I never wanted to hear it again.

Before I sat, I picked up my glass and drank deeply; it was good. I had a little more and then put it down, making sure it wasn't too close to spill *or be knocked over.* The thought of us actually having sex today hadn't even crossed my mind. However, I felt like a bride on her wedding night back in the 1950s - going from nothing at all to something pretty major. True, in the scheme of things her 'major' was more like a cliff face in lieu of my hill, maybe my mountain… We had previously been through the opening courtship and knew each other so well already; I was sincerely hoping he was on the same page. "Do you want some music on?" he asked.

"I don't need anything else at the moment." I went to him and he proved me wrong by taking me in his arms. His lips played with mine, tasting and moving, teasing.

"Hmmm," he purred, laying me across the sofa, sliding his leg between mine. I couldn't get enough of him, our kisses becoming more and more heated. I had to thank Elijah for bringing me out of my awkward shell; all the embarrassment and bravado I felt each time I initiated holding hands or kissing him was no longer an issue. Perhaps it came down to being with the right partner.

I ran my hands from his waist to shoulders, rucking the back of his shirt up in their procession. He lifted his weight from me so I could hook it up at the front and he sat up quickly to pull it over his head. I dragged him back to me, my hands ravenous for this new skin. With one arm, he held himself slightly from me so I could graze my fingers over his chest, down his arms and across his waist, causing him to shudder. He felt amazing, firm and muscular, full of power. I traced the outline of his bicep, thinking back to Bree's party when Lorien had removed his shirt, the shutter-clicks of him in Michael's pool, at the beach. He was always sexy, but it was nothing in comparison to what I was thinking now. He took my hand and placed it above my head, resting it on the sofa arm. He moved his elbow into the area it had vacated and brought his other hand up to caress my jaw, sharing deeper kisses.

He eased down, pressing softly into my stomach, caressing with his forehead, his cheek, his chin, slowly, enticingly. He nuzzled his face back up my body, resting it between my breasts. They seemed to swell under his hot breath. As he shaped his palm to my curves, he drew back to watch my face. His fingers crawled down my side to find the edge of my shirt, leisurely raising it. His hand trickled under and sought out my breast again, slipping his fingers into the cup - teasing across, underneath and around. My head was thrown back, my breathing escalating. He was intensely taking in my reaction as he slid his hand across to my other breast. "You have no idea of what you do to me Ash, you are just so *arousing*," he growled. He hooked his thumbs outside my shirt, lifting it higher, readying it for removal. I sat forward a little, eager to be against him. In the distance, a bell rang. "Great timing," he mumbled and stopped, albeit lamentably.

"What?" I asked feeling a little befuddled.

"School's out, Elijah will be home within five minutes." He sat up shaking his head. "I'm *so* sorry Ash, we should have gone somewhere in the car after all."

He looked around for his shirt, finally finding it near the dining room table. He ran his fingers through his hair as he came and sat next to me, fully dressed. I swung my feet back onto the ground, adjusting my clothing. "Not that I was *finished* with you, but we have all the time in the world." We got lost in each other's eyes again, but after only a few moments Lorien roused himself. "However, we don't have all the time in the world now. I don't want to be rude, but can we leave from the back door again?" It wasn't a concern to me, but I was curious why. We spoke simultaneously,

"Elijah." I hadn't stopped to think he was unaware of our newfound union. In fact neither was I until about an hour ago.

"I need to speak to him Ash, before this can become public."

"I understand Lorien; I don't want to hurt Elijah either. How do you think he'll take it?"

"I'm sure it'll be fine, it's not like you two just broke up. I want to be the one to tell him though, not have him find out or walk in on it."

We stood on the back verandah waiting to hear the front door open. When he called out Lorien's name, we stole across the street like a pair of thieves. He relaxed once we were back at my car. "Would you like to go on a date tomorrow?" he asked, moving my hair behind one ear, lingering his palm over my cheek.

"You love to ask for dates," I teased. "I thought we were a little past the friend stage, no longer needing to request formal *dates*?" He was still smiling at me, waiting for my answer. "I would love it," I answered breathily. "Do you want me to pick you up or should I meet you somewhere?" I asked with a little unease, thinking it may be best not to be pulling into his driveway tomorrow morning.

"It will be fine, come to the house. In a few weeks, I can pick *you* up all going well. I go for my licence soon."

We were oblivious to the cars pulling out around us, leaving for the day, and soon found we were the only ones left in the parking lot. "I should go…" he didn't move.

"Want to get in for a second?" I asked, unlocking the passenger door. He didn't answer, already halfway in.

I pulled into the driveway at about 10.30 am the next morning. The front door opened and Lorien spoke to someone inside before closing it behind him. "Hi," he said, climbing into the car, leaning over to kiss me tenderly.

"How did it go last night?" I asked, not as if the thought hadn't been *all* I had thought since we left each other yesterday.

"It was fine. I told you it would be."

"What did he say, what do your parents think of it, will we..."

"Shh," he put his finger to my lips. "First of all we need to make a stop. Pull in at the deli please," he directed. "Won't be a second." He jumped out of the car and disappeared into the shop. A few minutes later, he came out with a box in his hands and opened the back door to put it on the seat.

"What's in the box?"

"You'll find out soon enough my impatient one," he said as he climbed back into the car, pointing west. "Follow the black-tarred road," he instructed.

"I feel like I've been hit by a tornado," I said. We both laughed.

Every now and then, he told me to make a left or a right turn; we were working our way closer to the lake edge and were at Glassread reserve when he finally instructed me to stop. A few homes scattered the waterfront, weekenders mostly, and wooden baths were set into the lakeside in the distance. It was a beautiful and tranquil spot he'd picked; I knew it well. "How do you know about Glassread, I wouldn't have thought you'd have been out here before?" I asked.

"I grilled a few people," he grinned. "The boys were *more* than helpful." *Have you brought anyone else here*? I wondered. He grabbed the box and walked a few metres from the car, finding a level spot. "Damn, didn't think to bring a rug."

"Wait right there."

I trotted to the boot grabbing the blanket and I flicked it out, settling it in a balloon to the ground. He put the box down and sat cross-legged. "Lorien *please* put me out of my misery, what happened last night? I want all the gory details, including what your parents thought."

"What makes you think Mum and Dad would be worried?" he asked, his head tilted slightly to the side. I sat down, facing him.

"I don't know, doesn't it seem strange to them I was going out with Elijah and now I'm going out with you?"

"You," he started, taking my hands in his, "are the only one who seems to have a problem with it." He smiled and leant over to kiss me. It was glorious to be kissed on a warm, late-summer day, out in the open air; we were the only two people in the world.

When we returned to Earth, I continued with the questioning. "And?" I looked at him with my face twisted.

"*And* I spoke to Elijah. He didn't seem all that surprised really. He knew something had been going on with somebody as he'd noticed the glasses I left on the coffee table when we snuck out the back door. I asked him how he felt about it and what boundaries he expected. He didn't really have any, just that we cool it a bit when he's around until he gets used to the idea, especially at home." I could live with that. I still couldn't fathom how the twins were so mature about the circumstances.

"So it's OK for me to come to your house?"

"Of course."

"And be in your room like I would be in his?"

"Yes, well in small doses initially, but yes," he smiled. "Ash, life goes on as normal OK? I told you this has happened before, *Eli* told you before. Maybe it wasn't quite to this level, but it's not the first time we've been through this situation. Obviously," he drew forward again, "it *will* be the last." After a few more minutes of bliss Lorien said, "I think you'd better come in with me this afternoon, so you can see I'm being totally honest with you."

"I believe you Lorien but it's just so hard to comprehend. I suppose we have to face it sooner or later though, it may as well be this afternoon."

"You make it sound like you're lining up for the firing squad," he teased. "Hungry?"

"No, not really, let's go for a walk."

We walked around the peninsula for about an hour, taking in the beautiful day and each other. I told him about my Gran, going into detail about my holidays spent here.

We made our way back to the baths eventually and sat with our feet in the water. If we'd been in a more secluded setting, I would've had no greater pleasure than to strip off and lie next to each other on the warm boards. I settled into this daydream, imagining the sun playing off our basking skin, the gentle caresses and soft lips... the splinters... "You're smiling," he said softly.

"Am I?" I sighed, my eyes closed.

"I always wonder where you go when you're off in dream world," he said, drawing me close.

"You're always there..."

"And what are we getting up to today?" he asked gently, trying not to break my vision.

"Just lying here naked, soaking up the sun..."

"We can do that, there's no one around…," he said. I sat up,

"That you are aware of! Lorien I couldn't, what if someone saw us?"

"So?" I had to admit, it was a tempting thought.

He took my hand and we walked about halfway back down the baths. We sat again, with Lorien straddled behind me. "I can be your body armour." I understood his intent as he started to lift my shirt.

"Lorien, we can't!"

"Can't we?" He eased it over my head and pulled it free from my arms, capturing my bra in the same movement. He reached around and crossed his arms over me, his hands covering my breasts. "Perfectly sheltered, no one can see," he whispered into my ear. He slid one hand down to the button on my shorts, unfastening it and drawing down the zipper. I started to breathe faster, unsure whether it was fear, excitement or a mixture of both. He worked his thumb into the back of my briefs, easing down both layers. I raised my hips so he could continue unhindered. His arms and legs wrapped around my naked body, holding me against him in a safety net.

After a few minutes he asked, "Are you ready to jump in?" I nodded and he untethered himself from me. I slipped into the water; certain I could see the hiss of steam rise as my smouldering body was exposed to it. I turned to see him standing; pulling his shirt and shorts off, not concerned if every eye in the world was upon him. He slid in next to me. The feel of his naked body pressed against mine was exhilarating. The water was just above waist deep, but I was beyond caring about being half exposed. In fact his body covered me; he had promised me amour and shielded I was.

His kisses stirred me; his hands were restless and impatient, trying to take in my entire body at once. I moved my arms to around his neck and he hoisted me up, so our faces were even, backing a little further into the deeper water. I wanted to hitch my legs around his hips, but the sensation of déjà vu was too familiar, the fact there were no clothes between us also opened up a 'hole' new situation. Irrespectively, we were like the tide - flowing and ebbing against each other, rocked on occasion by the natural movement of the lake. His exquisite kisses captivated me, hungry and searching. His sensitive hands played me with the same talent he performed his music, but instead of the keyboard, it was my body he caressed.

I pulled back in surprise when I felt him against me. He looked at me inquisitively. "I didn't know that could happen in cold water," I said in all sincerity. He laughed loudly and this seemed to deflate him a little.

"When I have a sexy girl like you in my life it happens *all* the time - doing the dishes, washing the car, shaving, solving algorithms, taking a shower... that one is my personal favourite." He smiled knowingly at me.

"So you... you know..., and you're thinking about me?"

"Hmmm," he held me to him, rubbing his cheek against mine. "I take a *lot* of showers," he whispered.

We stood in the water for some time, continuing to explore each other slowly in an almost innocent way; taking in our curves and plains, delighting in each other's touch. I ran my hands down his wet hair; it felt as soft as I knew it would. When I brought my hand to his face, he noticed the pruning of my fingers and the goose bumps on my arms. "As much as I'd like to think I'm solely responsible for this, you're getting cold." He kissed me lightly, "Ready for lunch? Not that I couldn't just devour you all day." We found another few minutes of splendour before easing away again. Lorien smiled at me, "Wait there."

He waded to the side of the baths and pulled himself out, grabbing his shorts and dragging them on over his wet body before running to get the blanket. He stood at the water's edge and after carefully checking no one was in the immediate vicinity, I dashed to him and he enveloped me. When he had it wrapped around me securely, he jumped back up onto the baths to get the rest of our clothes. We walked slowly back to the car, Lorien's arm around my waist.

"I'm going to need that blanket back," he instructed, opening the mystery box. I laughed, tossing it to him bravely then turning to quickly dress, pulling my shorts and shirt straight on. "Well look who's starting to become more comfortable with Mother Nature," he commented in surprise.

He started to pull things out of the box, and I was amazed. He had brought so much food. There was chicken and coleslaw, ready-made rolls of various fillings and some juice and a cheesecake stored in a cooler bag. "Wait," he reached back in and grabbed some grapes and crackers. When all laid out on the blanket, he looked at me and grinned. "Nothing is too good for the girl I love." I started to laugh when I saw the cheesecake and explained the discussion I had with Michael on the way home from the cinema. "That guy is a classic," he said. We ate, hardly putting a dent in it.

Lorien laid himself across my lap, smiling up at me. He was still bare-chested, and I ran my hands languidly across his pectorals, marvelling in their smooth firmness. I traced the contour lines down his abs, now truly knowing where they ended. Although my appetite was sated, I could have still eaten him alive. When I looked back into his eyes, I noticed he'd been watching me explore his body. His eyes glinted as he raised his hand to the back of my head, lowering me down to meet his lips. All that could be heard was the sound of the trees confiding their secrets to each other and the occasional cry of a cormorant.

"You watch me." I said, running my fingers slowly through his curls.

"Is that a question or a directive?" he asked, and I laughed, imagining me ordering him to do just that.

"You do though, I've noticed."

"I'm watching you right now," he said.

"That's not what I mean, and you know it!" I scolded.

"You're going to have to explain yourself better than that Ash as I don't have a *clue* where you're going with this." He knew exactly where I was going with this, but apparently, I was going to have to spell it out for him, for his amusement no doubt.

"You know..." I started, and I knew this was *not* going to suffice and sure enough, he called me on it.

"Now the last time you said that I *think* you were alluding to my masturbating about you." I blushed deep red; he was so open and comfortable, and I felt like an infant in comparison. "You know...," he continued, "in the shower and that?" He chuckled lowly, totalling revelling in my flustered state. I decided to give it my best shot.

"I notice you *watch* me... when we're... you know," there I went again. He smiled and raised his eyebrows, obviously *not* going to help me get this out, or make it any easier. I cleared my throat and tried again, "When we are intimate, when I'm doing things to you or you to me... It's like you're watching my reactions to your hands and kisses, how it makes me feel…" I trailed off, nearly swallowing the last few words. My face felt hot.

"It's exciting," was his simple response.

"That's all you have to say?"

"You may have realised I *also* like to hear you talk about it Ash, as difficult as it seems to be for you. That's something we'll have to work on."

"You tell *me* something then."

"What do you want to know?" He drew me down, laying me on top of him, wrapping his arms around my lower back and locking us together. I folded my arms across his chest and looked down at him.

"What you're imagining when you're *masturbating*? Are you happy I can ask you that question?" It was hard not to lower my eyes when I *had* asked him.

"Very," he plied his lips softly against my throat. "There are a lot of things…," he murmured, his hot breath making a track across my neck. "It evolves and changes over time too…"

"I'm listening." He laughed and rolled us onto our sides, facing each other.

"A lot of the time it's what we're doing, no real background story, just *lust*. For example," he hitched one leg over mine and started to rapidly pump himself against me, "going at it hammer and tong - sideways, backwards, upside down, you riding me, me riding you…" he rolled his leg back off, we were both laughing. He moved a strand of hair to behind my ear and continued a little more intimately, his voice lowered. "And then there are times when I'm kissing you and you are *loving* it."

"We do that now," I told him. He ran his hand slowly over my breast then eased it down my body, softly massaging between my thighs, better emphasising his point.

"Maybe licking is a better word?" he suggested elusively.

"Oh." I was feeling heat again, but it wasn't from a blush this time.

"My favourite is the entire combination starting with you in the dress you wore to the end of year dance. You do *own* that dress, don't you?" he was nearly whispering. He'd been running his hand over my stomach all the while, raising my shirt higher with each sweep, eventually exposing my breast. He was waiting on my answer. I nodded and he brought his mouth down to torment me with his tongue and lips. I groaned, holding his head to me.

As I lay there sometime later, my thoughts drew back to the issue of his personal gratification. He must have been having those lustful thoughts about me *well* before we got together. "More daydreams Ash?" he asked quietly, playing his fingers through my hair.

"No, I was thinking more about *your* daydreams."

"Oh really, and what daydreams are you referring to?" he asked, amused.

"Exactly how long have you been *masturbating* over me?" I coaxed. "We've only been together since yesterday…" His smile widened, then broke into a laugh.

"There's a big difference between me masturbating *over* you compared to *about* you. And out of respect to you, the former will never happen without your permission." I laughed too when I realised I'd chosen the wrong preposition. It took us a few minutes to regain the composure required to continue this conversation. "Busted hey?" he said.

"Well?" I prompted.

"Day one."

"Day one?" I asked in disbelief.

"I was sitting next to you in History." My look was one of scepticism; there's no way I wouldn't have known. He understood my expression adding, "Not that I whipped it out and ripped the head off it in front of the whole class." I laughed again at the image. "You think I never get embarrassed? Well you tell me Miss Mercy, what could be *more* embarrassing than sitting next to a girl for the first time and getting an erection in the History class that is being taught by your mother." He shuddered for effect. "But it was the first of many erections I blame you for." He shook his head lightly, "I should have asked you out then and there instead of losing my chance to Elijah."

"Why didn't you?"

"If I'd been able to keep your attention off my brother for more than five seconds I would have. *And* if you recall, I did ask you out the very next day." He had.

"I'm here now…"

"Yes, you are," he said, his brown eyes were deep within mine. I melted when he looked at me that way.

When the trees had us fully cloaked in shadow, Lorien glanced at his watch and said, "Time to face the music." I didn't think I'd ever be ready for that. "Trust me Ash, it will be fine." As we pulled into his driveway he leant over and gave me a quick kiss, "It'll be fine Baby." I found myself getting out of the car so must have believed him. "Anyone home?" he called, opening the front door.

"Out here Lori," his Mum answered from the back verandah. He led me through the short hallway out the back.

"Look who I found," he said as I came through the door behind him.

"Ashlyn, it's so nice to see you again outside of school." I really wanted to believe her. "Did you enjoy your break over Christmas?"

"Well yes and no Mrs Standish," I answered, shrugging my shoulders and gesturing to Lorien. "It was a rather confusing time." She understood my inflection and smiled.

"You can call me Cara when we're out of school, same goes for Mr Standish – Nick." No mother who was going to tear out my jugular was going to be that nice about it at the onset. I relaxed a little, then turned to Lorien,

"Can I have a minute with your Mum?" He pulled a slight face and went to speak; his mother interjected.

"Ashlyn may like a drink perhaps?" Lorien got the message and disappeared back inside the house, leaning in closely, trying to hear the conversation I was sure.

"Mrs Standish…." I corrected myself, "Cara," she smiled at me and took her glasses off, setting them on the book she'd been reading. "I wanted to explain to you about the problem I appear to be having with your sons." She laughed saying,

"You turn quite the phrase Ashlyn." She patted the lounge for me to come and sit by her.

"Lorien has told me there is no issue with either yourself or Nick, but I wanted to talk to you about it, you know, woman to woman." She smiled at me in encouragement. I had no idea of the next words that were supposed to come from my mouth and after a few moments she interposed,

"You're very sweet to consider my and Nick's feelings in this but you don't need to worry yourself. Elijah doesn't have a problem with it, and I suppose other than the two of you, he's the only one that is affected in any case. The boys have their own way of working these things out," she finished, patting my leg warmly. I felt a lot better, and out of relief, threw my arms around her.

"Keep your hands off the History teacher," Lorien ordered as he came through the door, two glasses in his hands. I heard the front door open, Elijah was home, and my car in the driveway would have already alerted him to my presence.

"If you'll excuse me, I think I'll start dinner," Cara said, tactfully departing.

I heard him greeting his mother in the kitchen and she laughed. Elijah couldn't be in too foul a mood I assumed. He came through the sliding door. "Hi," he said and smiled at me. "I've hardly seen you all week at school, where have you been hiding yourself?" He looked at his brother with a glint in his eye and said with a grin, "Oh that's right, the Music room." I didn't know whether he was being funny or flippant so was unsure how to respond.

"Ease up Eli," Lorien said, before coming over to sit next to me. He took my hand before adding, "She's worked up enough over this without you paying out on her."

"I'm sorry Ash, it didn't mean for it to come out as sarcasm; I wanted to mess with your head."

"Mission accomplished!" I told him. Lorien put his arm around me in comfort. I thought we were supposed to be cooling it around Elijah.

"Seriously though Ash, I haven't been able to get anywhere near you since school started…" Lorien and I both looked at him. "I mean the Dobermans had you pretty well covered." He laughed at his own connotation of Michael and Bree.

"Dobermans…" Lorien chuckled. I knew it was going to be OK.

"Is one of those for me?" Elijah asked, picking up one of the glasses. Lorien looked at me for assurance before he got up to get another drink.

"You OK?" he asked quietly when Lorien had left. I smiled and nodded. There was that question again. "He'd better be treating you right or he'll have me to answer to." He puckered up his brow in a serious manner.

"He is," I told him.

"I miss you a lot Ash. I suppose I get the best of both worlds now, well in a second-hand smoke kind of way."

"I am *so* sorry Elijah," I dropped my eyes, feeling guilty once more; he could be making this extremely difficult.

"Hey," he said, cupping his hand softly under my chin, lifting my face. "It's OK. We had this discussion on the train that day, remember?" He gave me a quick kiss on the cheek as Lorien came back through the door. "And if I remember that conversation correctly," he turned to face his brother, "you were really ticked off with me that I'd even *suggested* you could end up with Lori." He tousled Lorien's hair, asking, "How do you feel about *that* little bro?" Lorien handed him the glass, choosing to ignore him before coming back to sit with me. His arm circled my waist, and he tilted his head to the side, *are you OK?* I smiled at him, nodding slightly, noting once again my feelings being validated. I suppose I shouldn't worry over such trifling things, it simply meant that I was loved.

"So are you going to make her part of the family Lori, ring and all that?" Elijah stirred.

"She already is," he said, brushing his lips to my temple.

"What fun we will have on Christmas days to come, swapping war stories hey?" All three of us laughed.

"Would you like to stay for dinner Ashlyn?" Cara called from the kitchen window.

"If it's no trouble Cara, thank you."

"First name basis now?" Elijah raised his eyebrows. "What will be next…calling her Mum? I can see Simon's face if you were to blurt that out in History." We laughed again. Lorien pulled me closer before saying to his brother,

"Are you done yet?"

"Not even warming up."

"We're going to my room then." He stood and when I hesitated, he reassured me. "It's OK Ash, will you tell her Eli?" He already had.

"That was a pleasant surprise," I said as he closed his bedroom door behind us.

"Only to you," he reconfirmed as he dissolved the distance between us. "Do you trust me now?" He wended his arms around me, his words pregnant with undertones. It felt as if every conversation we had was now drowning with innuendo.

"I'll always trust you Lorien," I said, my hands sliding around his waist. "It's still hard to accept that your *entire* family is just so cool about things."

"What do you think you're doing Madam?" he asked as I wrenched him forward against me. I was unaccountable; my hands were now solely responsible for their own handiwork. My lips slowly traced across his throat before coursing them up to his left ear, nibbling on his lobe and exhaling breathily. I knew what this did to me when Lorien used it as a weapon so expected a similar reaction. I found myself interrupting my own crusade however when my lips sensed his ear. His eyes opened slowly, questioning the unexpected interlude when he realised I'd moved away from him.

"I didn't know you had a pierced ear." He smiled, tugging at his left lobe.

"I forget it's there most of the time. Elijah and I were thirteen when we *begged* Mum to let us get them pierced. I haven't worn an earring in it for ages."

"Hmmm, I think it's sexy," I whispered, flicking my tongue over his lobe.

"I think *you're* sexy." He pushed me onto the bed, running his lips around my jaw before nuzzling them to my ear. "Do I need to check *you* for piercings?" He checked me for piercings.

"Ears…standard…" he confirmed, sucking a lobe into his mouth. "Nipples…" he exhaled into my ear, sliding his hand under my shirt. "Oh My God! So *incredibly* hard… but no apparent artillery in place…" His tongue made him a liar as he forged my already hard nipples into bullets – cold, hardened steel. "Princess Albertina…" he ran his hand down my stomach and into my shorts, his breathy inspection making me ache for him.

"You're nothing but a tease Lorien," I told him, sitting up, unable to cope with it any longer.

"Baby, I still need to check for tattoos!" he claimed, feigning innocence over his erotic checklist.

"What you need is a cold shower!" His smug look reflected the conversation we'd had earlier at Glassread. We both needed a cold shower when he was eventually satisfied I had no further piercings or tattoos.

Evolving

Music Selection: Diana Ross, 'Chain Reaction'
Diary Entry: How you make my body react when you touch me. You tease me and move on to tease me again and again...

THE TWINS WERE TURNING SEVENTEEN the following weekend and I was at their house on Monday afternoon when they were deciding on a theme for the party. "How about red since it's Valentine's day?" I suggested.

"We've done that," Elijah told me.

"But not here and it's an easy one to do."

"We don't *do* easy Ash," Lorien chastised. "However, it would give you an excuse to get that halter dress out you wore to the end of year dance. In fact both of you could wear what you had on." He looked at his brother. Elijah met his gaze and raised his eyebrows at him. "Maybe not," Lorien admitted, understanding. I'd noticed this interaction too and I agreed with Elijah. "Maybe I could wear it?" he suggested, trying to downplay the issue.

"I'm saving that dress for a *special* occasion," I reminded him, hopefully subtly enough in front of Elijah. Lorien's eyes met mine and I knew he understood my point.

They finally decided on 80s as a theme, surprise, surprise. "Can I come as a woman *in* her 80s?" I asked as an outside possibility.

"I'm not making out with a granny!" Lorien said, attempting shock.
"No matter how sexy she might be under the support hose." Elijah
laughed. Things had continued to be fine since Lorien told him; he'd
accepted us being together without a problem. I supposed the fact we
had broken up before Christmas helped. The irony of it all was he *had*
started seeing Keren about a week ago. It truly did look like this was
another example of them having had each other's girls.

Having settled the theme situation, we started on our homework
at the dining room table. Cara came in shortly after and asked if we would
like a snack. "Yes please Mum," the twins said in unison. She came in
several minutes later with a plate of five sandwiches and three glasses of
milk.

"Who is going to eat all that?" I laughed.

"Get in quick Ashlyn," she said. "They'll evaporate in seconds."
She was right. They ate their way through two sandwiches each, and
when the final two halves were alone on the plate, they both looked at me.

"Eat them, please." I pushed the plate towards them, laughing.
Where did they put it all? Lorien smiled at me as he took a huge bite.

An hour later, he shut his maths book and said, "That's enough for
today. Are you done Ash?"

"Just let me finish this problem." He got up and went to the fridge,
coming back with two apples, one of which he threw to his brother. As he
sat next to me, I looked at him and shook my head.

"What?" he asked through a mouthful of apple.

"You're like a machine." He waggled his eyebrows at me.

"Love machine!" he laughed. "Want one?"

"No thanks," I said and went back to my work. He moved in closer and played a tress of my hair through his fingers. I flicked it out of his hand, trying to concentrate. He leant forward and blew in my ear, drawing his tongue around the outer edge. I moved my head away. Apple finished, he got up and threw it in the compost bin, coming to stand behind me. He rubbed my shoulders, working himself down to my lower back and up again.

"You didn't carry the three," he said over my shoulder, watching me work.

"Looks like you're finished Ash," Elijah said.

"Lorien, you are so exasperating." I closed my book and he took my hand, leading me upstairs.

I loved Lorien's room so much. It was masculine but immeasurable of emotion. I wanted to lay star-fished on the bed with him having his way with me every time I was in here. "Would you mind telling me *what* is so amusing about my room?" He was not meant to have noticed my absurd reaction. I ducked my head avoiding his eyes, hiding the colouring to my cheeks. "There's something going on you aren't telling me," he reprimanded, lifting my face so he could look at me. "Ash, there's nothing you can't tell me, nothing." I sighed and said,

"This is uncomfortable, it's sort of another daydream I've been having, every time I walk into this room it seems."

"Maybe I can help, I love your daydreams," he offered. "But I need to know what it is first, don't I? Do you *want* me to help?"

"I don't know," I said truthfully. "It *is* a little full on," thinking back to the daydream - big mistake, there I was blushing all over the place again.

"Will it help if I don't look at you, or you don't look at me whilst you tell me?" I shook my head. "Well," he said throatily into my ear, pulling me close, "what about if you *whisper* it to me?" My head started to spin; I was going weak with wanting him already. "Are you never going to be able to express yourself to me without my insistence?" he asked gently. "Baby," he breathed, "I would never make fun or tease you about anything you thought or said, especially on this subject."

Feeling like an idiot, I whispered it into his ear. "Hmmm," he nuzzled against my neck, "that's something to think about..." He took two quick steps, backing me against the bed and knocking my feet out from under me. My hands became immobile as he grabbed and then pinned them above my head. "Something like this?" he asked, moving his knees between mine, sliding one and then the other of my legs apart. I was completely exposed to him, laid out, every nerve ending in my body throbbing in instant stimulation. He watched me carefully, not wanting to scare me by play-acting too intently. He had *no* idea.

"Uh huh," I bucked slightly, wanting to pull him to me and scratch my fingernails down his back. He swung himself from the bed and knelt on the floor, taking both of my hands in his right, allowing his free hand to lift my shirt, his mouth at my stomach.

"Hmmm, you taste so good," he mumbled. He watched me watching him as he started undoing my buttons. "Can I trust you to be still whilst we get this obstacle out of the way?" he asked. All I could do was nod. Lorien was really good at this or was really good at giving me what I wanted. I marvelled again at his lack of insecurity, always so effortlessly at ease. My shy moments still bubbled to the top at times. I didn't think I could have done this to him.

I sat up as he pulled his shirt over his head before moving in behind me. He eased my shirt over my shoulders and down my arms, throwing it to the floor. His breath was on my neck, hands moving my hair to the side, lips brushing around my ear and down to my nape. His breathing suggested that he was not as calm as I first suspected.

I raised my arms, holding my hair out of the way to allow him better access. The now two free hands slid around to cup my breasts; gently massaging, teasing his fingers slowly across them. It was torturous and delicious, heaven and hell wrapped up in one emotion. His lips continued to nuzzle and entice me from behind as he moved his hands to my back. He slid my bra straps down over my shoulders and unhooked it, his fingers gravitating back to their earlier position where he moulded and shaped me with his seducing hands. He hooked my loose bra with his thumbs and drew it down my arms, sending it to floor 'Coventry' with the other discarded castaways. I flicked my hair over his shoulder as I leant back into him, draping my arms around his neck. His hands ran down my stomach and lightly tickled across my pelvis, igniting my libido like a shock. If he lowered them, even for a mere second, I would detonate on contact.

I disclosed my eagerness and betrayed myself to him with the moan that escaped my mouth. He slipped an arm over mine and was suddenly beside me, our mouths hungry as he rolled me onto my back. I couldn't kiss him hard enough, deep enough. I wanted to crawl inside his body as he in turn crawled into mine. His burning was equal to mine - *It's going to happen,* I thought, *we're going to make love.*

My hands ran the length of his body, delighting in his warm, firm skin; moving myself slightly aside so I could nestle one hand between our stomachs. My searching fingers looked for and found him easily. This time Lorien groaned, rolling onto his back and taking me with him. The stony feel of him seduced me even further as I traced his contours. Our hearts were hammering, our breathing becoming more intense. I moved to the button at the top of his shorts, flicking it open and instantly his hand was on mine, stopping me. I broke the kiss, looking at him bewildered. "What's wrong?" I croaked, still panting, frustrated, and elevated. My breath was racing, my pulse exploding through my body.

"We should talk about this Ash." He wriggled into an upright position then drew me back to his chest, his arm around my shoulders. We lay like that for several minutes, allowing a slow diminish to the intensity. "You need to be sure, *we* need to be prepared. I don't want this to happen on the back seat of a car or on the sofa or floor somewhere, not even lying here, simply in the heat of passion. I want it to be special, to be worked like a song - the introduction, verses and chorus, working into the bridge and finally the crescendo finish." I smiled at his analogy.

"My strings bowed sweetly and your chords melodious and true?"

"Exactly!" he agreed, pulling me tighter. "I love you Ash and if this takes twelve months to get right, I want to take twelve months."

"I don't!" I told him severely, but smiled. "OK, we have the *how*, but what about the when and where?" He thought this over. I watched him, his deep eyes contemplative, hair hanging in them, gorgeous, sexy… I moved up to kiss him again. I couldn't help myself. He smiled and placed a kiss on my forehead.

"I'm trying to think here scrumptious…" he trailed off, laughing. "I can't believe we're sitting here like this whilst *I* am thinking of ways to get you into bed." When he put it like that, it was comical. "You can put your thought processes to work too please Ash," he said sternly, repositioning me into a more formal arrangement. In a sudden thought, I looked at him. "What?" he said, smiling warmly, his eyes glowing.

"Have you had sex before?" I asked in honest curiosity.

"Does it matter?" he said, brushing his fingers up and down my arm absentmindedly.

"You do realise *that* could bring on the next latent incident?" I teased. He smiled down at me but didn't stop the caresses. "You haven't answered me Lorien."

"Do you really want to know this Ash?" He sounded a little pained.

"Is it a problem to talk about?"

"Well no, of course not, but it's not something you usually go chatting about to your girlfriend."

"It's more of a mate conversation?" I razzed, and then felt terrible. I was taunting him, and he obviously felt badly enough as it was. He looked at me again, and with understanding in his eyes, he knew I was teasing.

"Well *mate*, it's the end of *this* conversation."

"No Lorien, I really do want to know. I'm sorry." I nestled my face against his chest; he didn't have a single hair, which emphasised the tone and shape of his torso. He was lithe and sexy, hard and supple. I ran a fingertip lightly across his chest, forming random circles. When he started to speak, it brought me back from my carnal fancies.

"Only one girl - *not* many and only two times..." I didn't interrupt him. "It was over before we moved here from Sydney, it was also very awkward, fumbling, and embarrassing looking back at it now," he added, laughing quietly. "We got together on my sixteenth birthday. Eli and I had a party and it just sort of happened – getting together, I mean, not having sex. We dated a few times and we both thought it was the right thing to do, the *next* thing to do. I won't say it wasn't great; first time and all, *wow!*" He looked at me to make sure I was OK with this; I was. "But it never really meant anything. The second time was just as clumsy, we weren't in love…"

"Like we are?"

"Yes, like we are."

We lay there quietly for some time, just being in love with each other. "Leave it with me Ash. I think I can work this into a magical experience, something for *you* to remember as your first time."

"You don't want my input anymore?" I pouted.

"Actually that depends…," he said, drawing back to better look at me. "Is this *your* first time?" He realised that this may not be the case, then frowned slightly, most likely thinking of his brother.

"It is, and I'm glad I waited, not that *I* have had the opportunities *you* have."

"Well that makes Eli a damned fool," he grinned. "What opportunities anyway? I just told you about my few meagre encounters."

"Yes, but you neglected to mention the many *numerous* occasions you chose *not* to accept."

"Oh?" He drew his eyebrows in, puzzled.

"Flipping through CDs in music stores at an inner-city suburb…" I dangled verbally at him. He sat bolt upright,

"I am going to *kill* him!" He looked around with a stormy face, then shook his head and smiled. "I suppose I have no secrets from you at all now," he sighed, taking me back in his arms.

"None," was my smug answer.

"I can't say the same though."

"There isn't much to tell with exception of Elijah and I doubt you want to know about *that*." I was sure he didn't want to know anything about that! His answer surprised me.

"What are you comfortable telling me?"

"Whatever you want to know, I guess." I sat up a little so I could see his face more clearly. I became very aware we were both still naked from the waist up.

"I'm happy to know whatever you're prepared to tell me," he said.

"This conversation could go on for hours," I laughed. "Come on Lorien, you must be getting at something specific here?"

"You've never shortened either of our names, have you?" he asked me tenderly, looking deeply into my eyes again. This was bound to get us side-tracked, yet I was happy to resign myself to that fate. His hands resumed their light tracings over my body.

"I never really thought about it," I muttered, finding myself locked by his gaze, ready to fall into another lustful encounter. I moved slightly toward him, moving slightly into a better position for passion.

"You know you can call me Lori, or Ree, *anything* you like."

"I like Lorien... I *love* Lorien; in name, body, mind and soul." He smiled at me, still wanting to discuss this. I put my feelings back into check, for now.

"How far did you two go?" he asked, a little self-consciously, returning to the subject. He wanted to know for a reason, some reason I couldn't fathom but he danced around instead of outright asking.

"I didn't know his ear was pierced," I smiled at him. He smiled back, waiting for me to continue. "Not as much as we have."

That was true; Elijah had been an all-but perfect gentleman. We had a few blissful moments of fairly heavy petting, but they were encased in their own moment of development. Nothing had happened that Elijah didn't allow me to accept and move *with*; he never forced, never jumped too quickly. It was all a natural progression with him, heated or not. The Standish's had raised their sons well, and here I was going through the same building of emotions, the same moment-by-moment construction of the relationship with another one of them. Could this possibly be what Lorien was trying to ascertain, whether it was the twin 'thing' again? I smiled bashfully at him, thinking back to our first date only two weeks ago.

"What?" he asked smiling.

"It was two months into my relationship with Elijah before he even *went* to second base, yet I believe it was our *first* official date you had me naked in Glassread baths. In comparison to you he was a saint!" I teased.

"Eli was always a bit slow on the uptake," he laughed, and let me continue.

"To what depth do you want me to clarify?" I asked, not wanting to share too much and make him uncomfortable.

"You know, I'm not really sure," he grinned. "I just need to know…"

"Lorien, as I told you at the coffee shop, only once did it really go further than what would be acceptable at say, a cinema. It was mostly lots of kissing and full body connections, clothed of course." He seemed OK with this information, but who knew what was going on behind those dark eyes? "I'll tell you something else..." I took his chin in my hand, turning him to face me fully, "I remember sitting in this very house wondering whether it was love and I knew it wasn't. I was expecting it to come eventually, but then I had the dream and that was the end of that. I knew from that waking instant I was meant to be with you. Elijah has already teased you about our first date in Castlebrook and it was true, I was so angry with him. It was when I first asked him about being a twin and he told me how you'd been with each other's more suited girls once or twice. The thought of *not* being with Elijah at the time made me want to cry right then and there. Little was I to know..." I looked up at him. He kissed my forehead again then picked up my hand and started to play his fingers in and out of mine.

"I think it's about time you told me about this dream, considering the changes it made to your life." My face flushed; I was mortified.

"No, I can't!"

"Not even a little bit?" he urged. "Come on Sweetheart, I would tell you." His face was so endearing, so open... I tried.

"I initially thought it *was* Elijah, as you know. I couldn't really see a face; it was more of a sensing... anyway, he was, *you* were... playing with me I guess." I was self-conscious hearing the words coming from my mouth.

"Really," he said. "What was I doing to you? It must have been rather illicit for it to have been considered such an erotic dream."

"You're teasing, aren't you?" I asked, looking up at him. He smiled slightly,

"I would never tease you," he answered huskily. "But *I* am feeling teased… I love it when *you* tease." He nodded, encouraging me to continue. I couldn't say any more; I was flustered and annoyed at myself. "I'm not sure why you can't tell me Ash, it was only a dream." After a few more minutes of silence, he accepted it was not going to happen today. "It doesn't matter; you'll tell me when you're ready, if you ever are ready." He rolled me on top of him, "I think we should work on creating our own dreams," he finished in a growl, which was silenced with his lips.

Turning Seventeen

Music Selection: Alison Moyet, 'Is this love?'
Diary Entry: I want to be pressed against you in rapture, ourselves spiralled and intense, but not our thoughts.

I ARRIVED AT LORIEN'S around 10.00 am on Sunday to help him and Elijah set up for the party that afternoon; him flinging the door open before I had a chance to knock. "Hi Baby," he was instantly aligned to me, kissing me tenderly, tracing the length of my arms trying to work out why I still had them positioned behind my back. "What are you hiding back there?" he asked, and I handed him his present, accompanied by a big smile on my face.

Lorien removed the wrapping and unrolled the soft length, looking at it curiously. "I love it of course... but what is it?" he teased.

"You've never seen one before?"

"Not one that looked like this. I'm guessing it's not a scarf," he said as he fingered the keyboard.

"Wow, that's surprised me." I shook my head in disbelief.

"Are you going to tell me what it is or not?" he laughed. I flipped the switch on the side of the electronic attachment and ran my finger up the keyboard.

"It's a roll-up piano." I told him, so much prouder of my sneaky purchase than I realised I would be when I bought it.

"You mean this is an actual keyboard?" he asked, his enjoyment unmistakable. He started to fiddle with the settings and a moment later, a mandolin was playing 'That's Amoré'. "Cool!"

"At any time you're struck by the composing bug you'll be able to whip this out of your pocket and go for it." I smiled at him. I knew he'd be able to use it, let alone like it. "Where's Elijah? I have something for him too."

"Still in bed," Lorien smiled. "Shall we go wake him?"

"No, let him sleep. I'll leave it here," setting his present on the dining room table.

"What did you get him?" he asked, picking it up, turning it over, sniffing it and finally shaking it to his ear, all of which was ludicrous, obviously being a CD.

"A kitten," I said with a hint of sarcasm and he smiled, putting it back down. "It's 'Chillout Sessions' by the Ministry of Sound."

"He'll love it; will probably drive me crazy with it after a few weeks."

"Your gift comes with headphones; you can block it out." He pulled me to him slowly, his chin on my forehead.

"It's such a thoughtful gift Ash and I love it, but you know it's nowhere near as much as I love you." He looked into my eyes, leaning in for his kiss.

Since our first day at Glassread, I was ready to rip his clothes off *every* time he kissed me. The organisation of my 'deflowering' was taking too long, and I was getting impatient, quickly coming to the realisation I was no longer concerned about it being special or romantic - I just wanted him, and in *such* a frantic way. I knew it was wearing itself on my sleeve, starting to get obvious, when Lorien said, "My, you *are* an aggressive one this morning." He kissed the tip of my nose as I smiled modestly at him. "Don't get me wrong, I *love* it," he growled, "but *what* is going on in that head of yours Ash? More delicious daydreams I hope."

"You could say that." He'd been rubbing my back and now started to wriggle his hips against me. "Stop it, that's just pure torture!" I pulled away, trying to look angry. He dragged me back against him, continuing the torment and purring into my ear. My breathing raced and I pulled completely away from him, frustrated and wanting.

"Whaaat?" he asked innocently. "Nothing wrong with a bit of friction in the kitchen is there?" I moved away and looked down at him. There was a lot more filling out his shorts than there had been a few minutes ago. I wanted to pounce at him from across the room, clawing the offending garments from his body like a panther. Instead, as he circled my body with his arms, drawing me to him, I slipped my hand between us, cupping him firmly. "Hmmm... Ash, you're going to be the death of me," he breathed into my ear, moving against my hand, welcoming me in... asking me to take a seat.

"When are we going to *do* something about this? I can't wait much longer Lorien, you're driving me crazy!"

"I'm driving *you* crazy?" he chuckled; like slate against me.

"Lo-ree-en..." I complained, my whining telling him of the torture he was causing.

"Soon my pretty, soon..." he pulled back from me. "Are you going to help me with this or not?" he asked, thrusting his hips at me. I stood there with my eyes and mouth wide, a slight smile on my lips. He laughed and drew me to him again, apparently only kidding. But, he didn't *need* to be.

"Would you like me to?" I asked a little shyly and started to run my fingers gently over him again.

"As tempting as that is, I can wait a little longer." He took a seat at the island bench. "It'll work itself out in a few minutes. However, I need a little space from you so it can... ahhh... think less sinful thoughts... He and I have a lot of trouble with it lately, especially when the sexy girl that taunts him is in my arms." I had noticed.

"He?" I asked, knowing what he was referring to.

"Mr Winky." I laughed loudly. "Before you go putting any ideas together that's how Mum referred to them when we were little kids."

"I think *Mr Winky* and I are going to be great friends."

"Oh you already are Baby." He took my hands and pulled me back to him. "To hell with it," he exhaled as he brushed my lips with his, "he can stare all he wants." He laughed softly and kissed me properly.

We reluctantly separated when we heard Elijah on the stairs. "Happy birthday!" I called. "That's for you," I told him, pointing to the gift on the table.

"Thanks Ash," he threw me a big grin. "Excellent!" he said when he'd opened it, and went to the stereo to play it. He came over and planted a kiss on my cheek, "You didn't have to do that."

"But you're glad I did, right?" I asked. He laughed and nodded.

"Look what I got, Eli." Lorien led him back to the table where his keyboard was laid out.

"Cool," Elijah agreed.

"That's what I said," he told him.

"Exactly what he said," I told them both. "You twins!" I said smiling. "So when are you going for your licences?"

"We're both booked in for Friday," Lorien answered. "And personally, you're looking at one happy driver."

"That confident hey? What about you Elijah?"

"Not quite as confident, yet still comfortably confident," he grinned again.

"Where are your parents?"

"We aren't supposed to know this but they're out buying us a car. We don't get it until we have our licences though so who knows where they'll keep it until then." They both looked at each other and answered in unison,

"Nanna's!"

I was about to go home and change when Lorien led me into the kitchen. "Happy Valentine's Day," he said, passing me a gift from on top of the refrigerator. I'd forgotten it was Valentine's Day; all I'd thought of was it being the twin's birthday.

"I didn't get you anything Lorien," I said, feeling disappointed.

"Ash, my birthday is *always* Valentine's Day. No gift is always more than enough." I smiled at him and opened my present. He'd bought me a ying and yang pendant on a silver chain. I loved it…

"Will you put it on for me?" I asked, turning and lifting my hair. He secured it at my neck and hugged me from behind.

"It's Valentine's Day *every* day now you're in my life Ash," he whispered and kissed softly behind my ear. My stomach rolled warmly, and I turned in his arms to face him.

"I love you Lorien, no matter how corny you are," I said smiling, leaning in to thank him and promising I would be back within the hour.

"You should have just brought your clothes over here and got changed," Lorien complained as he stood with me next to my car.

"Not on your life. I put a lot of thought into this costume, and I want it to be a surprise!" Climbing into the car, he stopped me, saying,

"Hey, what about a kiss goodbye?" I smiled, climbing back out.

"The problem is we can't just have a kiss or a cuddle anymore. Mr Winky and 'the Orchid' keeps trying to turn it into something more…rampant."

"The Orchid? I like it…" He grabbed me, leaning me backwards against the car into a kiss, enforcing exactly how much.

I really loved this costume and was glad I'd chosen it, going as Toni Basil from the 'Mickey' film clip. I'd hired a red, white and blue cheerleading outfit and pom poms from the costume shop in Sommersett and it was *really* cute. I was just putting my hair into pigtails when Mum came to my bedroom door. "Don't you look *adorable* Ashlyn," she crowed, and I did a spin for her. "Come and show your father," she said, leading me out of the room. I was pretty certain this was going to turn into a happy-snap moment again.

When they'd finally finished with me, I gave them both a kiss, telling them I would see them tomorrow night. Keren and I were staying at the Standish's and going to school from their place on Monday morning.

"Just remember it's a school night!" Mum called and I waved, clarifying I'd heard her reminder, backing out of the driveway.

When I pulled up, Michael, Bree, and Simon were being dropped off. They looked so cool, Bree was in three quarter tights with a tulle skirt and a midriff mesh top with a big cross dangling nearly to her navel. What seemed like hundreds of black bracelets were strewn up her forearms and she'd tied black lace into her teased blonde hair as a headband. "Madonna, right?" Like there was any other choice.

"What about me?" Simon asked. He was Prince, decked out in a crushed-velvet purple suit, which had been attacked with a Bedazzler and accompanied by a white layered puffy shirt. He had a black afro-type wig and had pencilled in a thin fake moustache. "The suit was some relo's from the 70s; Dad never thought it would be worn again."

"Me! Me!" Michael danced around pointing to himself. His blond hair formed stiff spikes and he was dressed in black leather pants and jacket, complete with many chains. He struck a pose and twisted his lip up.

"Bill Idol!" I laughed. He ran a few riffs off on his air guitar, confirming it.

"You look great!" Michael exclaimed. "Can we see a bit of your Mickey?" he said, laughing loudly, but it wasn't until Simon said,

"I certainly hope not!" that I understood him.

"Well come on, give us a cheer," Michael encouraged. Knowing they would all recognise the scene from 'Grease', I shook my pom poms and sang it out but stopped when I noticed Lorien standing at the doorway watching me. He looked delicious dressed in a black suit with matching fedora and sunglasses; one of the Blues Brothers I guessed, and no doubt Elijah was somewhere in the house with the exact same outfit.

Mrs Oates pulled up behind us and Frankie jumped out and ran around to Cyndi's door, helping her from the car. I could see why; she had come as one of the Robert Palmer girls from the 'Simply Irresistible' clip. She was wearing the highest black heels, stockings and the tightest short, black dress. Her bright red lipstick and gelled-back hair confirmed their duo. She looked hot and I was sure that 'Robert Palmer' helping her out thought so too.

By this time, Elijah and Keren had joined Lorien at the door. I was right, Elijah was the other Blues Brother, and they made a fine pair of bookends. Keren had come as Boy George and had plaited her hair through with ribbons, was wearing masses of eye makeup and the accompanying black felt hat. She had black pants on, and a white smock painted with numbers in red and black. "Hi guys!" she called waving. Elijah had his arms around her waist, and she was beaming - she finally had her man!

I grabbed my bag and school uniform out of the car before following them all inside. We went out onto the verandah and made ourselves comfortable. The twins disappeared. I heard Elijah's new CD start and a few minutes later they came out with a tray of drinks. Cyndi was looking at them inquisitively... "So are you The Police?" she asked them in all honesty.

"No, muso's!" they chorused together, both roaring with laughter; Frankie and Simon joined them. After their moment of frivolity, Frankie explained to Cyndi about the Blues Brothers and the infamous, albeit misquoted line from the movie.

There was a knock at the door and Lorien went to answer it; it was Alex and Cherilyn. She'd come as Pat Benatar complete with stiletto ankle boots, black tights and a sweat band around her forehead, and Alex looked terrific as Michael Jackson from his Black or White phase. He had on an open white shirt with a white singlet underneath and black pants, and a bandage around his right hand and forearm. Technically this Jackson period was from the 90s, but I didn't think anyone would argue this point considering Alex had come as *the* King of Pop for the 80s decade.

"OK, I'll be the official spokesperson." Michael stood and called Lorien outside; he poked his head through the door a few seconds later. "You'll notice that none of us have come bearing gifts this afternoon. All we offer you is this," and he handed each twin an envelope.

"Wow, this is too much guys!" Elijah said after tearing his open. They had all chipped in and given them each a gift certificate for one hundred dollars at Myer. I looked at Lorien to see his reaction and he was standing there just looking at me, winking when he saw me watching him. *What is he doing?* I wondered. I hadn't spoken to him since we got here, nor had I been given my greeting via his usual soft *or* demanding lips.

"Show them what I got you Elijah," Keren said excitedly. He flipped his sleeve back to show us the watch on his wrist.

"Jeez Keren," whistled Michael, "that must have taken a hit out of your savings." It was a beautiful watch. I looked to Lorien again, but he'd disappeared back inside.

"What did you get from your olds Elwood?" asked Simon, perching Bree on his lap.

"Lorien's Elwood, I'm Jake," Elijah corrected him, laughing. "We're pretty sure they were out buying us a car this morning. We go for our licences on Friday."

"Ix-nay on the ar-kay," Lorien muttered, coming to join us outside - his parents close behind him. He sat down next to me, taking my hand in his.

"Hi kids," Cara and Nick greeted us. "You all look great, takes me back years..." Cara said.

"That's a history teacher for you," Nick jibed her.

"We'll be upstairs if you need anything. The boys know where everything is... and we'll *try* to keep the noise down," Cara said with a laugh. I smiled back at them, as did we all, but it was hard to focus on any of the conversations around me; all I could think of was Lorien and his odd behaviour.

"You're quiet this afternoon Ash," he whispered.

"I'm trying to work something out," I told him.

"What's that?"

"You! I haven't even had a kiss since I got here," I griped. He laughed and pointed out the crowd around us.

"I didn't think you liked a great display of public affection."

"Well take me somewhere else then," I demanded. He raised his eyebrows at me.

"Isn't anticipation luscious?" he breathed into my ear. I couldn't agree with him. He ran his finger gently across my lips then kissed me sweetly but didn't linger. I sighed deeply and resigned myself into having to be patient.

Bree and Simon were talking about going to see the new Sandler movie next Saturday and were asking who else wanted to join them.

"Sounds good," I said, looking at Lorien to see if he wanted to come too.

"No, not next weekend," he shot out and then seemed to compose himself. "I mean we already have *plans* Ash, don't you remember?" I did not. "You know, *plans*," he reiterated. I was still not catching his drift. He took my hand and led me inside.

"Lorien… what?" He put his finger on my lips and directed me out to the back verandah. The first thing I noticed was the garden in bloom again.

"He watered," I said softly and smiled.

I turned to find him, and he was sitting on one of the lounges. He held his arms open for me and I went to him. He wrapped himself around me as I melted into him, finally where I had wanted to be since I arrived. "You're a hard one to please Baby," he chuckled lowly, running a hand over my back.

"Why?" I asked.

"After what you said this morning, I've been *trying* to be a gentleman, and I have to admit, with you in that costume it has been *very* difficult to do," he said, eyeing me over and licking his lips. He ran his hand from my waist to thigh and then slowly dragged it back up, bringing my pleated skirt with it. "These red scungies *do* something to a man," he confessed, sliding his hand around my curves and then playfully snapping the elastic at the waist. He teased his hand over me again and drew me against him tightly. "I wish it was Friday night," he sighed into my ear.

"What… what…" I had no idea what I was going to say. His eyes flashed at me and we succumbed to the fire that had been igniting since I arrived. He swung me up onto his knee and then gently lowered me to the length of the lounge.

"Oh God Ash," he moaned, running his lips and tongue down my neck, "I want you so much," he whispered.

"Well take me then, let's go up to your room," I suggested breathily, wanting to be taken in the worst way. I wanted him in the worst way too. If I kept burning like this in torment, I was likely to overcook and become charcoal.

"Friday night..." he mumbled against me. I sat up abruptly.

"Friday night?" I asked in disbelief. Had he finally set a D-Day, 'D' for de-flowering? That thought made me laugh. He raised his eyebrows at me smiling, sitting up next to me. The sliding door opened, and Elijah and Keren stood there.

"It's OK Mum," he called over his shoulder, "he still has his pants on." Lorien rolled his eyes at him as Elijah laughed at my reaction. "Just joshing," he said grinning. "Are you going to help me with the food bro?" he asked and then evaporated inside again.

"Friday," he confirmed, taking me back in his arms for another lustful kiss before we went inside.

Instead of Michael being the one to start the party games, Cara surprised us by bringing out a large, covered corkboard. When she removed the sheet it held photos of the twins taken at various ages; she explained the rules. Whoever guessed the most correct won the prize - pretty simple. The prize was a 'Best of the 80s' CD. Neither of the twins was obviously expecting this surprise game as they both complained loudly when their Mum initially uncovered the board. I couldn't help myself but to bill and coo along with the rest of the crowd, they were both so *cute*! Simon took great pleasure in pointing out the photo with the two of them about five years old, bare-butt naked, making mud pies; one was standing, the other sitting. We should have thought to check Lorien and

Elijah's reactions to work out which one was which, even though not identical twins, at this age they were hard to tell apart.

There were ten photos in all, only four of them containing both in the same image. That meant there were three single shots of each of them. Fortunately, these were closer framed photos, so I simply picked the three where there was a dimple in the cheek; Elijah at eighteen months in a sailor suit, at three years opening Christmas presents; and around two, screaming on Santa's knee. Lorien's photos had him at the same ages; sleeping in his cot, sitting on the bathroom floor covered in lipstick - howling; and perched on the potty with a Little Golden Book open on his lap. I wondered whether Elijah had applied the lipstick or whether Lorien had been caught and chastised for doing it himself. It was hard not to laugh.

I looked at Lorien and he smirked at me and said, "*You* have five minutes, make the most of it." The photos of them together included a school photo from kindergarten, their dishevelled return from the first day of kindergarten, them running around in a kiddie's blow-up pool at around the age of two; and the mud pie shot. The school shots weren't too hard to pick, as they looked a lot different by that age, as they still did now. However, you could tell them apart solely from the colour of their eyes.

The pool and the mud pies were a lot harder. I picked Lorien as the one standing making mud pies; if Simon or anyone else wanted to have a crack about me having seen one of them naked it was best it be the one I was going with. The two of them in the pool was going to have to be a 50/50 guess. Their hair was the same length and therefore had the same curl, it was too distant to see the colour of their eyes or a dimple, and their swimmers were identical. "Time's up Ash!" Lorien called and came to eject me physically from the playing area. I quickly wrote down Lorien as being the one on the right and tossed my answer sheet into the bucket before he reached me. Cara came out fifteen minutes later and removed all offending items, smiling sweetly at her twins.

"Thanks Mum!" they called to her together.

"So how many do you think you got right?" Lorien asked me cheekily, thinking I would be possibly stumped.

"Eight or nine," I told him smugly. He raised his eyebrows, not believing I would have done so well. "Well I guess we'll find out together."

The rest of the group were still paying out on them, it was hard not to join in. Cara came out a few minutes later to announce the winner and return the corkboard so it could be studied further after the answers were known. "Where are you Simon?" she asked, looking around the circle, finally spotting him. "You only got three right, how is that even possible under the law of averages?" Simon shrugged, saying,

"I don't look at them that much." We laughed with him, Cara joining in.

"First place got all ten correct, no surprises though as she's gone out with both of my sons..." *It's me or Keren*, I thought. "Ashlyn," she smiled at me, handing me the CD. Great, this would get a lot of use.

"Talk about insider trading!" Michael said. Cara went back inside and then the real tormenting began, as I had expected, and, as the focus was now on me and not the twins, they joined in.

"Why do you think I'm the one standing?" laughed Lorien. "I had something to show for myself even back then... tell them Baby!"

"I wouldn't know!" I cried. I glanced at Elijah shamefacedly and he grinned back. Having seen them both naked I could honestly say they were twins all the way. Keren wasn't the happiest looking person; I wondered how she had scored? Elijah, considerate as always, noticed her reaction and leant in to kiss her tenderly and she perked up immediately.

"Ash your face is as pretty a colour as the lipstick your twin is wearing," cooed Michael as he passed the photo to me.

"How did you tell us apart in *all* of them?" Lorien asked, still surprised at how well I had done.

"I guessed the mud pie and kiddie pool ones," I admitted. Not everyone believed me. "And I just looked for the dimple or eye colour in the rest."

"Having sucked face with both of them wouldn't have helped at all of course," Michael whispered, but loudly enough for those in our immediate vicinity to hear, namely Lorien and Bree. Bree and Michael howled with laughter; I looked at Lorien. He smiled at me and motioned for me to come and sit with him. As I climbed onto his lap, his mother came out with a birthday cake, candles burning. She passed me Lorien's new roll-up piano, and I plinked out 'happy birthday', which everyone joined in on, as their mother passed the twins a knife each. I went to get up but Lorien held me to him, reaching over me to take the knife.

"No mucking around this year please," Cara warned and took a step back. They traded a look and I wondered what family tradition was about to be played out. Sure enough, Lorien dragged a finger through the edge of the icing and proceeded to smear it down my cheek. He then ran his tongue up my face in one big lick, collecting it all.

"Yuck!" I said, rubbing a hand over my face. "That's gross!" He laughed and put some on the tip of my nose and licked that off too. Keren was in the midst of a similar scenario.

"Are you two ever going to grow up?" their mother laughed. "Thank God you girls are here; I usually get a dual application." Lorien reached over to get more icing and as he retracted his hand, his mother said, "No more!" and took the cake inside to cut it; Elijah followed her. Lorien sat there smiling at me widely, a dob of icing perched on his finger.

"And just what are you going to do with that?" I asked. He rubbed some of it across his lips then applied it to mine.

"Oh yeah, eat the cake, eat it!" called Simon, egging him on. I saw Bree nudge him with her elbow, but he found this hilarious and had no intention of stopping.

"If you'll excuse us," Lorien mumbled through his iced lips, lifting me to my feet and taking my hand, dashing me around the corner to the other verandah. He then proceeded to have his cake and eat it too, finishing by slowly licking my lips, ensuring he had it all.

"Hmmm, that was tasty - I could go for some more." So could have I. Friday seemed so far away...

A screeching feedback broke our lewd musings. "What on earth was that?" I asked Lorien.

"Karaoke machine." We then heard a rich gravelly voice sing the opening refrain from Nickelback's 'Favourite Damn Disease'.

"I wonder if he's actually singing this to Keren," Lorien laughed, taking in the opening lyrics.

"Is that Elijah?" I asked, amazed. Lorien nodded. "He's excellent!" I wondered if it was Elijah's natural voice, or whether he had added the rasp to sound more like Chad Kroeger. I knew either way he'd be hamming it up.

"Are you going to have a go?" he asked.

"Are *you*?" Karaoke didn't worry me; I could sing in tune. He obviously expected me to be difficult about it.

"I will if you will."

"I will if *you* will," I teased back.

"Wait there!" He disappeared inside. Shortly after, Bree and Michael started belting out Beyonce's latest hit. Lorien came back out with a book containing the song lists.

"Do you sing as well as your brother?" I asked him cheekily.

"I do everything better than my brother."

"There is *one* thing you don't do as well as Elijah," I said.

"And what would that *one* thing be?" he asked as his eyebrows rose.

"Science." He laughed with me.

"Any requests?" he asked, flipping through the pages.

"Surprise me."

"Can I pick the song for you too?" An innocent look was his expression.

"Do I have a choice?"

When I heard the introduction to the Pussycat Dolls' 'Don't Cha' I was hoping there was already someone standing with the microphone; that this was not the song Lorien had selected for me. Yet, here was Lorien's amplified voice, "Please join me in welcoming the erotic song stylings of Miss Ashlyn Mercy." I stood, resigned to my fate. This was my fault - I should have picked my own.

I got through it painlessly and even managed a few dance moves. The worst part of the song was the self-proclaimed vanity in the lyrics, not keeping to the melody. When Michael stripped his jacket off and threw it at me screaming, I was laughing too hard to sing much more of it anyway. During the applause, I turned to Lorien and handed him the microphone. He sat on one of the dining room chairs and pulled me onto his lap as Robbie Williams' 'Angels' played its opening tune.

I couldn't believe what a breathtakingly rich voice he had. He sung to me as if we were the only two people in the room, his emotion and intent making my heart flutter. During the instrumental, he lifted my leg and played it like an air guitar, fingering the chords at my ankle and strumming his fingers over my thigh. As he sung out the final sustained note I cried, "Oh Lorien!" and kissed him, my hands running through his hair, forcing his face to mine. He wrapped his arms around me, carrying me back outside, ignoring the applause, wisecracks and jibes from the rest of the group. I couldn't hear anything...

At some later stage, there was a tap on the back door. It was Nick, interrupting us as politely as he could. Lorien gestured him out, whispering to me, "We're out here a lot, aren't we?"

"Do your mother a favour Lori," he said. "Come and do acapella with us, she would love it."

"Have you run it by Elijah?"

"Would I be out here bothering you if he'd said no? Sorry Ashlyn," he smiled at me. I got up off Lorien's lap; I couldn't wait to see this!

"I don't know if I'll be able to manage the falsetto Dad, our voices hadn't broken the last time we tried this," he told his father with a laugh.

They performed the Beach Boys classic 'Don't Worry Baby' with Nick clicking his fingers, counting them in and they all came in on tempo. I'd already been impressed with both of the twin's voices, but this was something even more special. Nick was bass and Cara took the lead with the twins as backups. I could see why Cara loved this song; it was a true family rendition with her leading all three of her men. They sang at times in four-part harmony, alternating into main and backing vocals. It was an exceptionally professional performance and we deservedly clapped and cheered loudly when they were done.

Elijah told his parents to stay where they were and went to the karaoke machine, putting on a selection. Cara and Nick then did the Kiki Dee and Elton John hit 'Don't Go Breakin' My Heart'. I could see where the twins had gained their singing ability - they were marvellous. Everyone had several goes, even I had another turn singing a duet with Lorien, 'Baby It's Cold Outside'. It was a big hit with the crowd, his parents especially loved it; they were having as much fun as the rest of us. Cara then picked a selection for her boys, the Frank Sinatra and Bing Crosby vernacular duet and 'What a Swell Party This Is' resounded. I was certain that the Standish selections were ones that had been performed many times over in the past several years as they had them so well perfected.

All good things come to an end some wise man once argued, and indeed everyone had left by 11.30 pm. Cara and Nick bid us goodnight shortly after, hugging their sons before taking to the stairs. Keren and Elijah disappeared onto the side verandah, so Lorien and I stayed in the comfort of the sofa to say our goodnights. I had never known two people who loved to say goodnight as much.

Keren and I were sleeping in Lorien's room and the twins were in Elijah's. She had been on at me for fifteen minutes wanting one of us to swap rooms, finally saying, "Well if you aren't going in there, I am." She got up and slid the bathroom door open quietly, fading into the dark. A few moments later the door slid shut and I sat up, curious to see who would be coming through. It was Lorien.

He crawled up the bed, leaning over and kissing me. "Hi," he breathed.

"Hi yourself," and then I silenced him with my lips, my arms encircling and drawing him down to me. In an attempt to roll me on top of him we pulled away, laughing quietly. It was nearly an impossible feat as I was under the covers and he was on top of them; he'd nearly dragged the entire bedding with me. He climbed in and I nestled against him. "I love sleeping in your bed," I murmured.

"I love that you're sleeping in my bed." He brushed a soft kiss over my forehead. "I love you," he whispered.

"I love you too Lorien and I can't wait until Friday night. When did you arrange it?"

"Finalised it this morning after you left. Do you think you can wing it with your parents to not be home until Sunday afternoon?" He'd made extensive plans for 'Friday'.

"I think so," I said. "What are we doing?"

"Well, other than the obvious," he looked at me and smiled calculatingly, "you'll just have to wait and see." He leant in to kiss me again, both of us stirred up over the nearing situation. "This could be dangerous, so near and yet so far," he rasped, pulling me closer. The last words spoken that night were, "Don't forget the dress," then there was only the harmony of our rising breathing.

Keren woke us at 5.45 am. "Did you have an alarm set?" I asked, rubbing my eyes.

"I haven't been asleep," she whispered. She apparently was not able to dress herself properly either, as her buttons were askew. Lorien kissed me once more and snuck through the bathroom door. I drifted back to sleep, dreaming again of what lay in store for me on Friday night.

The Name of the Game

Music Selection: Olivia Newton-John, 'Xanadu'
Diary Entry: Blink and look around, what is here, is here. It's true and our location is Utopia.

GETTING THROUGH THE DAY AT SCHOOL on Friday was nearly impossible, knowing the crescendo we were building up to all day. It was obvious to the others too I was to realise eventually. Whilst Lorien and I were locked at the mouth over lunch, Michael commented, "Are you two out to break an Olympic record or are you about to pop her cherry, twin?" I pulled back from Lorien and looked at Michael, dumbfounded. His playful smile turned into a knowing grin and I was certain he had worked out what we were up to this weekend. "Why is it again you aren't coming to the movies with us tomorrow? I don't remember what you said you were doing instead," he asked pointedly.

"We have other plans," Lorien said, and sealed his lips back to mine, dismissing him.

In English, Bree caught my eye and mouthed, *we want a full run-down Monday*. I blushed and had to turn away, unable to hide the impish grin that spread across my face. My whole body was smouldering; the fact that Lorien's hand was stroking my outer thigh under my skirt was not helping either.

He was at my door, right on time. "Enjoy yourselves!" Mum called as I closed the front door, handing my bag to Lorien. I could still hear Dad snoring in front of the TV. "Hi," I said breathlessly as I climbed onto the front seat.

"Hi," he purred as he climbed in and slid over, wrapping his arms around me. I could hear my breath catch as he leant into me for the first kiss of the evening. The awakening kiss, the first kiss of maybe thousands. My head started to spin, and what seemed like fifteen minutes later, our faces slowly parted. I could see his wonderful smile lit up by the dashboard lights. He laughed as he straightened up; we'd nearly ended up horizontal on the front seat without realising it. Such a passion. "You wore the dress," he said, eyeing off the cherry-red halter.

"Was there ever any other option?"

He was behind the wheel of a Buick LaCrosse that included a bench seat instead of the optional buckets. He'd received his licence today, whereas Elijah had not. "Where are we going?" I asked.

"You'll soon see, Sweetheart." He took my hand and held my palm to his lips, and then placed it on his leg, running his hand over it gently. After several minutes, he moved his hand to my leg, slowly caressing up and down between the split of the dress.

Not long after, we pulled into a restaurant carpark in the township of Rondo, about halfway between Sommersett and Castlebrook. "But before the delights on the menu, a few more delights in the car," he crooned and slid his way over to me again.

We kissed, as before, long and deep, slowly, but intensely. This time he gave me more of promises to come as he slid his hand under the split, running it firmly up and down my thigh. I sighed into his mouth, still kissing, breathing, and stepping up a notch. I hitched my leg over his, trying to roll around into a better position. His ardour was equal to mine and then he said, "Ouch," and started to laugh. I just looked at him, waiting for my head to cool.

"What happened?" I asked, swinging my body back into the upright position, not unlike the requirement to do so on a plane when approaching turbulence. He rubbed his lower back, grimacing slightly.

"Gear-stick." We both laughed, realising the depths of oblivion we faced to the outside world when we were in the throes of even 'above the clothes' passion.

He got out and came around to open my door. "Madam," he stated officiously, and I stepped from the car. "One more," he growled and grabbed me again. Leaning against the door of the car, we spent our next five minutes.

"Get a room!" Someone shouted from a passing car, this finally snapping us out of our reverie.

"I have," he grinned at me malevolently, pretending to twist an invisible moustache, "but first, we eat."

He'd brought me to an expensive, candle-lit, lakeside restaurant, oozing with romance and ambience. My appetite wasn't great. Possibly because of nerves, or alternatively I just wanted to get to *dessert*. I smiled at this, causing Lorien to raise his eyebrows at me in question. "Never you mind," I told him. He beamed his wonderful smile at me. I could look at that forever.

After our meal, we were finishing our drinks, a little coyly. Well I felt that way, and thought he did too as I watched him finger the edging of his napkin aside his discarded plate. It was the first time I'd ever seen him unsure of himself. "Ash," he said, a little reservedly, "I just want you to know something, before we end up in another public-ignorant embrace, or before we go any further…" He stopped and looked around sheepishly. I waited for him to go on. When it appeared he wouldn't, I took his hand from across the table.

"Go on Lorien, I'm listening, my love." I couldn't imagine what he was about to say.

"Well…" he started. He looked up at me and saw my warm smile, giving him the strength to go on. "I know I've told you many times I love you, and I know you love me too?" This ended as a question more than a statement.

"More than anything Sweetheart," I breathed, hoping the stormy undercurrents of lust and desire were shining back at him from my eyes, taking in the understanding I did truly love him. Could I find the right words if he was indeed questioning this, the words to explain myself fully to him with no confusion resounding?

"Seventeen years old is well and truly old enough to… 'express ourselves physically'," he coughed a little embarrassedly, again scanning the restaurant, then continued. "I just wanted to instil in you I do indisputably, unquestionably, find myself more and more head over heels in love with you with every passing day. But I know you are aware of this." He looked to me, and I nodded, smiling. "I hope, no, I know you feel the same, as you keep confirming to me… I just want to make sure you're here with the right brother, the correct and truthful brother in your heart. I won't bear any ill-will if there is still *any* cause for doubt or indecision." He had dropped his eyes to the table as he spoke the last words, softer than the other already quietly spoken sentences.

I was completely flabbergasted where this had come from, and why now? His response was simple, "Your dream Ash," he replied. "I know after you had that dream you were unable to look at either my brother or myself in the same light again, much to my benefit." He grinned, but fleetingly. "I don't want you basing your choice between us on a dream that may not have subliminally meant anything."

"Lorien, my Sweetheart..." I started, "my angel, my heartbeat, my heart. You need to accept that 'this, us, we', has nothing to do with anyone else. It's not about the twin thing, it's about Lorien and Ashlyn, OK? I think it's time I told you the whole dream; you can then judge for yourself." He nodded in agreement, and I commenced what would have had to be the *most* embarrassing ten minutes of my life. I ensured I didn't leave out one moment, one breath. I wanted him to know the exact emotions I was feeling at all times in my subconscious. He was finally getting his wish – me talking about sex and emotions, things I'd been struggling with for so long. But this time, I had to do it, do it for Lorien.

At the onset, it was difficult, especially at the beginning as originally, I thought this dream *was* about his brother. But, knowing the outcome, I replaced *the* hands, or *his* hands, with *your* hands in the replay. He sat there looking intently at me, enjoying and savouring the moment. At one stage he snaked his tongue slowly over his lips, which left them shining in the dim lighting. His eyes grew hungry; on occasion, a growl-like purr escaped his lips, one eyebrow raised salaciously at me.

I realised I'd been unconsciously moving in my seat, feeling the heat building again. As I spoke the final words leading up to my waking, he took my hand saying, "Let's go." He went to get up and realised he was in a bit of a discomforting position. He sat back down abruptly. "Ah, I *may* need a few minutes before we can go anywhere Ash," that wonderful smile back on his face. I knew he now understood exactly where we were, and we were there together. It wasn't about Elijah from that moment on, only Lorien. "Cheque please waiter," he called, working into his tighter than usual pants to get his wallet.

I awoke Saturday morning with a smile on my face, stretching and basking like a kitten in the sunshine. I looked at my lover; he still slept. I noticed the same smile playing on his lips that I'd also woken with on mine. I revisited the night, delighting in the intensity of the memories.

We'd fallen through the doorway already in full fervour, open lips, panting breathing, urgent hands - our minds exploding and imploding in an impossibly inverted creation of the universe. We writhed, standing in the centre of the room, wobbling against gravity, then against the walls. We were pressed into the couch at one stage, and another rolling on the floor.

Eventually Lorien sat up, looking at the surroundings, noting where we were. "Let's take this to the bed Ash," he said through softer lips, still formed to mine. "I don't want you getting cold," he looked down, "or bruised." He scooped me into his arms and tossed me onto the bed before I had a chance to answer. "Now," he exhaled breathily, crouching above me, "let's try this from the start of the dream." He re-enacted it perfectly.

When he reached the part where the dream stopped, he was relentless, and finally the centre aching of my being was found. His lips were on mine; our breath hot and vital as he teased and separated, feeling his way through his sightless fingers. Eventually, his insatiable mouth took over.

When I started to cry out, he stopped, looking up at me with concern. It took only a second for him to realise what was happening as my body started to buck and shiver, to twist and contort. I tried to repel him and hold him closer at the same time. It was not enough, it was everything, it was too much, and the heavens burst alive in patinas of colour never realised. There were low cries and whimpers, and finally my spasms were subsiding into a wave where before the tsunami had raged.

He smiled at me teasingly as he moved up alongside me, nuzzling at my ear and throat. "I love you so much Lorien." His reply was gestured through his lips, back on mine, softly, tenuously, caressingly. His hands moved down my body, foraging and finding. He stopped momentarily and I heard him tearing something open with his teeth. He rolled quickly onto his back and his hands disappeared out of sight.

"Where were we?" he muttered, rolling back towards me.

He watched my facial expressions react to his touch as he grazed his fingertips across my nipples. I closed my eyes and slightly arched my back, forcing my body into his hands. He lowered his lips to mine once more. As he listened to my breathy moans, the lightly feathered kisses became more urgent. Unable to withstand the delicious torture any longer, he moved across me, and finally, into me.

My eyes flew open, and I gasped, making him freeze instantly. "Are you OK Baby?" he asked, tracing his fingers over my cheek, a look of concern on his slightly drawn brow.

"I'm certainly not a virgin anymore," I said, and smiled at him, drawing his lips back to mine. He chuckled lowly and deepened our kiss.

We moved together, slowly at first, with him at times transposing me fluidly from top to bottom in a sporadic, flowing dance. Finally, with me still on top, his motion became more critical, his hands on my hips bringing me into his rhythm. A hiss escaped his lips as he threw back his head. The tendons and muscles in his neck straining as his massive final force bucked me upwards, bringing on my second tremor for the night.

We lay entangled in each other with the heat subsided for now, neither of us moving. I looked through hooded eyes and noted random pieces of our clothing scattered around the room. Limp, worn, dishevelled; this was the image projected back at us.

He trailed his lips across my brow and face, gently combing his fingers through my hair; my previously harried lips soothed with soft kisses. I think we dozed at one stage, drifting on a calm ocean under starlight, they guiding us on the course chosen for us to follow. I don't know how long we lay like that, but I eventually looked up into Lorien's eyes. His were already riveted on me. "Lorien," I murmured, smiling demurely, "can we do it again?" There were no further words.

We'd slept and made love many times over in the past twelve or so hours. My musings drew me back to remember waking, still dark, with Lorien spooned behind me, kissing my neck and lightly brushing his fingers over my arm, ready again and hard against me. Another delicious instance saw the sun rising over our flaying bodies with small tendrils of his hair plastered to his fevered brow, repeating my name over and over in his urgency.

I was assessing the damage to myself, still replaying the night in my head when Lorien stirred. "Good morning Baby," he crooned and rolled over to me.

"Ouch," I winced.

"Are you OK Ash?" He was so worried, it made me smile. "How can you be smiling at me, you're hurt." He scanned my body for a sign of injury, almost frantic was his examination.

"Lorien," I said, pulling him back to my side, "It's just a part of... the aftermath ... I'm a little sore is all." I smiled at him again, soothing as best as I could. "You have to remember that the ahhh... previously unexplored territory," he smiled back at me in understanding, hugging me closer, "has been discovered and the new inhabitants have been partying all night." I laughed at my own analogy. "Not to mention the frantic 'hammer and tong' action that accompanied them," I added softly. He chuckled then looked at me,

"I *am* sorry Ash."

"Don't be sorry Lorien. How can you be sorry for something that introduced me to such high plains? I didn't think it was possible, but I'm even more in love with you than I ever thought I could. Is that something you want to recant?" He shook his head, moving up to rest on his elbow, smiling at me from above.

"Are you sore here?" He brushed his lips over mine.

"No," I breathed, sealing myself to him. His fingers trailed down to my breasts, teasing me back into rigidity.

"Here?" he murmured from the corner of his mouth. I shook my head, not trusting my answer to come out evenly. His mouth took over, freeing his hands to continue their wandering. He started to caress me gently, causing a groan to emanate from my lips. "Oh Baby, I'm sorry," he whispered, stopping. He looked at me and realised from my sultry smile it had been out of response to him, not in pain. "I think some warm water will help, don't you?" He lifted me from the bed, not waiting on my response. "Let's take a shower," he suggested with a wicked glint in his eye.

The hot water felt wonderful against my skin and looked wonderful cascading over his. He lathered his hands and slowly started to work his way over my body. When he eased between my legs he was trying to be as gentle as he could, not realising this was out of both our controls. My body reacted, wanting him – it was as simple and carnal as that. However, I moved his hand after a few minutes when it started to sting a little. "It's OK," I told him, "it's just the soap." He slid down to his knees and rinsed me thoroughly.

"Poor Orchid," he crooned, pulling me to him, kissing her directly. He darted his tongue out, once, quickly, looking up and smiling at me. I started to lather my hands in readiness for his turn as he worked his mouth back up my body.

I enjoyed the slow procession my hands made across his chest and back, down over the firm curves of his rear. Running my foamy hands over him were a treat unto itself, his body was so sexy. When I started to massage my soapy fingers around the best-till-last part of him, I could tell he agreed with me.

Lorien threw his palms against the shower tiles several moments later, his entire body stiffening. I lazed myself back up him, coming to rest in between his splayed arms with my back against the tiles. He was still panting, his eyes half closed. "That was fun," I smiled at him beguilingly, running my hands across his pecs again. He laughed breathily and pulled me to him, kissing me under the jet of water.

"Hmm hmm," he agreed. His stomach interrupted him, growling noisily. "Time to refuel," he said, turning off the taps.

We walked hand in hand along the waterfront until we found a café still serving breakfast. I was famished and made short work of my

Eggs Benedict. Lorien had ordered the big breakfast, and it was huge, but all that was left on his plate was the parsley garnish. "Making love sure does give you an appetite hey?" he laughed. He took my hand and dipped my finger into the leftover hollandaise sauce, slowly sucking it into his mouth. "Hmmm, good," he murmured, looking at me intently. "I'd like to eat this off a few other places I know." My face was hot, and not from embarrassment. Lorien made me feel so aroused when he used his subtle flirtations and I think he knew it too. Sore or not, I wanted him again right now.

"Let's go back to the room!" I said. Lorien was already halfway out of his seat before I'd even finished the sentence. As he paid the waitress, he asked her something I couldn't hear and when we exited the café, he took me in a different direction from the way we came. "Where are we going?"

"To get more condoms," he smiled at me. "I only have a pack of twelve and the way we're going, we'll definitely need some more." I couldn't believe I blushed at that. "Still so easily embarrassed," he grinned at me before stopping in front of the chemist. He traced a finger across my hot cheek before leaning down to kiss me. I didn't care we were on the main street of Rondo and people were passing us by, I kissed him right back. "Do you want to wait out here?' he asked, knowing I would possibly go through the procession of pink to purple when faced with our actual purchase.

"No, I'll come with you."

"I've noticed," he teased into my ear, my body buzzing again in anticipation.

He left me standing in front of the condom display whilst he went and spoke to the Chemist. I wanted the floor to open up and swallow me whole. I shook myself a little, realising I was being stupid, and every sexually active woman had a right to be standing here. I think that was what embarrassed me; people would understand I *was* a sexually active woman. *So what*, I reasoned and started to flick through the boxes.

I didn't realise Lorien was behind me until he asked, "Find anything you like Madam?" I smiled at him then asked,

"What was that all about?" referring to him speaking to the Chemist.

"I explained you were a little sore and asked for his advice on the best condoms to buy."

"Oh Lorien, you didn't." I peeked around him to look at the Chemist; he was not paying any attention to me. Lorien pulled a box from the shelf. He showed me the front and then surveyed the water-based lubricants.

"What do we need *that* for?" I whispered. He matched my speaking level replying,

"Not that you need any help in the lubrication department, you sexy little minx," I felt my body flush again when he looked at me, "but the softer condom and the water-based lubricant will make it a lot gentler for you, less abrasive. Considering our ages and the fact I've never had unprotected sex, HIV and STIs aren't really an issue here so the softer condoms will be perfect." I was glad he'd thought to ask and once again found myself amazed he was unfazed by it. "I need you again right now," he warned as he led me to the cashier. We were going to have to run back to the room...

The urgency and incitement that had resonated through our first bout of lovemaking was replaced by a more delicate and sensitive aura. The gentle and soothing replaced the cymbal crashes and lightning strikes, sculpting my excitement to an ever-deeper level. His hands and lips were soft and slow, working their magic on me in an entirely different fashion. My breathy sighs soon spiralled into loud groans. Lorien kissed me deeply as I started to climax, covering his hand with my own.

"Baby, you take my breath away," he purred. "I'm yours forever if you'll have me." He slowly entered me. "Do you know how I long for you?" he crooned in my ear, maintaining his languid pace. Did he know what he was doing to me? "I can't stop thinking about you; you're always on my mind." He stopped his motion and gazed into my eyes, "I'll never let you go." My breathing was shallow, my pulse racing again; his words caressed me like his skilled musician hands. He kissed me more aggressively as he started the delicious grind again. His tongue ran lightly over my lips before sucking the bottom one into his mouth, gently biting it, his controlled tempo unwavering as he moaned into my mouth. All these little nuances were amplifying me whilst his tongue lazily traced my own.

"Lorien, you complete me," I murmured, playing light kisses to his throat, my hands running through his hair. His mouth moved to my ear, his breath hot,

"Hmmm," he sighed, holding me tightly as he rolled onto his back, putting me in control of the pace.

All of my self-consciousness was gone - I had never felt so much a part of anyone else. As I writhed atop him, my hands found their way to my breasts, fondling them for both his pleasure and mine. "Oh God Ash," he panted, sliding his finger around my self-destruct button. Seconds later, I was going over the edge again, so deeply, so intensely, nothing like the other orgasms had been. Lorien's slow, tormenting and sensual exploration had brought me to the highest of crescendos, which quickly became a duet. He sat up, laying me slightly backward, our connection becoming horizontal. Shortly thereafter he clung to me tightly as his body went rigid, his breathing erratic.

We stayed like that for several minutes, just drawing off each other's ebbing intensity. "Ashlyn Mercy, you have captured my heart," he confided, drawing me back down beside him, holding as much of me as was possible against his body.

When we checked out on the Sunday, I said to Lorien as we approached the car, "I don't want to go home."

"Where would you like to go Ash? I'll take you anywhere your heart desires."

"You've done that all weekend," I smiled, but only a little shyly this time.

"It's been amazing hasn't it?" When we reached the car, he drew me into an embrace.

"That's my point," I told him, "I don't want to go home, period. I want to live forever in our little secluded Garden of Eden; walking around naked, feeding each other grapes, and hopefully avoiding the whole snake situation this time," I laughed, lightly grinding my pelvis against him. "With exception to this one of course." He gently moved my hair back from my face before leaning in to kiss me.

"We'll just have to make *my* garden the Garden of Eden for the time being," he suggested quietly, drawing back and looking into my eyes.

"Our parents will end up getting sick of the sight of each other," I laughed.

"Where do your parents think you are anyway?" he asked.

"With you, of course."

"So can I expect to be met at your door with a shotgun," Lorien laughed.

"I'm nearly eighteen and they're not idiots. They also let me out of the house *twice* in that red halter, the second time to spend a whole weekend with you," I smiled. "You won't officially be sleeping in my bed when you stay over, but what they don't know won't hurt them right? Same situation as when I'm at your place."

"I think my parents will be OK with it," he mused.

"Well that's something you can ask them when I'm *not* around thank you," I instructed. He opened the car door for me, and I sat down gingerly.

"Would you like to come back to my place with me?"

"Yes Lorien, there is nowhere else I want to be but with you. But," I warned him, "If you have *any* ideas in that head of yours about just *how* cool your parents are, I have disconnected the gas at the mains for the moment. *Mrs* Winky is going to need a few days to catch her breath."

"What happened to my Orchid?"

"I like Mrs Winky better, don't you?" He nodded, smiling, and said,

"Like two pieces of a jigsaw." Now where had I heard that before...?

I was deep in my own thoughts for much of the car ride back to Sommersett. Lorien didn't interrupt me, although he would have been accurate in guessing I was thinking about him, of course. I'd been going back over his comments about his few attempts at awkward lovemaking in the past. After the weekend I'd just spent with him, it was difficult to believe that had ever been the case. I knew he wanted me to be able to discuss these things with him openly, and I did agree. After what we'd already shared so intimately it seemed ridiculous in hindsight that I could ever have a problem asking him anything, telling him anything. "Lorien, can I ask you something?"

"Always Ash, you know that." I expressed my thoughts as explicitly and honestly as possible.

"That's an interesting point." He pondered it for a while before saying, "I suppose it comes down to the simple fact that I love you, am *in* love with you. What we shared over the weekend was just a natural flow, I hadn't come here with any 'planned scenarios' or anything... although I would have been *majorly* disappointed if I had to shower alone... again," he smiled at me suggestively. "You bring out the best in me, or possibly the beast in me," he concluded. It was as he had done also, to me.

Elijah and his father were sitting at the dining room table when we entered the house, doing homework and reading the paper respectively. "So did Mr Winky get a feed?" Elijah asked Lorien smugly over his shoulder.

"Elijah Nicholas Standish!" Cara exclaimed from the kitchen. "You're not too old to put over my knee young man!" Nick suppressed a smile. Lorien approached his brother and leant to his ear speaking quietly,

"Several times in fact. What did *you* do over the weekend Eli?" This silenced him for the moment. I went into the kitchen to leave the men to their banter.

"Did you have a nice weekend Ashlyn?" Cara asked me genuinely. It was strange to have his family so acceptant when they obviously assumed I'd been having unbridled sex with their son all weekend.

"Yes, I did, thanks." I could hear Elijah quietly sniggering, imagining the look he was giving Lorien.

"Looks like you're going to be a permanent fixture around here from now on," Cara said. "I think I'll give your parents a call and see if they're free for dinner on Friday or Saturday night; it's time we got to know each other better."

"They would like that very much."

Lorien came into the kitchen and his mother handed him something small, so small it fit into his closed palm and I couldn't see what it was. He took my hand, leading me out to the back verandah. "I have something for you..." he opened his hand to reveal a box. Before I opened it, I teased him about getting his mother to buy gifts for me.

"I paid for it, she just chose them," he said. Inside the box was a pair of small diamond earrings.

"Oh Lorien, they're beautiful." He took the box from me and removed one of the studs.

"This is to represent *our* ying and yang, one for you and one for me. That's also why they're rather small, I would have bought larger ones, but I didn't want a diamond rock hanging off my lobe." He threaded the earring into the second hole of my right lobe and the other into the hole in his left. I looked at Lorien's earring and thought they were a perfect size. They winked in the sun but were otherwise unobvious; something that we knew was there, reminding us constantly of each other without drawing attention from others.

"Why didn't I get these over the weekend when I could've thanked you *personally*," I asked, inflecting my intent.

"I wanted to have something else to give you once we got home. I knew it would be hard when we eventually had to leave our 'love grotto'. This will always serve as a reminder of us; our love, our union, and of each other." He kissed me softly, his fingers playing through my hair in a gentle caress. "Will this Eden suffice for the time being?" he whispered, then drew back to look into my eyes. I pulled him back to me, letting our silence answer his question.

THE END

EPILOGUE

IT WAS THE TWENTY-NINTH OF JULY, not only my eighteenth birthday but also our six-month anniversary. I was having a party on the weekend, but was currently lying in my bed with Lorien making plans, not only for the weekend but also for our futures. He'd written a lot of music over the past six months, calling me his muse. It included the usual arrangements for keyboard, bass and electric guitar, but also the violin. When he'd composed several additional pieces, he wanted us to run some auditions to find a drummer and another guitarist. He couldn't play all the instruments at once.

It was during one of these previous discussions I found out Elijah could also play bass and lead guitar. As he'd not taken Music as an elective, I assumed he didn't play an instrument, so was surprised to find there was already another member to this group, and Lorien had already teed his brother up for it. He had this planned to fall into place by the time he turned eighteen so we could play the pub and club circuit as a start. He likened us to 'Bond' meets 'Nickelback'. I loved him so much for his enthusiasm and knew with his musical ability, wonderful singing voice, and the plethora of instruments he could play, we could be a success.

"I haven't given you your present yet," he whispered.

"You just did," I smiled, and rifled through the bedding to find the red ribbon he had bowed around Mr Winky, much to my great enjoyment when I discovered it. He took it from me, tying it around my wrist and kissing my palm before holding it to his cheek.

"Don't you want your present before your parents get home?" he asked. I teased my hands over his chest in response, moving myself down to harass his nipples with my lips.

"So soon?" I murmured against him. Although we were going on five months of lovemaking, not that I was counting, we were still insatiable and could never get enough of each other.

"Ashlyn Mercy!" he reprimanded, snatching the covers over himself, feigning prudish shock. "You can't keep your hands to yourself for more than five seconds, can you?" He leant down and kissed me, letting me have my way for a few more minutes. "Come on Baby, I want to show you what I have for you," he crooned, then added, laughing as he sat up. "And keep the sexual innuendos to yourself!"

He went to my wardrobe and pulled out a large box. He was comfortable in my room. He kept some clothes in the wardrobe, and I'd emptied out a drawer for him to keep his toiletries and underwear in. There was a similar setup for me at the Standish home. "How long has that been in there?" I asked. He finally had my attention.

"I hid it whilst you were on the phone to Bree." He passed me the box saying, "Now this is from all of us Standish's, not just me." He climbed back into bed beside me and angled himself so he could see my reaction as I opened it. Inside was a violin case, and inside that was an electric-blue, Carlo Giordano electric violin.

"Oh Lorien!" I took it gingerly from the case, not wanting to get even a fingerprint on it. "So 'Bond' meets 'Nickelback' hey?" I smiled at him.

"I've even thought of a name, how does 'Listening at Keyholes' sound?"

"Like number one material to me," I leant over and kissed him lightly. "It's so beautiful," I said turning it over in my hands.

"*You're* beautiful, I love you..." I looked at him and put the violin back in its case, handing it to him to put out of the way.

"I'm going to need some proof," I smiled, drawing him down to me.

GLOSSARY OF AUSSIE SLANG

- And that: more things of a similar kind. Informal, and can be playful in its use. 'and the like'.

- Beating around the bush: to talk about non-important things, to avoid discussing the actual point.

- Blank: as in come up with a blank / draw a blank – unable to remember something.

- Boardies: abbreviation of board-shorts. Knee length quick drying swim shorts, worn by all sexes, but predominantly males.

- Bombshell: to make an unexpected or shattering announcement.

- Boot: car trunk.

- Briefs: panties, underpants (also known as undies in Australia). Briefs is a unisexual term.

- Bucketed down: poured down with heavy, soaking rain.

- Bummer: disappointment, as in darn it! Or damn it!

- Bush telegraph: grapevine, rumour mill.

- Busted: caught in the act, guilty.

- Canteen: snack bar. Also known in Australia as a tuck-shop. Where food and drinks can be bought, often run by mothers of the students. No formal seating is in place, but rows of benches are often located outside of the canteen. Canteens are also found at local sporting grounds.

- Card (for public transport): Since the late 2010s Australia has used a 'tap on' and 'tap off' system for each time you board or alight from a train, tram or bus. This is either by a pre-paid 'opal card' (in NSW) or a credit card.

- Centimetres: 1 inch = 2.54 centimetres.

- Choke down some chow: to eat something.

- Cooler bag: a firm or soft-sided smaller insulated bag or container used to keep food and drinks cold at a picnic, etc. Much smaller than an esky.

- Demountables: portable school buildings (classrooms or toilets) put in place as the enrolments for the school grow larger than the solid classroom or toilet structures can accommodate.

- Electives: non mandatory school subjects once past Year 8, such as languages, music, history, geography, woodwork, art and home sciences (excludes English, Science and Maths).

- Esky: portable cooler, cooler box, ice box, chilly-bin, igloo.

- Eyeing off / Eyeballing: checking out, considering, reviewing, estimating, sizing up.

- Funny one: as in 'you're a funny one'. Odd, strange, weird. Not meant as a derisive comment, but as a musing.

- Get a rise: get a reaction, provoke.

- Getting / get it: as in 'I am getting you' – understand (I understand you). Get it – cop it, as in you will get it tomorrow! To be punished or spoken to severely.

- Green bin: the green bin takes all compostable green waste. We have a yellow bin for recyclables, and a red bin for other garbage.

- Hammer and tong: to go hard at something, put all of your effort in.

- Hang on: wait. 'Hang on a sec'. Wait for a second.

- Heaps: as in 'heaps of time' – a lot, plenty.

- Lemonade: what the US would call 'Sprite'. Sprite is a brand in Australia. The Aussie lemonade is a clear, carbonated, colourless soft drink, barely represented by lemons. Lemon squash, or pub squash, or squash is the Australian equal of the USA (cloudy) lemonade.

- Lend: as in 'having a lend'. To lie to someone, for your own amusement. It is taken in a light-hearted way.

- Main drag: prevalent shopping area of the district, where you'd find the best stores and fast food chains; usually the main road of a town.

- Mate: friend, buddy, pal. You can refer to anyone as 'mate', from your best friend to a complete stranger. However, 'a' mate, or 'my mate', is someone you know and like.

- Mickey: this can also be in reference to the vagina, in Australia. Along with Mickey hair, or mickey whiskers, being pubic hair.

- Mobile phone: cell phone.

- Muck around: waste your time, fail to achieve anything.

- Muso: musician.

- Myer: an upmarket department store.

- Out of bounds: an area forbidden to enter, prohibited.

- (The) oval: the school sports field.

- P1s: driver's licence where you no longer need a licensed driver to be present in the car. Speed is capped at 90KM/hr.

- Paying out: as in paying out on someone. Teasing, joking. Similar to stirring someone.

- PE: physical education. USA equivalent of gym class.

- Pegged: as in 'I pegged the orange at him'. Threw.

- Perving: checking someone out in an erotic way without their knowledge. Not considered overly crass or depraved, but girlfriends don't like to catch their boyfriends doing it, and vice versa.

- Piped up: started speaking, and/to make their presence known.

- Quad: quadrangle. A rectangle-shaped outdoor courtyard, and in this instance, the school buildings occupy three of its sides.

- Queenslander Verandah: High and wide external verandahs built to enable movement from one side of a house to another, to catch a cool breeze and stay out of the heat or sun. Most Queenslander verandahs wrap around at least two sides of a house.

- Reckon: think, as in - What do you reckon? What do you think?

- Relo: short for relative, member of the family.

- Ripped the guts out: stripped, as in renovating.

- Road service: this is additional to comprehensive vehicle insurance, most often used in cases of break-down. A mobile service comes to your vehicle and either tows, or repairs the car, depending on the malfunction. The most commonly known road service provider in NSW is the NRMA.

- Scungies: sports knickers -- pants girls wear over undies, under sport skirts:

- Sheep stations: as in 'playing for sheep stations'. When used in the negative form, it is to encourage players of a game to do so in a friendly and non-competitive environment. Usually, the term would be used as, 'Hey, we aren't playing for sheep stations!' meaning, lighten up. 'Playing for pinks'.

- Slow on the uptake: not process things easily, dim-witted.

- Smack bang: directly, encountered. In this instance, both weren't looking where they were going, and basically collided without warning, into each other. Wham! Whammo!

- Soft drink: soda, pop. In various part of Australia, this may also refer to cordial (as in a concentrated sweet syrup to be mixed with water before consumption).

- Spunk/s/y: a sexually attractive person.

- Stirred: to tease or joke. Can also mean to come out of a trance or begin to wake up.

- Sunblock: sunscreen.

- Swapping saliva: French kiss, make out.

- TAFE: Technical and Further Education – a lesser version of University   Completed with a trade certificate moreso than a degree.

- Tea towel: dish towel, drying towel.

- Tee (to a): exactly.

- University: University in Australia is the equivalent of USA College.

- Ute: abbreviation of utility. Pickup truck.

- Wet one: a juicy kiss.

- Year 8: equivalent to USA final year of junior high (middle school).

- Year 10: equivalent to USA sophomore.

- Year 11: equivalent to USA junior. Year 11 and 12 are the senior years and is mandatory attendance unless you are starting a full-time job or are enrolling in TAFE.

This glossary of Australian slang was developed to assist non-Aussies with any terms they find confusing in the novel. This could range from another country having a different understanding of the same word or phrase, to not understanding the term whatsoever.

The glossary outlines the reference to how the slang is used in the novel and is not all encompassing of every use of the word or phrase in Australia. Slang can also vary from state to state, which is why immigrants who have lived here for decades still look at we born and bred Aussies in total confusion when we speak. Who can blame them! ☺

A special thank you to my dear friend Jennifer D McLaughlin, my USA mate and pen-pal since we were 13 years old. Her input into this glossary from an American perspective has been immeasurable. Thanks Jen!

THE STANDISH HOME FLOOR PLAN
Northern Side

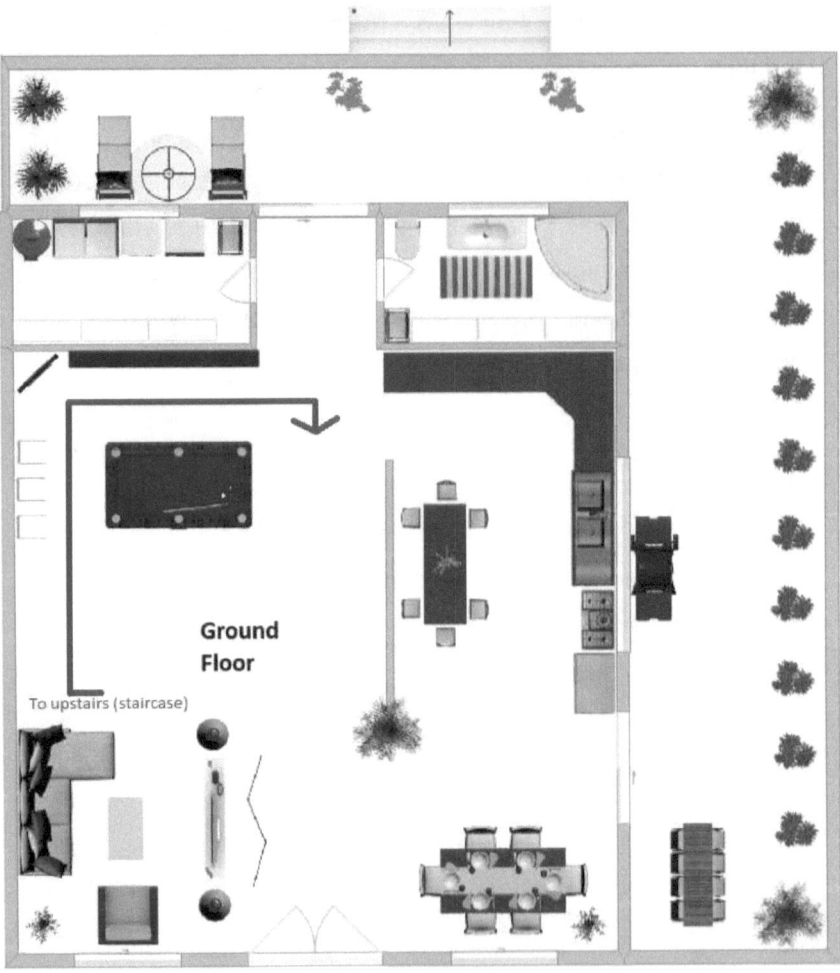

Ground Floor

To upstairs (staircase)

Eastern Side

(Not to scale of Ground Floor – rotate 90° to the right to sit on top of ground floor correctly)

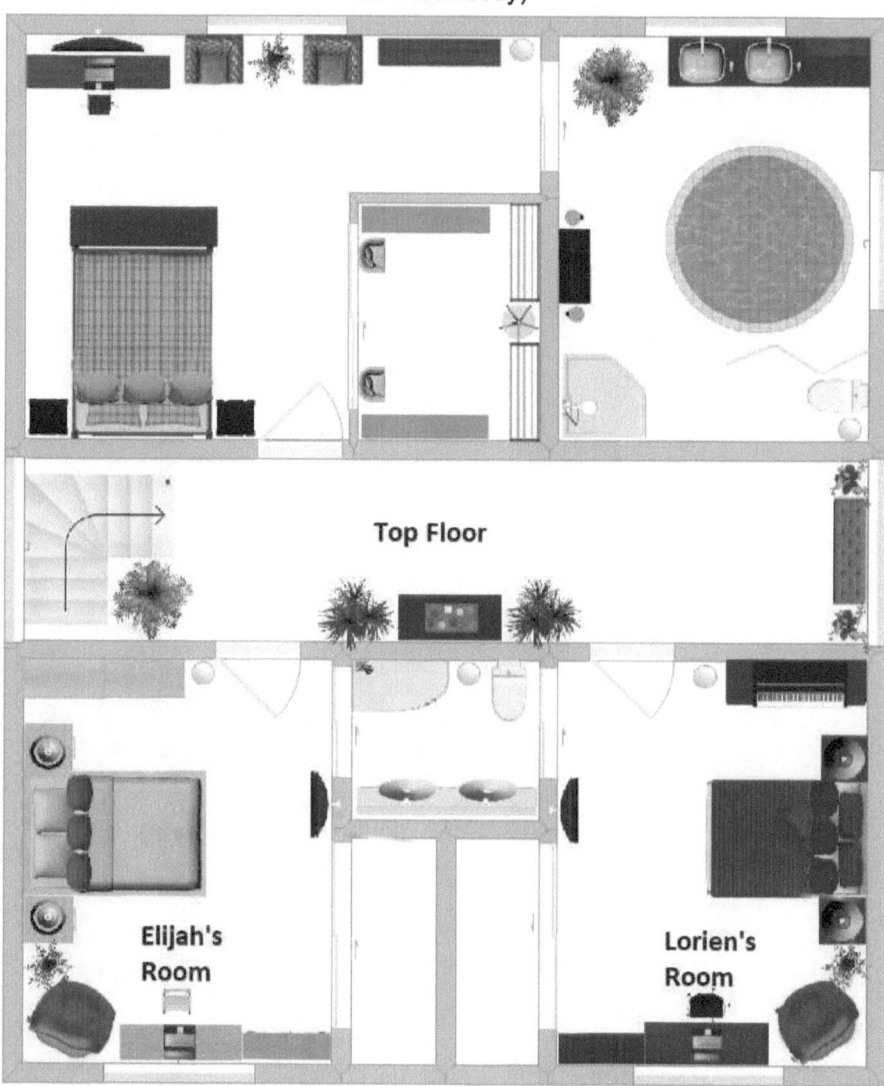

Top Floor

Elijah's Room

Lorien's Room

About the author

Cassandra Ann Frew (nee Souter) was born on a July winter's night in Hornsby NSW. At the age of three, the family moved to a dairy farm outside Lismore NSW where she spent the majority of her childhood. At ten years old, the family moved to Lake Macquarie NSW.

Cassie found her love of romance writing during her high school years, and her first several 'novels' were hand-written exercise books, passed around for her friends to read.

Her career in business and administration has led her into further self-education including web design, IT, professional proofreading and editing, creative writing and industrial psychology. She is also a Justice of the Peace and a Civil Celebrant.

Her most rewarding achievement to date is what she has in common with the residents of the Standish household – their love of music, playing an instrument and the 80s. What a decade!

These stories belong to my readers, and to Ashlyn and the Standish family. This is how love should be, can be, is.